Rebel Alpha

Book 5
Aloha Shifters: Pearls of Desire

by Anna Lowe

Twin Moon Press

Editing by Lisa A. Hollett

Covert art by Kim Killion

Contents

Other books in this series

Aloha Shifters - Pearls of Desire

Rebel Dragon (Book 1)

Rebel Bear (Book 2)

Rebel Lion (Book 3)

Rebel Wolf (Book 4)

Rebel Heart (A prequel)

Rebel Alpha (Book 5)

visit www.annalowebooks.com

Free Books

Get your free e-books now!

Sign up for my newsletter at *annalowebooks.com* to get three free books!

- *Desert Wolf*: Friend or Foe (Book 1.1 in the Twin Moon Ranch series)

- *Off the Charts* (the prequel to the Serendipity Adventure series)

- *Perfection* (the prequel to the Blue Moon Saloon series)

Chapter One

Cynthia sat in the rocking chair on the west porch, fingering her pearls. A bee buzzed, and a bird whistled from a nearby tree. Another perfect Maui day on the outside. Another stormy day in her soul.

She turned to check the mountains, sure there must be dark clouds creeping down the slopes. But there was nothing — not even a foggy crown around the peaks. Just pure, golden sunlight, bringing the colors of Maui to life. So why did she have a feeling of such foreboding?

She wrung her hands and looked north. Joey, her son, was over on Koa Point, the neighboring estate. A stab of fear went through her, but she chased it away. Joey was as safe there as he would be on Koakea Plantation, their home. Both places were populated with battle-hardened shifters who would lay down their lives for Joey if the need arose, and there was no reason to believe he was in any danger. Just a mother's paranoia, she supposed.

Still, it was hard to shake the feeling of something afoot. Of destiny moving pieces over a chessboard, preparing for its next assault. After all, the day she'd lost everything three years ago had started out just as peacefully as this. Then enemy dragons had swooped down out of nowhere, and shouts had filled the air.

Take Joey. Run! Run!

She squeezed her eyes shut, but that didn't stop her late husband's voice from ringing in her ears.

I can fight, she'd insisted.

You have to protect Joey. Now go!

1

She wrapped her arms around her stomach the way she had curled them around her son that day, and though she was barely moving, it felt as if she were fleeing again. Her long black hair whipping behind her, her bare feet racing across the lawn. She could hear the crackle of dragon fire and feel its lethal heat reach for her. The air rumbled with the beat of dragon wings as a battle raged overhead, and Joey's panicked cries stabbed at her heart.

Her eyes snapped open, and she gulped for air, forcing herself to calm down. All that was in the past. Joey was safe. Together, they'd found refuge under an assumed name in Maui, where fate had introduced her to a rough, tough, and incredibly loyal group of shifters — shifters just as much in need of a fresh start as she. Together, they'd turned a temporary safe house into a long-term, comforting home and formed a new weyr. A pack, in other words, if a ragtag one.

That, at least, made her flash a bittersweet smile. What would her mother say about all that? The heiress to a mighty dragon clan living among bears, wolves, lions, and a handful of dragons from inferior bloodlines?

There's nothing inferior about them, Mother. If only you knew.

A sigh escaped her lips, and she shoved the memories into a corner of her mind. She owed it to Joey to look forward, not back. If only she didn't have so many regrets...

She caught herself rocking and slammed a foot down to stop. She was far too young to be rocking away her days — even a day off, like today. Normally, the plantation grounds would be bustling with activity. Hailey and Sophie would be out in the fields, weeding another row of coffee plants free from decades of neglect. Dell, the lion shifter, would be making truck noises in the sandbox with his daughter Quinn and Cynthia's son Joey. In other words, acting like a third child, even though he was a full-grown man. Meanwhile, Chase's dogs — all five of them, for goodness' sake — would be sniffing around the shrubs. Jenna would be sanding away at her latest surfboard creation, while Connor would be helping Tim with improvements to the grounds. Although none of them owned the ten-acre property, they got to live there rent-free as long as they kept up the place.

But it was Sunday, and everyone had agreed to keep that day work-free. Which was great, but Cynthia just couldn't relax.

A low hum sounded from the distant road, and she whipped around, listening intently. But the sound died away, leaving only the rustling of bushes and the murmur of the ocean.

"Damn it," she muttered, turning away.

It used to be she could identify the sound of a Triumph Thruxton from a mile away. These days, every motorcycle made her head turn in hope.

She rose abruptly and walked into the house, looking for something to keep busy with. But the parlor was neat as a pin, and the dishwasher was already running in the kitchen. She glanced in the direction of the whiteboard where she posted the week's duties. Once upon a time, that duty roster had been a bone of contention between her and the men of Koakea. Now, everyone pitched in without protesting — except for Dell, who still ribbed her about it, though only for show. They'd all become more disciplined, while she'd learned to relax ever so slightly.

She frowned, looking past the billowing curtains to the sea. Why couldn't she relax now? She'd barely taken a few steps around the house, and yet her pulse was racing, her nerves jittering away.

What? she wanted to scream. *What is it?*

Something... her inner dragon murmured.

The feeling was vague, but so insistent, it was killing her. Should she call Connor, the co-alpha of their pack, and tell him to alert everyone? Or was it just a case of nerves?

She banged a fist against her own thigh. Damn it, she was not the nervous and flighty type.

Well — okay. She could admit to being a little high-strung.

A little? the others would joke.

A little, damn it. But she restricted herself to worrying about real issues, not imagined ones, and she certainly wasn't prone to panic attacks.

So why did her fingers fidget with the pearls of her necklace? Why did her body alternate between heating up and chilling all over?

I know why, her dragon murmured.

Cynthia scowled. Okay, she'd had a few X-rated fantasies last night. So what? She wasn't even thirty-five, and she'd gone far too long without the company of a man.

Not just any man. Her dragon's hum was sultry. *My mate.*

She closed her eyes as emotions roiled and collided inside. Lust. Guilt. Loyalty. Desire. The problem was, each of those emotions was tied to one of two different men.

You know who I mean, her dragon growled. *Our mate.*

Mate was a term that could be interpreted several ways. It applied to the decades-older man her parents had arranged for her to join in the dragon equivalent of marriage. That would be Barnaby, the father of her son. But while she'd grown to respect and appreciate Barnaby, her feelings had never gone beyond that. The dear man had known and accepted that from the start, and she'd never forget how willingly he'd made the ultimate sacrifice for Joey.

So, yes. Barnaby had been her mate in one sense, but never the mate of her heart, body, and soul.

I mean our destined mate, her dragon whispered. *Cal.*

A hot flash racked her body, and she gripped the banister that led to the upper floor. She hadn't seen, heard from, or — more to the point — touched Cal in twelve lonely years. She'd never stopped thinking about him either. But lately, her fantasies had blown out of control. Every night, she dreamed of racing down a tree-lined highway in the Adirondacks on the back of his Triumph, surrounded by fall colors as fiery as the passion that still burned in her heart. She dreamed of wrapping her arms around him as they lay in bed, sweaty and satisfied from making love. She dreamed of gazing into dark, mysterious eyes so full of love, they made her ache.

"Cal," she whispered into the silence.

She closed her eyes, reliving the sights, sounds, scents. So intensely that she imagined the crunch of gravel under motorcycle tires in the driveway. She even imagined the scent of leather and sandalwood wafting through the air.

For a few quiet minutes, she let herself pretend that it was all true. That she'd never been forced to part with her true love. That everything had worked out the way her twenty-year-old self had so desperately desired.

Then a quiet voice broke into her thoughts, snapping her out of her reverie.

"Cynthia?"

She didn't turn until the burn of a blush faded from her cheeks. As co-alpha of this mixed shifter pack, she wasn't supposed to act like a cat in heat — or a lonely widow who still pined for her first love.

"Yes?"

She turned when she'd finally composed herself, linking her hands at her waist like the prim lady her mother had raised.

Anjali stood on the porch, peering in without actually stepping inside, which was strange. The first floor of the house was communal space, and everyone came and went as they pleased. Only Cynthia's private quarters on the upper story were off-limits. So why did Anjali — calm, confident Anjali — seem so nervous and unsure?

Anjali glanced back as Dell came up the stairs behind her. His shoulders were squared, and his usual smile was gone, as was the habitual sparkle in his eyes. Another heavy step sounded on the porch stairs as Tim, the bear shifter, joined him.

Cynthia stood straighter. Something was definitely up. But what?

A flash of panic made her think of Joey, but when she reached out with her mind, she sensed laughter and joy as he played on the neighboring estate. So Joey was safe, thank God.

"What is it?"

"Someone is asking to see you," Anjali said.

Dell shot his mate a concerned look. "I was going to turn the guy away, but Anjali thinks. . . "

He trailed off, and Cynthia frowned. What did Anjali think?

"You know I would never bring an outsider here," Anjali explained. "But I think—"

"I think he's trouble," Connor growled from outside.

He? Who, he? Cynthia stepped to the doorway, surprised to see everyone there. Hailey and Tim, the bear shifters, were on the porch stairs, looking fierce. Jenna and Sophie were on ground level, shooting Anjali bolstering looks. The women appeared to be in favor of the visitor, whoever it was, while the men were all on edge. Including Chase and Connor, who stood in the driveway, holding another man in place. Together, they pinned his arms behind his back like a criminal caught in a dastardly act.

Anjali moved aside, and Cynthia strode to the edge of the porch, looking down. The visitor stared silently up at her, and—

It was a good thing there was a porch column for Cynthia to grab for support.

There really was a Triumph Thruxton parked in the driveway, and the man who'd arrived on it was a vision straight out of her dreams. He was older. Wearier. Wiser — like her, no doubt. Handsome as ever, in that roguish way that kept most people at arm's length. He was harder and tougher than when they'd first met, as if the invisible armor he wore had grown even thicker in the intervening years.

Had he pined for her the way she'd pined for him? Had he shed even a quarter of the tears she had? Or did he loathe her for what she'd been forced to do, the way she loathed herself at times?

Cal Zydler. Road rider. Wolf shifter.

Mate, her dragon cried.

"Cal," she whispered in spite of herself.

His smoky gray eyes gave nothing away, and neither did his deep, unwavering voice.

"Cynthia," he murmured in a tone so low, it might have been a whisper on the wind.

Chapter Two

Cal took the longest, deepest breath of his life and held on to it. Who needed air, food, or water when he could just drink Cynthia in? His heart pounded, and his throat went as dry as the desert roads he'd crossed aimlessly after she'd broken up with him, all those years ago.

I love you more than anything, but I can't have you, she'd said, pleading for him to understand.

He'd just about thrown her over his shoulder, jumped on the Triumph, and sped off to someplace where no one would ever find them. But, no. The moment they'd met, he'd known his heart was destined to be broken. Make that, shattered. Make that, exploded to pieces. Make that—

He cut off the thought. Cynthia was the one with the fancy vocabulary. He was the one with the hole in his chest where his heart used to be.

Please don't make this harder, she'd begged through her sobs. Then she'd done her best to explain why she had to marry a decades-older dragon shifter she didn't even know.

Family honor... Tradition... Bloodlines...

All kinds of things that made no sense to a lone wolf like him. A lone wolf with the shit luck to fall — hard — for a woman like her.

He'd spent the first two years apart from Cynthia in agony and the next ten in a numb, emotionless state — so much, he was sure he'd lost the ability to feel anything at all. But seeing Cynthia now made everything rush back. The yearning. The loneliness. The need to hold her and never let her go.

So maybe it was a good thing he was locked in place by two guys — a wolf and a dragon shifter, judging by their scents. Otherwise, he might have rushed up, hugged Cynthia, and given his inner wolf reason to hope.

Why not hope? his wolf protested. *She's single again, right?*

Cal clenched his jaw. The day Cynthia had turned him away was the day he'd died inside, and there was no coming back from his own personal hell.

A sea gull cried overhead, and Cal squinted, following its flight. It was midday, and the sun was high. Not a breath of wind, not a shadow to hide in.

His inner wolf let out a long, mournful howl. *Don't want to hide. Want to claim my mate.*

Yeah, well. That was life, wasn't it? He stood perfectly still, making sure the firestorm inside him didn't show.

The guy on his left — the dragon — twisted his arm, making Cal wince. Whoever that asshole was, he sure was protective of Cynthia. So were the other men, from the wiry wolf shifter to the sunny-boy lion and the burly bear shifter half a step away. Every one of them appeared ready to rip his head off, which was a good thing. Cynthia needed all the protection she could get. Several of the guys sported Special Forces tattoos or wore dog tags around their necks, which meant she was surrounded by a formidable defensive force.

The women had been friendlier, if wary. Still, they were the ones who'd talked the guys into letting him in. Of course, women had that mysterious *intuition* thing, and their eyes had bored into him as they decided whether to let him in or kick his ass back out onto the street. Those women were shifters too, and it was obvious they were not to be messed with any more than the men.

Clearly, Cynthia was surrounded by a healthy combination of brawn and brains. The question was, would that be enough? And was Cynthia aware of the imminent danger closing in?

"Cal who?" the pushy dragon shifter at his side hissed in his ear.

"Cal Zydler," Cynthia whispered as she had the day he'd revealed his full name.

His lips quirked in the tiniest possible smile. She'd left out the *Calvin* part, thank goodness. It didn't bother him that she'd revealed his last name, because who cared about names?

His inner wolf sighed. *Dragons care.*

Cynthia had about eleven middle names and three family names, as he'd eventually learned. All carefully chosen to reflect an illustrious family tree. A tree that had to be made of fucking gold, the way her parents talked about it the only time he'd ever met them, when they'd stiffly explained why it was impossible for him to mate with her. Hell, even loving her from a distance was a crime in their books.

He grimaced. They'd gone so far as to try to buy him off. As if he were more interested in money than his mate.

"Connor. Chase," Cynthia whispered to the men locking his arms in place. "Let him go." Neither made a move to obey until she added, "Please."

The big shifters looked at each other before finally relaxing their iron grip. Still, they pinned him with murderous looks and kept their arms at their sides, ready to attack if he so much as twitched.

Cal shook out his arms, and he could tell the exact moment when Cynthia noticed the burn scars, because she cringed.

Oh God, her expression cried. *What happened?*

Shit happened, he wanted to say.

He watched her closely. Did she loathe what she saw, or could she see past the scars to the real him? The Cynthia he'd known over a decade ago had that ability, but fate hadn't been kind to either of them. Of course, she was just as gorgeous as ever — maybe even more so, what with those noble, chiseled features and perfectly shaped lips. Those fierce, dark eyes. That proud bearing that practically screamed *royalty.* Hell, even her long, shiny black hair was swept up into an arrangement that resembled a crown.

Still, for all her blue blood, Cynthia had never exuded a single snobby vibe. Her eyes had always sparkled with curiosity, and she listened — really listened — to every person she met, from roughshod vagabonds like him to plain old humans on the street.

But now, sadness hung over her shoulders like a shadow she just couldn't shake. She twirled her pearls nervously before straightening her shoulders and beckoning him up the stairs.

He clomped right up, hiding the little bit of a limp on his left side. The others stepped aside, but only barely, remaining alert. Cal braced himself as he reached out to shake her hand, being as businesslike as he could. But a crackling force field zapped his body the moment their hands touched, and he nearly wobbled on his feet.

Christ, lady. What you do to me...

He used to say that in a good way, like after they'd made love and sank, sweaty, into the sheets — if the heat of the moment had allowed them to get as far as a bed. Now, the sentiment only highlighted how much had changed.

Cynthia shuddered ever so slightly, and her lips parted enough to make his body ache.

"Good to see you again," he said.

The thing was, seeing her again was going to kill him, and he knew it.

"And you," she replied, so quietly he couldn't tell what she really meant.

Then he forced himself to utter, "Sorry to hear about Barnaby. He was a good man."

He meant it, too. Barnaby had turned out to be too good a man to hate, much as Cal had tried. Not that he would ever tell Cynthia how well he'd come to know her late husband.

Her eyes blazed, and he stared back. Didn't she know that was as close as he would ever come to acknowledging she'd had to sleep with another man?

Apparently not, because her jaw jutted the way it did when she got mad, and she just about spat back, "He was."

He ached to tell her the truth — the whole truth, and nothing but the truth. But damn it, he'd sworn to guard those secrets forever. A man didn't have to be a blue-blooded dragon to know an oath was an oath.

Footsteps rushed up behind him, and before anyone could protest, a little kid whisked by, bowling right into Cynthia's arms.

"Mommy! Mommy! Look at the shell I found!"

Cal glanced at the kid, then aimed his gaze at the floor. Damn it. The redhead — Joey, Cal knew — was the spitting image of his father. Which meant old Barnaby would always be there to haunt Cal.

Cynthia kneeled and cupped the shell in both hands. "It's beautiful, sweetie."

Her voice wobbled, making Cal glance over. Was that a tear fighting to escape her right eye?

She brushed at it quickly, then hugged Joey long and hard.

The little boy laughed. "It's just a shell, Mommy."

Still, Cynthia held him. It was almost a minute later that she gulped and extracted herself. "Yes, but it's a beautiful shell, and it comes from the person I love more than anyone in the world."

Cal squeezed his lips in a sharp line. If that wasn't a hint, what was?

Cynthia straightened and shooed the boy into the house, then smoothed the wrinkles in her blouse. When she looked at Cal again, her gaze was soft and unguarded, and he swore her eyes brightened. But a moment later, she stiffened, and her face went cold again.

Cal shook his head. How right he'd been, all those years ago. That the flustered, inexperienced college girl he'd met on the side of the road would become a hell of a powerful alpha someday. Not that her perfect nails and silky hair suggested as much — just her steely nerves. The sharp discipline. The ability to make coldhearted decisions from time to time.

"Joey, right?" Cal murmured. "He looks just like Barnaby."

Cynthia's eyes narrowed. "How do you know my son's name?"

Cal wanted to snort. If only she knew.

The moment her voice rose, the shifters beside him inched closer, and their hands balled into fists. Cal wouldn't have minded taking on one or two. But four angry males, plus another four females who looked equally capable of tearing his eyes out? Maybe not.

11

He shrugged. "I know a lot of things."

Yeah, that made Cynthia wonder, all right. She looked him up and down slowly.

"You look just like your mother when you do that," he couldn't help murmuring.

Her head snapped up, and his wolf growled to his human side, *Quit riling her up.*

He hid a bittersweet smile. It used to be, he'd rile her up for fun — just a little, and only when her blue-blooded upbringing showed. The same way he used to lean into turns or slalom his bike over the median line, just to make her squeal. Teasing used to be part of the game of love.

Not a game any more, his wolf mourned.

"What brings you to Maui?" she asked, watching him closely.

"You," he said.

Her eyebrows shot up.

The bear shifter behind Cal let out a low growl of warning, but Cal ignored it. Circumstances might force him to keep some secrets from Cynthia, but he would never lie to her. Besides, he was too fixated on the thin, dark lines of Cynthia's eyebrows. The hollows of her cheekbones. The tiny creases at the corners of her eyes. God, she was beautiful. But she looked...tired. Empty. A little like him, he supposed.

Her eyes wandered over to his Triumph. Yes, it was the same bike he'd owned way back when, shipped over from the mainland. And yes, the scarf she'd once given him was still wrapped around the handlebars. But one of the men moved closer, blocking Cynthia from getting a full view.

Her brow furrowed, and she cleared her throat. "And what exactly have you been up to over the last few years?"

He snorted. "Do you really want to know?"

She pursed her lips. Was she as surprised as he was to discover he still had that cocky, roguish side?

"Yes," she said. One clipped syllable — an order, not a question.

Against his better judgment, he replied.

"Killing dragons."

Her mouth fell open and her eyes went wide. An unguarded expression he wouldn't have minded relishing for a moment or two, just like in the good old days. But the lion and dragon shifter grabbed his arms again and wrestled him back.

"That's it. You're out of here, asshole."

"No!" Cynthia cried.

Everyone froze and stared.

"I mean..." she stammered, flustered, perhaps, by the sheer need her tone had revealed. "I mean..."

The men looked at each other like they'd never seen their leader caught so off-balance. Then the big dragon shifter spoke decisively.

"Take him to Silas." He leaned in close and let his eyes flash death and destruction. "Dragon killer? We'll see about that."

Chapter Three

Cal didn't bother dragging his feet as the two shifters hauled him off. Part of him was still flying high after catching what he'd seen in Cynthia's eyes. Love. Hope. Yearning — for him.

Of course, all that was way in the back, behind a decade-plus of regrets — and even worse, mistrust. But love was still there. Enough to make him hope.

Which was bad, but his stupid wolf couldn't get some things through its thick, lovesick mind.

Mate loves me! She still loves me!

Well, of course, she did. They were destined for each other. But things didn't always go according to destiny's plan, especially when the fucked-up traditions of noble dragon clans intervened.

He sucked in a deep breath and hauled his focus back to his surroundings. Maui, huh? Even as a woman on the run, Cynthia had managed to end up in some pretty amazing digs.

"You know why I'm not killing you outright?" the blustery dragon growled as he bustled Cal along.

"Must have something to do with my charm," Cal shot back. The lion shifter twisted his left arm, and Cal winced, then went on. "Or because you're dying of curiosity."

"Dying, huh?" The dragon wrapped a thick hand around Cal's neck. "Don't give me any ideas."

Cal snorted. Way back when he'd first met Cynthia, he'd been a little wowed by dragons. Even a powerful wolf shifter had to respect a creature with wings, talons, and the ability to breathe fire. But dragons had their weak points, too. His right arm might be covered in burn scars, but the dragon who'd done that to him was dead.

He twisted, trying to break away — more to test the shifters who held him than to actually get free. A test they passed with flying colors, which was good. Cynthia needed real protection, not just a bunch of amateurs in muscle shirts.

"Do you have to be so rough with him, Connor?" the woman following them complained.

A she-dragon, Cal decided, judging by her scent. A scent with a lot of salt air and ocean mixed in. He sniffed again, then glanced back.

"Whoa. Sea dragon?"

She grinned, but her mate jerked Cal's arm hard enough to make his teeth rattle.

"What's it to you?"

If Cal's hands had been free, he would have stuck them up to show he meant no harm. Not to these dragons — or the lions, bears, and wolves they lived among. Hell, if this bizarre little pack had a koala shifter, he'd be fine with that too. The more and the fiercer, the better, because they protected Cynthia. That much, he'd picked up from the very first glare.

Apparently, the rumor of Cynthia being holed up with a bunch of Special Forces veterans was true. Maybe she had a fighting chance against the shitstorm he knew was bound to rain down soon.

"Connor. . . " the sea dragon warned.

"Jenna. . . " her mate replied in exactly the same tone.

But a moment later, the dragon released his grip on Cal's neck. "I don't trust him."

"You don't trust anyone," Jenna sighed.

"I don't see why you and Anjali insisted on letting this guy in."

"Call it a hunch."

Cal would have loved to turn around and study Jenna's expression, but Connor would probably tear his arm out if he tried. Did she know more than she let on? It had been impossible to interpret the looks she and the other woman — Anjali — had exchanged when he had first asked to see Cynthia. They'd almost turned him away, but Anjali had looked him over intently and whispered two words.

What if. . . ?

The women hadn't said a word after that, but he could sense them pushing thoughts into each other's minds as all closely bonded shifters could.

What if, indeed. Women talked, right? Had Cynthia told them the whole long, sad story during a boisterous evening of girl talk? Had she described the lone wolf who'd come out of nowhere and swept her off her feet?

The more Cal considered, the more he doubted it. Cynthia didn't do girl talk. She didn't drop hints. She was a dragon, after all, and the only thing dragons hoarded more than treasure were secrets.

"We'll see what Silas thinks of your hunch," Connor muttered.

Other than the stomp of their footsteps and the occasional whoosh of branches swatted aside as they walked, the next few minutes passed in silence. Cal looked around, trying to get his bearings. The coastal highway he'd cruised in on was somewhere to his right, making a long bend away from this huge property. The shoreline had to be to his left, judging by the murmur of surf rolling over pebbles and sand. That left a long, thickly wooded strip between the shore and the road. The perfect shifter hideaway.

One stand of forest gave way to another, and he had the sense of crossing an unmarked property line, because everything changed. The underbrush was thinner, the woods tidier — more like a private estate than an overgrown farm. They even passed a clearing where neatly trimmed grass hemmed in a helipad, complete with a brown chopper with red and yellow stripes.

He stiffened, and his head snapped around to the left. Someone was stalking them from the bushes. A pair of tigers?

He nearly whistled. Maybe Cynthia had a bigger army at her disposal than he'd thought.

Finally, they emerged onto a patch of manicured lawn. Footpaths converged from every direction, leading to an open-sided, thatched building where several burly men stood, thick arms crossed over their chests. There were women too, and each looked just as capable of defending the place as the men. A row of tiki torches marked the main approach to that meeting house, and though it was high noon, he could picture them crackling and swirling at night.

All in all, a pretty impressive sight. Every subtly flexed muscle, every sure stance told him this was not a pack to be messed with.

Then a calico cat wound between the legs of those cold, uncompromising men, and Cal had to hide a grin when one or the other glanced down with a soft, indulgent smile.

So they were tough, but they had heart. Another good sign, at least as far as Cynthia was concerned. Still, that didn't change the fact that there were about a dozen of them and only one of him.

In other words, the usual shitty odds. His wolf sighed.

Connor and the lion shifter marched Cal directly up to the tall, dark-haired man at the apex of the phalanx of shifters waiting by the meeting house.

"Let me guess. Silas Llewellyn," Cal said, oh so casually.

The man's dark eyes flickered, but he answered smoothly. "To whom do I owe the pleasure?"

Before Cal could answer, Connor gave him a shake.

"A dragon slayer — or so he claims."

Cal kept his head high as Silas's dark eyes swept over him, taking in every detail.

Yeah, look at me, dragon, he wanted to say. *And don't hold your breath waiting for me to be impressed.*

If Cal were honest, he *was* impressed. Not so much by the man's wealth, power, or reputation — yes, he'd done his homework before coming out to Maui — but by the solid wall of loyalty and respect Silas commanded from those around him. Up to that moment, Silas Llewellyn had only ever been a name to Cal — another name on a long list of snobby dragon clans. But now...

"Release him," Silas murmured.

Cal pursed his lips. Logic dictated there had to be some decent dragons in the world other than Cynthia. It was just that he'd rarely met one.

18

The dragon shifter frowned, and the lion protested outright. "Silas, man. Did you hear what Connor said?"

Cal considered, impressed all over again. Soldiers who thought for themselves and didn't hold back from questioning crazy orders, even if they respected their commander? The world could use more of those.

Silas nodded gravely, and the others complied, though they didn't back away. They stood there bristling, ready to pounce if Cal tried anything.

"Dragon slayer? The one we've been hearing about?" Silas turned his head this way and that, studying Cal from different angles. "The one who strikes then disappears, leaving no trace?"

Cal grinned. Funny how a reputation could be a good thing sometimes.

He shrugged, playing it cool. "I'm one of them."

Everyone's jaw dropped, and even calm, collected Silas did a double take. Typical dragon — trying to hide everything, still revealing too much.

"One of them?"

"A dragon slayer who takes innocent lives?" a tall redhead on the right demanded, unimpressed.

"There's not an innocent bone in the dragons I kill." Cal's voice went all gritty, and he chastised himself for letting a tiny hint of emotion slip out.

"And which dragons might those be?" Silas demanded.

Cal made a face. "Believe me, I specialize in killing bad guys."

"That depends on your definition of bad," the redhead said, crossing her arms. Her eyes were as green as the emerald that hung from her necklace, her face stony.

Cal swung his jaw left and right. "How about dragons who steal away women they have no business putting their dirty claws on? Or two-faced dragons who show the world how rich and generous they are, while earning major drug money on the side? Dragons who kill a man in front of his kid's eyes and laugh while they do it? Do any of those meet your definition?"

He didn't mean to glare but, hell. He usually kept the memories locked away, but mentioning each of those bastards made it all come back. "Believe me. They deserved it, all right."

The next few seconds ticked by in utter silence, and Cal took several deep breaths. Seeing Cynthia had gotten to him more than he thought.

"And what about Bartholomew James?" Silas demanded.

Now it was Cal's turn to do a double take. James had been a close associate of Cynthia's husband, Barnaby.

"Hell no. His only crime was being a snob. You know, like all dragon shifters."

Connor glared. "We're not all snobs."

Cal shot him a sidelong glance. That, he had to give the guy. While Silas had a measured, aristocratic air, everything about Connor screamed *rebel*. He wondered what the guy's story was.

Cynthia's not a snob, his inner wolf said dreamily. *She's special.*

Yes, she was. Like Silas Llewellyn, if he were honest. By reputation — and all outward appearances — Silas was one of those rare dragons who, despite a strict upbringing with hopelessly outdated traditions and manners, turned out to be more classy than snobby. The kind with heart and a sense of principle that made them look beyond their own fortunes every once in a while.

"Hang on," the lion shifter broke in. "How exactly does a wolf kill a dragon?"

Cal flashed his best roguish grin. "Trade secret."

Silas frowned. "The how doesn't concern me. It's the why, and the suggestion that there may be more than one dragon slayer out there."

Cal snorted. "Dragons have more feuds running than any other shifter species. Is it so surprising that one of them has turned to hired guns?"

Silas narrowed his eyes. "Is that what you are? A hired gun?"

Cal made a face. Who the hell did they think he was? "No, I have my own personal vendetta."

"And that would be...?"

"None of your business."

The lion shifter let out a low, grumbling growl, and a whiff of sulfur wafted over from Connor's direction — a sure signal of how close the man was to shifting into dragon form. But the slightest motion from Silas made them back down again.

Cal decided he liked the guy. For a dragon, at least. And the mixed shifter pack Silas led was... interesting. Very interesting, to put it mildly.

Another quiet moment ticked by before Silas spoke again. "And what exactly is your business with Ms. Brown?"

It took Cal a second to realize who Silas meant. Then he burst out laughing. "Cynthia? Brown?"

Silas gave him a sharp look, and everyone frowned in confusion.

Cal shook his head, incredulous. "A she-dragon as classy as Cynthia named Brown? I know she's in hiding, but who the hell is going to buy that? You and I both know she's a Ba—"

Silas cut him off with a grunt, and Cal stared. Everyone else did too, and it dawned on him that while he and Silas knew exactly who Cynthia was, the others might not.

He glanced at Silas with renewed respect. So that was the level of security the man was trying to offer Cynthia. Well, good on him.

Cal cleared his throat and went back to Silas's question. What business did he have with Cynthia? He motioned toward the adjoining property. "Why don't you ask her?"

His voice was raspy, damn it, and he wondered what Cynthia might say if Silas asked. Would she admit that she'd once loved a lowly wolf like him?

She still loves us, his wolf growled. *You'll see.*

"Anyway," Cal added, moving on quickly. "Cynthia is not my target, and she never will be. Neither is her kid. You either, for whatever that's worth."

Silas seemed willing to take him at his word, but Connor snorted. "We're supposed to accept that?"

Cal rolled his eyes. "Dragons kill dragons all the time. But when another shifter does it, you all flip out."

"I only kill when I have to, and only the bad guys," Connor snarled.

"Just like me, asshole. Just like me."

When Connor bristled, Jenna put a hand on his arm then turned to Cal. "Why do you do it? Why get mixed up in dragon business at all?"

Something in Cal snapped. Not so much at Jenna's words but at all those disbelieving faces. "Because I swore to protect Cynthia. I swore to hunt down the dragons who killed her family." His voice grew louder with every word. "Because I would die for her, all right?"

The silence that ensued was thunderous, and Cal cursed himself. Now, why had he gone and admitted that?

But, hell — it was the truth. He *would* die for her. In fact, he already had, at least in his heart.

So why did it thump that hard when you saw her? his wolf pointed out. *We still love her, and she loves us.*

Cal frowned. Hope. The most dangerous emotion of all.

An awkward moment passed in which everyone glanced at each other or studied him. Some suspiciously, while others seemed to see him in a new light. Were they starting to get that they didn't have a monopoly on love and honor? That a guy like him might be in on those qualities too?

When Silas spoke, it was in a gentler, quieter voice. "And Cynthia is in danger because...?"

Cal cleared his throat. "Moira is building her forces."

Several people groaned at the mention of the name, and he didn't blame them. That she-dragon was the scourge of the shifter world.

Conceited... arrogant... greedy... his inner wolf ranted.

Don't get me started, he sighed.

"We know," Silas replied, unimpressed.

Dragons. Thought they knew everything.

Cal faked a yawn. "Okay, so you must also know about Kravik and the gang he's moved into North America with."

The way Silas narrowed his eyes suggested he knew exactly how much trouble those old-world dragons had brought with them.

"The Lombardi clan? How do you know that?"

Cal grinned. "I know a lot of things."

"Believe me, I've been tracking them closely," Silas said.

Cal laughed outright, touching his scars. He'd been doing a lot more than tracking the bastards. He'd been hunting them down, one by one. But fresh arrivals had quickly filled those gaps, eager to follow a promising new leader.

Kravik, his wolf grumbled.

Cal's burn scars itched. He'd faced Kravik once, but the bastard had gotten away before Cal could work out a plan of attack.

"I don't know what's worse," he said. "The idea of those bastards starting an all-out shifter war against Moira, or joining forces with her in some kind of deal."

Silas's face darkened. "Moira won't stick to a deal."

"I know that and you know that, but does Kravik know? You have to consider the possibility."

"I don't like it," Silas said, looking grim.

The lion shifter at his side made a face. "What's to like?"

Silas gave Cal a long, hard look, then turned to the others.

"Gentlemen, ladies," he announced, looking around slowly. "I'd like a private word with Mr. Zydler, please."

The others looked surprised, but one after another, they stepped away — out of earshot, if not very far. All but that stubborn lion shifter who stayed put with his arms crossed.

"Mr. O'Roarke," Silas murmured.

The lion shifter shook his head in a gesture that said, *Not going anywhere.* Cal could have sworn Dell's beard grew thicker and longer, hinting he was on the verge of shifting.

"We all want to protect Cynthia," Silas said.

"And Joey," Dell added, not giving way one inch.

"And Joey," Silas agreed. "But if you respect Cynthia, you'll respect that she has certain... secrets."

Cal wanted to laugh. Oh, she had secrets, all right.

Dell didn't look impressed, but Silas went on. "I swear I'll share anything you need to know. But until then..." He raised his eyebrows in a not-so-subtle dragon command.

Dell jutted his jaw from side to side, then pierced Cal with a murderous look. "I'll be watching, you got it?"

Cal rolled his eyes. Lions. Always acting like kings of the goddamn jungle.

Finally, Dell retreated, and Silas leaned in.

Cal kept his face masked when Silas began to speak in low, earnest tones, though it was hard at times. Silas knew more about Cynthia than Cal had guessed. Then the tables were turned when Cal told Silas exactly what Kravik and his European clan had been up to.

The more Cal revealed, the more he questioned himself. Was he nuts to trust a dragon with knowledge he'd nearly died to acquire? But, hell. Cynthia trusted Silas. Cal would trust the guy too. He had to if he wanted the dragon alpha to reciprocate.

Their private conversation didn't last more than three or four minutes, plus the long, silent minute Silas used to size him up at the end. Finally, the dragon spoke.

"Mr. Zydler, I offer you a choice. Leave now, and go in peace. Turn your back on this matter while you still can, and leave it to us."

Cal snorted, but Silas shook his head.

"There is much you have discovered, but there remains much you don't know."

There's much you don't know, asshole, Cal nearly growled.

"Or..." Silas continued.

Cal couldn't help leaning in. "Or?"

"Stay, and work with us to protect Cynthia and her son."

"I don't need you to do that," Cal scoffed.

Silas tilted his head. "If you truly care about her — and I sense you do — you'd recognize we're better off uniting our efforts. If this matter is as serious as I suspect, we need to use every resource at our disposal."

Cal's rebel blood boiled at that one. "I'm not your resource, and I'm not at your disposal."

Silas leaned away. "So you choose the first option? Turning your back?"

Cal scowled. He'd sworn to protect Cynthia, and nothing would make him leave. But staying — even worse, cooperating — was out of the question. He wasn't a team player, for starters.

Could have been, his wolf grumbled.

He made a face. If he'd been born into a halfway stable pack with decent leadership, he would have been tracked to become alpha when his time came. But his mother had bounced from pack to pack throughout his entire childhood. Just when Cal had finished fighting to establish himself in one pack, his mother would join a new one, and the whole tedious process would begin again. By the time he'd turned sixteen, he'd had it with packs and had hit the road. Being on his own was so much simpler. So much easier.

So much lonelier, his wolf snipped.

Yes, it had been. But then he'd met Cynthia and found new purpose in life. To love her. To woo her. To make her laugh. She'd been engulfed by college studies at the time — Yale, no less — and insisted that he give her space. But every weekend, he'd cruised into that snotty college town, picked her up, and spent the next forty-eight hours giving his destined mate everything her gilded cage lacked. Freedom. Laughter. Love. His body heated at the thought of all the times they'd holed up somewhere together and made hot, hard love.

Then he remembered Silas was half a step away.

Cut that out, he cursed his inner wolf.

Cut what out? the beast asked all too innocently.

Cal cleared his throat and forced himself back to the matter at hand. Choice A — leaving — was a no-go. But Choice B was even worse. Staying meant more fighting. More suffering. More heartbreak. He had to walk away if he wanted to stay sane.

Will never leave my mate, his wolf declared.

Cal's hands formed fists at his sides. There was a third option, of course. He could stick around and do whatever the hell he pleased regardless of what this shifter pack demanded.

But Silas was right about uniting forces. In fact, the dragon was right on most counts. It was just that Cal's rebel blood rejected the proposition for the sake of defiance.

In the end, the answer was a no-brainer, and he knew it.

Cal frowned at Silas. "All right. But no ordering me around, dragon."

Silas stuck up his hands. "You'll have to abide by our rules, but beyond that, you move as you wish and do what you deem best. Every day, you will report to me."

"Report?" Cal's frown deepened.

Silas sighed. "Call it a meeting, then. You may be a born alpha, but I'm in charge here, you got that?"

Cal wanted to laugh. A born alpha? Ha. He was a loner, and he liked it that way.

What about the prophecy? his wolf rumbled.

He wanted to laugh. *Prophecy, my ass.* Just because some old woman claimed to have had a vision when he'd been born didn't mean he had to believe it. Him, becoming a warrior who accomplished great things? A warrior who would extinguish a great evil and herald in a new era of peace in the shifter world?

His heart thumped harder, but he pushed the notion away and glared at Silas. His choice was made, and they both knew it.

Begrudgingly, he stuck out a hand. "You got yourself a deal. I just hope you're right."

Silas shook his hand while casting a worried eye at the sky, as if he expected a dozen enemy dragons to come hurtling over the ridgeline at any moment.

"I hope I'm wrong," he murmured. "For Cynthia's sake."

Chapter Four

Cynthia wrung her hands as she moved from room to room. The sun had long since set, and her heart was pounding, her palms sweaty. She'd pined for Cal for so long, and now...

Hours had passed since he had first arrived, but it felt like mere minutes. She was still in shock and seesawing between feeling thrilled and mortified. Destiny had brought back her true mate, but it was too late.

Guilt washed through her at the thought of her late husband. If only Barnaby had been a selfish, greedy bastard. Then she could hate him and move on. But Barnaby had been a true gentleman who'd loved, honored, and offered her every kindness — the ideal partner, really, if she had come from a different generation.

What about love? her dragon insisted in the same tone she'd once used to protest to her parents. *Being mates means loving — deeply, madly, passionately.*

Her heart ached, and regrets gnawed at her soul, but she pushed them away. Nothing would make her undo the past, because that would undo Joey's existence, and nothing was more precious than her son. Not the comfortable living she'd lost, nor the treasures locked out of her reach. Not even the self-respect she'd sacrificed by marrying a man she didn't love.

She fingered her pearls, and their cool, comforting presence made a bittersweet smile play over her lips. They were the sole reminder of two vast fortunes — her parents', which she'd been slated to inherit, and the fortune she'd married into. Now, she didn't even own the dishes she ate from. Funny, the games destiny played.

Not so funny, her dragon cried.

She made a face. No fortune could buy freedom, let alone happiness. Cal had taught her that.

Footsteps sounded on the porch stairs, making her straighten quickly. It wouldn't do for one of the others to see her in such a state. Not when she'd worked so hard to establish herself as co-alpha of this pack.

"Cynthia?" Hailey called quietly.

"Come in."

Cynthia sniffed deeply as the scent of fresh-brewed Kona coffee wafted into the house one step ahead of Hailey. Anything to erase the scent of her mate — er, Cal — from her mind.

"Hi," Hailey said. "Would you like a coffee before you go?"

Cynthia glanced at the sky. Damn. She'd almost forgotten it was Wednesday — her regular night out. Not a fun night out — God forbid — but a night out flying. Training. Learning. Not that she needed to learn anything about flying, but fighting. . .

She frowned. As the daughter of an affluent dragon shifter family, she'd had a strict education in all the lore and lessons of dragondom. But fighting was left to male dragons, with females sticking to slightly more traditional roles. They could run the family business or take the lead when it came to diplomacy, but never, ever fight. There had never been a need. But now. . .

Cynthia shivered and glanced at the waxing moon. The past years had ushered in a major changing of the guard in the dragon shifter world, and nothing was as it had once been. Moira was building an empire, and a powerful group of European dragons was rumored to be spreading their sphere of influence, too. Cynthia couldn't afford to stand by and hope for Silas, Connor, and the other shifters of Koakea to protect her — and more importantly, Joey. It was high time she learned to fight. So, for the past month, she'd been honing her fighting skills with her fellow dragon shifters.

"Thanks." Cynthia nodded and took the steaming mug Hailey offered. Hell yes, she could use a coffee.

Then she nearly put a hand over her mouth. What would her mother think if she heard such words coming from her only daughter? And worse, what would her mother say about all the training and sparring?

It's just not ladylike, the woman would surely cry.

Cynthia frowned into her coffee. No, it wasn't. But she'd do anything to protect Joey.

Anything, her dragon agreed in a low growl.

Then she remembered Hailey — and her own manners. Had she just accepted a coffee with little more than one single syllable of thanks? Hailey wasn't a servant, and she wasn't simply a packmate. Like all the women of Koakea, Hailey had become a friend. Over the past months, Cynthia had found herself slowly letting down her guard and finding a new balance between her role as co-alpha and as a friend.

"This is delicious." She shot Hailey a smile. "You could open a coffee shop."

Hailey laughed, and her cheeks flushed with pride. "The world's smallest coffee shop, going by the size of my crop. But next year..."

Her eyes shone as they always did when she dreamed her dream.

Cynthia drank the coffee in several grateful sips and chatted for a minute or two. Then she briefed Hailey, who'd be keeping an eye on Joey in her absence.

Call it practice, Hailey had once joked, hinting that she and Tim were thinking of starting their own family.

As Cynthia spoke, it hit her all over again how lucky she was to have friends like Hailey and the others. She'd never thought she could entrust Joey to anyone, but these days, she did it all the time. Her packmates were people she could count on through thick and thin — something that had never been clearer than in their reactions to Cal's arrival. Everyone had been on high alert, ready to tear Cal to pieces if he'd shown any intention of harm. At the same time, the women had been determined to give Cal a chance. Had they sensed that he was the one?

She grimaced. Whatever magic she and Cal shared, it was all in the past, and there was no going back.

Maybe not, her dragon hummed. *But starting over...*

She snorted. There would be no starting over. She'd reconciled herself to being a widow for the rest of her life, and that was that.

"Hey," Hailey whispered. "Are you okay?"

Cynthia forced a quick smile. The one that insisted she was fine even if she wasn't.

"I'm perfect. Thanks so much for the coffee — and for watching Joey."

Hailey smiled. "My pleasure."

Which left Cynthia no option but to stride across the porch, over the lawn, and behind the barn to reach a rocky outcrop — a place perfect for taking off and landing.

Usually, her dragon would be pushing to escape to the skies. But all the way over, she dragged her feet and fretted. About leaving Joey, for starters. About Cal. Because Silas — drat him — had agreed to let the wolf shifter stay.

There may be more afoot than we know, he'd explained when he dropped in earlier. *And I believe he can help us defeat the enemy.*

Cynthia frowned into the balmy night. An unseen enemy who might be planning an attack on beautiful Maui at any time.

"Cal," she whispered into the night.

Why, why, why? Of all the people fate could have sent to protect Joey, why him? She already had an entire Special Forces team on her side, not to mention their equally fierce and protective mates. Did she really need Cal?

Of course we need him, her dragon insisted. *The way he needs us.*

Her steps faltered, but she pushed on, shedding layers as she walked. A dark shadow swooped overhead, barely making a sound, but a voice sounded clearly in her mind.

Ready to fly?

It was Jenna, as exuberant as ever. Cynthia looked up wistfully. Ah, to have been born the daughter of a surfer, footloose and fancy-free.

"I'll be right there," Cynthia called softly.

She held out her arms, shifting as she walked. She spread her fingers wide, letting the folds of skin between them stretch until she was sporting a pair of leathery wings. Scents grew sharper and more layered as she shifted, and her keen dragon eyes caught the slightest movement in the shadows. When she hopped onto the rocky outcrop, she nearly released a thunderous call into the night. A dragon clan as ancient as hers had every right to bellow their presence to the world, or so she'd been taught. But she forced herself to cough away the instinctive call. Her fortunes had changed, and she couldn't go announcing herself like a queen.

Just a princess, her dragon sighed.

She flexed her legs, flicked her tail, and sprang into the air, reminding herself not to get all snooty about that. Her family had left Europe generations ago, so the *princess* part was a stretch, at best. And even if it was easy to feel superior to most folks on earth when she was up in the air, that wasn't the way things worked. Cal, Connor, and the others had taught her that honor and dignity weren't qualities exclusive to noble clans. Birth was an accident, and shifters born in ordinary — or even adverse — circumstances could prove themselves more noble than those born into privilege and power.

She shot toward the moon with a few powerful beats of her wings. Whatever legacy she left in life, it would be one she earned with her own blood, sweat, and tears.

Her dragon snorted. *Well, we've got the tears part nailed.*

She flew faster, trying to outrun ugly memories. Opening her mouth, she spat fire into the inky night. Just a thin stream so as not to be noticed by any humans who happened to be out that evening.

In the distance, a burst of fire lit the sky, and she tensed. But it was only Kilauea, a simmering volcano way over on the Big Island. The behemoth had been active over the past months, and the huge ash cloud it sent up was as clear as a beacon marked by little outbursts of fire.

Fire. Like the passion that used to burn between us and Cal, her dragon moped.

Then, *whoosh!* Jenna dive-bombed past Cynthia's right wingtip, chasing those thoughts out of her mind. It was time to train, not to feel sorry for herself.

She sped after Jenna, looping and twisting in the air every time her fellow dragon dodged or rolled. It was exhilarating. Freeing. Empowering.

And not at all ladylike, her dragon grinned.

Jenna twisted to nip at her wingtip, but Cynthia veered right.

Good, Connor's voice boomed in her mind. The big green-brown dragon hovered to one side, studying their moves the way a boxing coach might. He'd been helping them train ever since Tessa had stopped joining them, making vague excuses.

Jenna had winked to Cynthia about that. *I bet she's pregnant — just not quite ready to announce it.*

If that was true, it would be great news. Tessa and Kai, the dragons from Koa Point, had been hoping to start a family for ages. Because shifting could harm an unborn baby, Tessa would be constrained to human form for another few months.

Cynthia hoped Jenna was right. She trained even harder, fueled more than ever before by a desire to protect her pack.

That move you just used worked fine, Connor said. *But there's an even better trick you should learn. Jenna, come and repeat that with me so I can demonstrate, okay?*

With pleasure. Jenna chuckled, shooting up toward him.

Cynthia pursed her lips. Jenna and Connor made great coaches, but the mated pair had a way of turning every move into a sensual dance. Still, she studied them closely.

Like this, Connor said when Jenna nipped at his wing. Instead of jolting away from her, he folded his wing tightly and rolled, dropping directly beneath Jenna. Then he flicked his wings open and shot upward, spitting fire at her belly. Just a tiny little spark, barely enough to tickle his mate. In a real fight, he would release an inferno that would inflict major damage.

And if that doesn't finish off the enemy, you do this, he said, dashing for Jenna's neck. But instead of attacking, he nuzzled her, and they both erupted into hearty coughs of dragon laughter. Cynthia sighed and turned away to practice the move. Once Connor and Jenna went goo-goo eyed, it was hard to get their attention back.

Sure enough, after a few more halfhearted maneuvers, Jenna cleared her throat and swooped off to the right.

Um, I think I left the kettle on at home.

We'd better check that, for sure, Connor agreed, following right on her heels.

Cynthia watched them go. Within minutes, the couple was bound to be back at their rocky lair, locked in the throes of passion. But who was she to spoil the fun of a couple of giddy lovers?

That used to be us, her dragon mourned, replaying images from the past. Such as a younger version of herself squeaking and clutching Cal's waist as he revved his motorcycle along a leaf-covered New England road in fall. The wind whipped at her pink scarf, and Cal's body heat made her nestle closer to nuzzle his neck.

She scanned the ground, unconsciously checking for wolf tracks. Then she swooped over the rooftop of her home exactly the way her father used to do when she was a kid. That memory, she smiled at, thinking of how she would lie in bed, counting the days until she could be a mighty dragon too.

She let out a bittersweet huff. Fate didn't always let things unfold the way they ought to have.

But I am a mighty dragon, her inner beast insisted, admiring the golden wings stretched out at her sides.

Cynthia didn't bother answering. How mighty was a dragon who hid out on a private estate, dependent on the help of her friends?

Then she caught herself. As a mother, her priority wasn't about showing off her power. It was to keep her son happy, healthy, and safe.

She circled the plantation house a second time then headed north, climbing over the jagged West Maui mountains. Finally, she glided out over the ocean, reminding herself of what the newest member of her mixed shifter pack would say.

The world is full of love and beauty.

33

Cynthia repeated Sophie's words as she slowly looped back. Love and beauty. For Joey's sake, she had to remember that. And, heck. Maui made it easy to keep in mind, with its dramatic skyline, swaying palms, and long strips of golden sand.

As she flew back over the plantation, ready to call it a night, a movement drew her attention to a rocky point. When she made out a lone wolf, her heart leaped. It wasn't Chase or Sophie, nor Boone or Nina, the wolves from Koa Point.

Cal, her dragon cried.

In her excitement, she nearly flew over, but she observed from a distance instead. The wind direction was in her favor, and Cal hadn't spotted her yet. Which meant he probably hadn't been watching her fly, and part of her mourned. When they'd first met, they'd made a game of going out at night in their different animal forms. She would soar through the skies while Cal loped along the ground. Eventually, they'd meet on a hilltop and circle each other a few times, then set off again and continue the tease. Eventually, they would shift back into human form and let the fun take a sensual turn.

She inhaled deeply, hating that she sounded like an old maid in a rocking chair. The kind who sighed and said, *Those were the days.*

Cal lifted his muzzle, and that was like the good old days, too. But instead of howling in glee, he let out a long, mournful cry. To human ears, the sounds were nearly indistinguishable, but she'd learned the difference, and it gutted her. His howl was lonely and devoid of hope. Resigned and empty instead of proud and optimistic, the way it used to be. Had she caused that?

She let out a tiny puff of hot air, reminding herself that Cal hadn't kept the promise they'd made to remain true to each other to the end of their days, no matter what. The moment she'd been forced to leave him, he'd taken off and shacked up with the first she-wolf who'd come along. Some tramp named Sheila, or so Cynthia had heard.

She beat the air with her wings, putting distance between her and Cal – or between her and the past. Whichever. It was time to get home to her son and to the new pack she had worked so hard to become co-alpha of. It didn't matter that her soul was crying or that her heart felt like it had just been stabbed all over again. That was all part of her old life, and she had finally succeeded in starting anew.

She glided in the slow circle, murmuring to herself the whole time.

A new start... A new start...

Sure. Go ahead and pretend, her dragon sighed.

Lining up her landing, she checked the wind one more time. Then she curled her wingtips, lowered her tail, and stuck out her talons. Moments later, she came to a skipping landing not far from where she had taken off. Then she held her wings wide and shook them before shifting back to human form. When she pulled on her clothes, every layer felt like a piece of armor being fitted into place. Back she went to being cool, aloof Cynthia, co-alpha of this pack. A person who couldn't be seen moping around.

Not moping, her dragon insisted. *Trying to find a way to make things work with Cal.*

"Well, it won't work," she said, striding toward the house.

That led her past the barn, where the door was ajar. Somebody had left the light on inside.

"What, again?" she muttered, glad to have something else to fuss about. She stepped inside and headed to the workbench to turn off the light. But before she could, something glinted, catching her eye. She stopped short as moonlight shone off chrome — Cal's beaten-up Triumph.

Her pulse skipped. Just looking at the classic lines of the Thruxton brought back so much. How many times had she ridden on the back of that bike? Her arms tight around Cal's waist, her cheek warm against his back...

So many good times, her dragon whispered.

Riding with Cal had always been an escape from the stiff, proper world in which she'd been raised. They'd broken speed limits and made too much noise. They'd ridden roads marked *No Trespassing* to reach hilltops where they could lie back and count the stars. With Cal, anything seemed possible – even the impossibility of their love.

35

Then she remembered Cal zooming out of her life on that bike, and her shoulders stiffened. That had been the last time she'd seen him, a week before the ceremony in which she was forced to bond with the dragon shifter her parents had chosen for her. Had Cal gone straight to Sheila that night?

She bowed her head, fighting the lump in her throat. An owl hooted outside, telling her...

Telling me what? she wanted to yell. Should she swallow her pride and grab the chance to love Cal again, or should she defend the walls she'd built around her heart?

Grab the chance, her dragon whispered.

She glanced at his motorcycle then froze, spotting the pink scarf wrapped around the handlebars. The one she'd given him the very first night they met. It was a ragged mess now, and more brown than pink. The ends were frayed, and it was splattered with mud. But it was still there. Why hadn't he ripped off that old thing?

Because he still loves us, her dragon said. *Always has, always will.*

Cynthia's knees wobbled. Never had she felt more ashamed of what she'd been forced to do, nor felt such regret. What if Cal hadn't given up on her, even though she'd given up on herself?

But what about Sheila? she wanted to protest.

We heard that Cal took off with her, but we don't know for sure, her dragon pointed out. *Ask him. You'll see.*

She fingered her necklace, trying to take comfort from the smooth, familiar surface of her pearls. The middle one, she rubbed extra hard. Something was wrong with that one — it was turning a pale, burnished blue. Or was that just the moonlight?

The soft pad of footsteps sounded behind her, and she whirled.

"Cal," she breathed, staring at the wolf standing at the barn door.

He was just as dark and dashing as ever. Just as big and wiry, and just as defiant. In short, exactly the wolf shifter she had fallen in love with, right down to the tiny scar on his lip.

The only real change was the burn scars — and the cloud of sorrow he carried with him.

The wolf glanced between her and the Triumph, and she could sense him remembering too. All the good times, all the hopes... and all the regrets. They stared at each other for a few minutes, eyes glowing, saying more than they ever could in words.

I wish...

I want...

I missed you so much, it hurts.

But just when she was sure Cal would shift into human form and speak, the wolf gave himself a firm shake and padded wordlessly off into the night.

Cynthia opened and closed her mouth, fishing for words. But really, what was there to say?

How about, I still miss you, Cal, her dragon whispered. *I still love you. Can you ever forgive me?*

She couldn't get so much as a peep past her too-proud lips, but she did rush forward to watch him lope silently off. She found herself clutching the sliding barn door, holding herself back from running after him. What was over was over, and that was that.

It was never over, her dragon cried.

The wolf shot her one last, sad look then moved on. His path took him through a shaft of moonlight, and she watched him slip from darkness to light and back to darkness before disappearing for good.

Cynthia drooped against the barn doors, feeling lower, lonelier, and more lost than she had ever been.

Mate, her dragon whispered. *That wolf is my mate.*

Chapter Five

Cal selected a piece of ironwood, settled back on the tree stump he was using as a stool, and went back to whittling. A moment later, he wiped his brow and looked around, holding back a sigh. His second day on Maui. The first had been hard enough, but this was shaping up to be a doozy too. Everyone was eyeing him like he was a traitor, and every time Cynthia walked by, his body felt on fire.

He shouldn't have come. Why torture himself?

Silas's words echoed in his mind. *Leave now, and go in peace. Or stay, and work with us to protect Cynthia and her son.*

He swung his jaw from side to side. He was in Maui to see things through, dammit. No matter how much it hurt.

Timber, the bear shifter, was sawing a sheet of plywood not too far away. Chase, the wolf, was chopping wood. At least, that's what they pretended to do while keeping an eye on Cal. If it hadn't been for Silas ordering everyone to leave him be, they'd probably run him the hell out of there. As it was, suspicion hung in the air like an invisible fog, but Cal just sighed. All his life, he'd turned heads as the big, bad wolf shifter from the wrong side of the tracks. A little uncouth, a little unkempt, and a lot rebel. The kind of guy who made people jump to conclusions about how much danger he posed.

Well, let them think what they wanted. He was here to protect Cynthia, and that was that.

He searched through the woodpile until he finally found a long, straight branch that might work better than the first. He tested its weight, balance, and strength. Yes, that one just might do. Settling back again, he laid the stake across his knees and started whittling a sharp point at one end. The set of his mouth grew more and more grim as he pictured the task he had in mind for it. How much time would pass before he was forced to use it? He glanced at the sky, wishing for some sign from above. Would he finally rid the world of the evil that had been hounding Cynthia for so long?

Sophie, the she-wolf, gave a friendly wave as she walked by. Anjali was with her, holding a blond baby that looked a lot like Dell.

"Hello, Cal. Did you have a good night?" Anjali called.

He could sense the men tense up. It was just like the previous evening — the women of Koakea were willing to give him a chance, but the men were ready to rip him apart.

"Couldn't ask for more," he murmured.

Tim and Chase exchanged looks, which was fine with Cal. He wasn't there to make friends. He just needed them to give him space and to do their part in keeping Cynthia safe. And from the looks of it, they were doing a pretty damn good job. He'd prowled the perimeter of the property early that morning — hounded by that overly zealous lion shifter the entire time — and confirmed his impression that the defenses were solid. The shifters kept a constant lookout, and there wasn't an amateur among them.

Still, no one could rest easy, even in a place like this. He looked out over the sea. That land-water boundary was a mixed blessing. On one hand, it formed its own line of defense, what with the fringing reef and surf. On the other, the sea could be used as an avenue of surprise attack. So could the mountains on the inland side. It didn't take much to imagine a squadron of dragons swooping in out of the blue, Pearl Harbor-style.

He scanned the jagged ridges, making a mental note of rocky outcrops that might suit his purpose. Later that day, he'd head out for a closer look. Scouting was the first step. Establishing extra defenses – and arming them – was the second, and who knew how much time he had?

He bent over the wood and whittled faster.

Dell laughed as he walked past. "Don't tell me you're planning to take down a couple of dragons by hand."

Cal didn't bother looking up when Dell's footsteps came to a sudden halt.

"Are you crazy, man? You can't slay dragons with darts."

Cal kept on whittling, and finally, the lion shifter sauntered off, muttering, "I think he really is crazy."

Cal snorted. No, he wasn't crazy. Not *too* crazy, at least.

"Heya, Joey," Dell called.

Cal's head snapped up. He hadn't seen much of Cynthia's son the previous day. But there he was, a little redhead with bright green eyes. The spitting image of Barnaby.

Cut that out, Cal ordered his inner wolf when it started to growl. *That's just the kid, not Barnaby.*

The man who stole our mate, his wolf growled.

He gritted his teeth, getting himself under control. He'd despised Barnaby, going so far as toying with the idea of murdering the guy. He'd come close too, sneaking into Barnaby's office to catch him unawares. That was a year after Cal had been forced to leave Cynthia, when everything had seemed so clear.

Kill Barnaby. Find Cynthia, his wolf had insisted. *Race her off to the farthest corner of the world where we can finally live in peace.*

But Barnaby, damn him, had simply rotated his huge leather chair and spoken casually.

"Mr. Zydler. I've been expecting you."

Cal's jaw had nearly dropped, but he'd done his best to fake nonchalance.

"That must mean you're expecting to die, too."

Strangely, it hadn't appeared as if Barnaby resented the notion much. After looking Cal over once, he'd waved to a chair.

"Take a seat. Please." Barnaby's voice had been weary, his eyes pained.

Cal had obeyed, mostly out of curiosity. He could listen first and kill later. That would be fine too.

At first, Barnaby just sat there, silently regarding the books that filled the floor-to-ceiling shelves. Most of them were old, leather-bound volumes, making the place smell like a goddamn library. Books on shifters, science, history — you name it. Cal spotted an entire section devoted to ancient Rome, and his wolf snorted. Not one book on engine repair, not a tool in sight. Didn't dragons concern themselves with real-world problems?

But finally, Barnaby spoke. Slowly at first, then faster and ever more passionately. The more he revealed, the more Cal's astonishment grew, and the more his assumptions crumbled.

Barnaby wasn't the arrogant ass Cal had thought him to be. He was just as reluctant about mating with Cynthia as she had been. Of course, Cal would have been happy to kill him anyway. But then Barnaby had uttered four words that would change everything.

"I need your help."

Cal had snorted and waved around the man's opulent office. Barnaby ran a business worth millions of dollars. He owned an estate in Connecticut that came with a stable and private guards. Hell, the dragon shifter could hire an army of mercenaries if he chose.

"What do you need me for?"

"To protect the woman I love. I do love her," Barnaby added quickly. "If not in the way you'd expect."

Cal might have scoffed, but Barnaby went on, laying it all out. All the hidden intricacies of the dragon world — details Cal had never even guessed at. All the feuds, all the vendettas gradually coming to a head. The tightening noose Barnaby sensed closing around his world. A great new force was rising in the dragon world, and even a shifter as well-connected as Barnaby had to be on guard.

"Believe me, I'd love to hunt Drax down and fight him myself."

Barnaby's fingers had flexed, and it was easy to picture them turning into claws and tearing into Drax, the ruthless dragon intent on dominating the shifter world.

"But I can't," he finished. "I have Cynthia to think of now — and our little one."

A shock wave had thundered through Cal's body. Cynthia was pregnant? With another man's child?

If he'd thought his world had fallen apart the previous year, he'd been wrong. His wolf howled inside, and he'd come close to falling to his knees. Cynthia living with Barnaby was bad enough. But Cynthia bearing Barnaby's child... The two of them would be bound together in a way that could never be undone.

"Yes, our little one," Barnaby had murmured. A bitter-sweet smile played across his lips, but the *bitter* outweighed the *sweet*, and Cal had to wonder why.

Then Barnaby cleared his throat and went on. "In any case, our enemies are multiplying. Worse, they are turning to methods we dragons have never stooped to before."

For the first time, disdain crept into Barnaby's voice, and a little bit of old-world arrogance showed. He scratched at the leather blotter on his desk with nails that lengthened in front of Cal's eyes, gouging the soft material.

"I need your help," Barnaby repeated, sounding more reso-lute than ever. "I will not soil the family name by stooping to such means myself, but I am willing to adopt... shall we say, unconventional weapons?"

Cal's eyes had just about popped out of his head. Did Barnaby mean him?

He'd barely caught the rest of what Barnaby had said that night. Cynthia really was lost to him forever. But he would always love her, and that meant protecting her.

Doesn't mean we can't kill Barnaby, his wolf had tried one more time.

But he'd extinguished that fantasy immediately. Killing Barnaby would make Cynthia's child an orphan, and that was wrong, no matter how badly his wolf cried for revenge.

That unexpected encounter had turned into the strangest evening of Cal's life — one that threw him into a whole new level of turmoil. But instead of drowning in emotions as he had over the previous year, he'd discovered a new purpose in life: protecting Cynthia. She might never find out about his secret role, and that hurt. But nothing mattered as long as she was all right.

Cal blinked in the soft, tropical light of Maui and focused on the child approaching him. Joey. Just seeing the boy made his heart ache.

The little redhead skipped across the driveway, circled by a hyperactive dog. Cal silently did the math in his head. Joey had to be going on six. The "little one" Barnaby had referred to at their first meeting, over a decade back, had been miscarried early on, and Joey had only come along years later.

"Buzz and I played catch," Joey called to Chase, looking happy as can be. Then he caught sight of Cal and walked over.

The air went perfectly still, the way it might in the Old West when a gunslinger walked into town and everyone in the streets scattered — including the dog, who took one look at Cal and ran off with his tail between his legs. Everyone, in short, except that one innocent kid who didn't know enough to get the hell away.

Well, if anyone thought Cal posed a danger to the kid, they were wrong. He'd saved the kid's life — twice, in fact, even if neither Cynthia nor the boy knew it.

"What are you doing?" Joey asked, coming right up to the point of Cal's stick.

Cal stared, amazed that such innocence still existed in the world. Not only did he have a six-inch blade in his hand, he had the makings of a pretty sturdy spear, but the kid didn't consider either a threat. Which, Cal supposed, reflected well on Cynthia and her friends. The boy had every right to grow up suspicious and afraid. But somehow, they had managed to let Joey be a kid.

"Wow." Joey leaned in, studying the point of the spear. "Can I touch it?"

"Not sure your mom would like that," Cal murmured, glancing toward the men ready to rip him to shreds.

His mind spun, and his stomach flipped. It was crazy, the effect that child had on him. Joey was a living legacy of the man Cal had tried – and failed – to hate. The symbol of destiny laughing in his face. At the same time, that child was the most precious thing in Cynthia's world.

"Whatcha making?"

"Just messing around," Cal bluffed.

He set the spear down, making sure to keep the point away from the child. Then he picked up a forked branch. Within seconds, he had the branch cut down to a size that would fit in the kid's hand. Joey watched, fascinated. Cal smoothed the edges, figuring the kid's hands weren't half as callused as his, and cut two slits into the ends of the Y. Then he motioned over to the shelf built into the barn.

"Get me that big rubber band, will you?"

Why his voice was so gritty, he had no clue. It was just a kid, for goodness' sake.

Joey skipped over on command, and Cal watched his every move. The boy didn't have a hint of Cynthia in him. Not on the outside, anyway — not with that flaming red hair and toothy grin.

"This one?" Joey called.

Cal cleared his throat. "Yeah. That'll be fine."

The kid scampered back so eagerly, it frightened Cal. It wouldn't take much for an enemy to trick this child and do who knew what. No wonder the other men looked ready to pounce.

"Hold it out, will you?"

Joey did as he was told, stretching the rubber band. Cal carefully cut it, exaggerating his movements to show he was moving the blade away from the kid. The last thing he needed was for the shifters around him to spring into animal form and attack. The kid would be terrified, for one thing.

"Okay. Now, we do this. . . " He tied one end of the rubber band to the left branch of the stick.

It was funny, how a simple movement could dredge memories out of a man's mind. More often than not, they were bad ones. But this time, Cal smiled. His father was an utter deadbeat, but his uncle had always been calm, quiet, and patient. Out of nowhere, Cal had a flashback of crouching by his uncle's knee, watching him whittle just like Joey did. Cal even found himself uttering the same words his uncle had once used.

"Now, we stretch that side over there..."

"A slingshot!" Joey clapped in delight.

"Yep," Cal said, just as coolly as his uncle once had. "You want to try it out?" The kid nodded eagerly. "Well then, go find yourself a rock." Cal jutted his elbow out to point.

The moment Joey's eyes caught on Cal's arm, the redhead's bright eyes went wide.

"Wow. You have a lot of scars."

The fact that Cal's heart started pounding harder had less to do with the remark than with the fact that Cynthia walked up at exactly that time.

"Sweetie, it's not nice to say things like that," she said, gently touching her son's shoulder.

Cal peered up into those amazing black eyes. *Cynthia*, he wanted to whisper. *Can we talk? Please?*

But instead, he shook his head and murmured, "I don't mind."

"How did you get them?" Joey asked, entranced.

Cal mulled that one over. He couldn't exactly say, *Fighting dragons.* Not to a kid who'd lost his father in a dragon attack.

"Just a burn. Now, did you find some ammo for your slingshot?"

Joey squeaked and jumped back into action, scouring the ground.

"Joey, honey..." Cynthia called.

"It's okay," Cal whispered, as much to himself as to her. Because damn, his hands were a little shaky, and his voice was about to crack, just from being close to Cynthia. A damn good thing Joey came running back with a couple rocks a moment later.

"Okay. The first rule is never to point your slingshot at anything you can hurt or break. It's just for fun, okay?" Cal said.

Joey nodded, and the deep furrows in Cynthia's brow eased slightly.

"You load it like this, and then you pull it back like this." Cal demonstrated, then handed the slingshot over.

The kid took it with a look of such delight that the achy, conflicted feelings in Cal's chest eased. He grabbed a can of nails and set it down a few paces away. Then he walked back to Joey and pointed.

"See if you can hit that. But make sure you check that nobody gets in the way."

Joey nodded and drew back the slingshot, focusing intently. Cal watched, fascinated. Maybe the kid did have a little bit of Cynthia in him, after all.

Joey's first shot missed by a mile, but Cal shrugged. "I couldn't get it my first time either. It takes practice, that's all."

He picked up a rock and motioned for Joey to give him the slingshot. Then he took aim, doing it slowly so the kid could watch.

"When you release, make sure you keep your fingers clear so it can fly straight."

He released and, *bing!* The rock bounced off the can and tumbled across the driveway.

Joey looked on in awe. "Wow. You're good."

Cal hid a smile. If only the kid knew how accurate his shot was or the size of the targets he'd managed to take down.

Walking out again, Cal dragged his boot through the gravel, marking a wide circle around the can.

"Try again. Five points if you get inside the circle, and ten points if you hit the can."

Cynthia tilted her head, looking at him in a way that was hard to decipher. Cal turned away quickly, telling himself not to think too hard.

Joey let another stone fly, and Cal nodded. "Five points. Way to go, man."

Joey looked pleased as punch, and the other men smiled, too. Were they finally getting that Cal wasn't the enemy?

"This is fun," Joey announced.

Cal's gaze traveled across the driveway and down the gentle green slopes. It was fun, actually. The sun was shining, the air was scented with tropical flowers, and nobody was threatening to kill him — for now, at least. Koakea was a nice place, especially for shifters, who had a closer link to Mother Earth than most humans did. It was a nice place to raise a kid too.

Cal glanced at Joey. The poor kid had lost his father, but he had a loving mom and, from the looks of it, several doting uncle types. He lived in a beautiful, quiet place, sheltered from the dangers of the shifter world.

But a cloud passed over the sun, casting a shadow, and Cal frowned. It didn't matter how sunny or warm a place was. Danger could strike anywhere, anytime.

Hailey came up and motioned Cynthia over with a question of some kind.

"You could make a really big slingshot. A bunch of them," Joey said, grinning. "And put them all around, so if the bad guys come, we could get them."

Cal froze for a moment, then covered up with a weak smile. "I guess you could."

Smart kid, his wolf murmured.

"Like up there." Joey pointed to a cliff.

The others had tuned in to Hailey's conversation with Cynthia, so Cal leaned closer to Joey and jutted his chin. "There's a better spot. See that ledge? Now that would be the perfect place to position your defenses. Don't you think?"

God, he was pushing his luck. But, hell. It felt good to hint at this plan, even if it was just to a kid.

Joey nodded a mile a minute.

Of course, we'd need different ammo, Cal's wolf hummed.

And just like that, his mind veered off into all the preparations he had to get moving with. More spears. Parts for the weapon he planned to build. More—

"Joey, sweetie," Cynthia called.

Cal snapped his eyes back to the ground before he gave anything away.

"It's time for some schoolwork. I promise you can play with the slingshot as soon as we're done."

To Cal's surprise, Joey didn't so much as groan. He just took his mother's hand and fell into step beside her. "What are we doing today?"

"Some math, some spelling..." Cynthia said.

Cal looked from Cynthia to her son. Homeschooling, huh? It figured. One, because whatever Cynthia did, she liked having control over. Two, because she did a damn good job at anything she set her hand to, and being *supermom* was right up her alley. And three, she couldn't send her son to a regular school, where he would be vulnerable to enemy shifters.

Cal's chest tightened. His childhood hadn't been a barrel of laughs, but he'd had his freedom. He looked at Cynthia and Joey, finding himself mourning for them both. Cynthia's childhood had been just as restricted as Joey's. Was that why she had reveled in the time they'd shared?

If I tasted freedom, it wasn't for long, her sad eyes reminded him.

But to Joey, she said, "After spelling, we'll read our book."

"Yay!" Joey smiled. "The history of dragons."

Cal tilted his head and caught Cynthia's eye. *Seriously?*

She turned away, leading Joey by the hand. "That's right. Let's go."

"Bye," Joey called, waving as he went.

When the pair disappeared around the corner, Dell walked over to put away the can of nails. Then he paused next to Cal, looking slightly less murderous than before.

"She's seriously teaching him all that dragon bullshit?" Cal asked.

Cynthia had once confided how she'd been forced to memorize dragon histories that went back for thousands of years. She'd even recited noble dragon bloodlines to him one night after making love. They'd laughed about it at the time, but he couldn't summon a sense of humor now.

Dell sighed. "Yep. But we've gotten her to cut homeschooling hours down from four hours a day to two, so that's progress. Poor kid."

Cal looked at the lion shifter, who was just about his height and weight, though the bun Dell wore his golden hair in made him appear an inch taller.

Dell flashed a smile. "You're good with Joey, I'll give you that." His eyes darkened. "But one false move..."

Cal stuck up his hands. "No false moves from me." Then he scanned the skies and muttered, "But, yeah. Don't let down your guard."

Chapter Six

Cynthia flew over the plantation grounds, eyeing the ground below. Days had passed since she'd heard Cal's haunting howl, and she'd been out every night since, looking for him.

No, wait. She'd been out every night honing her fighting skills, right?

Sure, her dragon murmured. *Right.*

Well, the fighting part wasn't entirely a lie since she really had been out sparring. She'd even caught Jenna off guard often enough for her friend to go wide-eyed and say, *Wow. You're getting really good. You must be more of a natural than you thought.*

Even Connor had been impressed. *Holy crap, Cynthia. Have you been training on the side?*

No, she hadn't, but she'd been reading up on aerial combat in a book she'd borrowed from Silas's library and rehearsing the moves in her mind. Cal's arrival had heightened an inexplicable instinct to be prepared — something she'd felt for a while, but never as urgently as now.

Prepared for what? she kept asking herself.

But neither instinct nor destiny bothered filling her in. They just left her worried, wondering.

A gust of wind funneled between the mountains, and without thinking, she dipped, rolled, and shot off to one side. Then she blinked, realizing what she had done.

Wow. Maybe Jenna was right. She really had mastered her new moves. She glanced down toward the plantation house. When she pictured a foe swooping in, she couldn't help spitting fire, if only briefly. She would never allow anyone to harm her son.

Once upon a time, that *anyone* had been Drax, the ruthless dragon who had murdered Barnaby and other members of the shifter establishment. Silas had finally killed Drax, putting an end to that evil. But a new force had arisen in Drax's place — his mistress, Moira, who was growing ever bolder in her bid to rule the shifter world. Moira had gone so far as to stage several attacks on the shifters of Koakea, and it seemed only a question of time before her attacks escalated.

At the same time, a whole new threat was rising with the influx of evil dragons from the Old World.

Cynthia allowed herself to spit a little more fire. She wouldn't let anyone harm her son. Not Moira, nor her henchmen, nor Kravik. And if they so much as tried. . .

For the next few minutes, she kept a sharp lookout and practiced her moves. Far in the distance, something glowed red, and she couldn't help but picture dragon fire. But that was just Kilauea — the volcano over on the Big Island, putting on another display of Mother Earth's power.

She turned her attention to the landscape below. A dark shape moved on the north end of the estate, and her heart rate rose. Was Cal out roaming on four feet? When she flew closer, she spotted Tim, lumbering around in bear form. She dipped her right wing and cut away, feeling foolish. She wasn't a love-struck twenty-year-old any more.

But the moment she caught sight of a shadow in the hills above the plantation house, her pulse skipped, and her spirits soared.

Cal. Her dragon cheered. *It's him.*

She headed for the mountains, flying at low altitude so as not to be seen. Then she circled around, watching.

It was Cal, and he was getting ready to howl again. She could tell from the way he braced himself on those massive paws and squared his shoulders. Then he took a deep breath, lifted his muzzle, and howled.

Aroooo. . .

The sound was long. Low. Mournful. His voice didn't just sound sad — it was tragic. Every stretched-out note gutted her. Full of pain, sorrow, and regret. So much, she nearly joined in.

We could have had a life together, her dragon whispered. *We could have had it all.*

Cal's voice cracked then steadied as his lament went on. *Aroooo...*

Cynthia bowed her head. Why had fate brought her and Cal together all those years ago, only to tear them apart? And why had it reunited them now that it was too late?

Dragons didn't cry, but her eyes sure did burn.

It's not too late, her dragon insisted. *It can't be.*

Aroooo...

Cal held on to another long note, giving his years of suffering a voice. But suddenly, he snapped around to peer south. His ears perked up, and one of his paws lifted off the ground.

Cynthia blinked, following his eyes. What had he sensed?

An instant later, Cal took off down the slope. Cynthia followed, keeping her distance. What had set him off? And why was he sprinting toward the center of the grounds? Sprinting toward her house, in fact.

At first, she watched, curious. Then his urgency jumped over to her, and a growing sense of fear made her joints tense.

Joey! she cried as Cal made a beeline for her house.

Precious seconds ticked by before she managed to shoot off in pursuit. Had Cal detected an intruder? Worse, was he after Joey? Her heart thudded as she raced along. But Cal had just enough of a head start to arrive at the house before her, and he sprinted up the front steps in wolf form.

"Hey!" Hailey shouted, jolting out of a chair. The hand she reached toward Cal started turning into a bear paw, but by then, the wolf was inside.

Fueled by a burst of adrenaline only a mother could summon, Cynthia rushed after Cal. The moment she touched down on the front lawn, she shifted and ran into the house. Up the porch steps, then the inside steps, where she hurried past Hailey.

Cal, stop! she wanted to scream, but her throat had seized up. He was sprinting right for Joey's bedroom.

"Mommy!" Joey cried.

The wolf burst in a moment later, and time slowed down for Cynthia. Every step stretched into the quagmire of eternity, the way it did in nightmares.

"Joey!" she screamed.

She reached, ready to turn her hand into a dragon's claw to fight the enemy — whether that turned out to be an intruder or Cal. But when she reached the open doorway of Joey's bedroom, she froze.

"Joey?" she whispered.

Cal was there, still in wolf form, right by Joey's bed. No intruder in sight, just her son, flailing in the throes of a bad dream.

"Mommy," he wailed in his sleep.

The blankets had fallen to the floor, and Cal brushed up against Joey's body — comforting her son, not threatening him. When the floorboards creaked under her uncertain step, Cal whirled and bared his teeth. Huge, ivory teeth that glinted in the shaft of moonlight illuminating the dim room. A drop of saliva extended from his canines, and the hair along his back stood in a sharp ridge.

Most of the time she'd spent with Cal, he'd been a surprisingly fun, tender lover, if a little short on the kind of social graces her family would approve of. She'd only seen Cal angry — really angry — a few times, and mostly when his possessive, alpha side came out to protect her around other men. But she'd never seen him look as murderous as now.

Come one step closer to this child, and you will die, his eyes dared.

She stared.

I will lay down my life for this child, those wolf eyes said.

An instant later, his eyes softened as he recognized it was her and not an intruder. Then they hardened again when Hailey appeared at the door in bear form.

Cal growled. Hailey chuffed a grizzly warning. Joey tossed in his sleep. Cynthia's hands fluttered in the air, not knowing whom to calm down first.

"It's okay," she assured the others before running to Joey. She fell to her knees and hugged his slight, sweaty body. "It's all right, sweetie. Mommy's here."

Her heart was tearing apart at the seams. Joey was afraid. Cal ached for something he could never have, and as for her... It was a good thing she had Joey to comfort. Otherwise, she might have broken into sobs as all the hopes and shattered dreams of the past hit her again.

Cal nudged the blanket toward Joey, and Cynthia spread it over her son.

"Everything is all right, sweetie. Everything is all right."

But it wasn't all right, because her heart was breaking all over again. All the more when Cal huddled his furry flank against her side.

Hailey chuffed in a question, but Cynthia waved her hand. "It's all right. We're good."

If Hailey had asked her who *we* meant, Cynthia would have been hard-pressed to answer. Her and Joey? Her and Cal? All three of them? That shouldn't be possible, because Joey represented everything that had driven her and Cal apart — as well as everything destined to keep them apart forever.

Joey flung his thin arms around her neck, crying. "Mommy. The bad dragons were back."

Cal tensed and sniffed the air as she rocked Joey.

"It's okay, sweetie. It was just a dream. Daddy fought the bad dragons, and they'll never come back."

The moment she said *Daddy*, Cal edged away, and the warm, powerful presence that had reassured her ebbed.

"Never?" Joey whimpered.

She gulped and cast an eye toward Cal, whose wary look asked the same thing.

Never would be lying, but she had to comfort Joey somehow.

"We're safe here, with lots of powerful dragons to protect us. Bears, lions, and tigers. Wolves too."

Her gaze snuck over to Cal, and their eyes locked. She'd meant the wolves of her pack, of course. But the image in her mind included Cal, and the oath in his gaze backed that up.

I will protect your son as I protect you, those smoke-gray eyes said. *With my life.*

Cynthia closed her eyes and went back to rocking Joey. It helped him calm down, and it helped her too.

Are you sure you're all right? Hailey asked, shooting the question into her mind.

Cynthia nodded. Which was definitely fibbing, but heck. Even Hailey couldn't help her now.

False alarm. Thanks so much. We'll be okay, Cynthia replied.

Hailey's hesitant step suggested she was weighing up the danger Cal posed, and again, Cynthia's heart warmed. All her life, she'd been taught that dragons were superior to all other shifters. But few dragons exuded the kind of warmth Hailey and the rest of Cynthia's packmates did. They were so unabashedly loving and loyal, they made her ashamed of her own species. Would a dragon race to the side of another shifter's offspring at the slightest hint of trouble?

She gulped and glanced out the window. At least it was just a nightmare and not the real thing. Then she buried her face in Joey's fair hair and held him tightly, murmuring, "Everything is all right."

Her dragon huffed. *For now, at least.*

Chapter Seven

It took half an hour for Cynthia to get Joey back to sleep. By the time she wandered downstairs, Hailey had gone home, but a dark, brooding form sat on the porch steps, looking at the sky exactly the way the lonely wolf had not too long ago on that rock ledge.

Cynthia leaned on the doorframe, tightening her grip on the robe she'd thrown on. How did she feel about having Cal there? Happy? Sad? Intruded upon — or comforted? She gave up trying to decide. She was too exhausted to feel anything, which was probably a good thing.

Cal had only shifted out of wolf form a few minutes earlier — she could tell from the intense, woodsy scent. As always, silence was his companion. He just nodded and rested his head against the porch banister, watching her.

"You okay?" he murmured so quietly, the words were a whisper on the wind.

She hugged her robe closer. Dear, sweet Cal. Saying something for her sake, not his. She nodded dumbly.

"What about Joey?"

She nodded again. "He's asleep."

Cal's chin bobbed, making her ache. It was an echo of conversations she'd once had with Barnaby. She would come downstairs after tucking in their son and take a seat across from Barnaby, doing her best to resign herself to her fate.

But now Barnaby was gone, and as for fate...

Cynthia gazed at Cal, trying not to think of what might have been.

"Does he get nightmares often?" Cal asked quietly.

Cynthia balled her fists, wishing she could let them fly at the bastards who'd traumatized her son. She nearly said *yes*, too, but when she thought it over, she changed her mind.

"Not so much since we came here," she said, making a mental note to thank Dell and the other men. They'd made Joey feel comfortable and secure from day one. "He's so resilient, it amazes me. This is the first time in a while."

She frowned, thinking it over. Had that been just another dream or some kind of premonition?

Don't be silly, she ordered herself. Still, she might ask Anjali her thoughts on that soon.

Cal stretched as if to stand, and her heart thudded. "Are you leaving?"

He shrugged. "You don't need me, right?"

There was nothing rebellious in his tone, just resignation, and all the ghosts in their past seemed to rattle their chains at the same time.

"You can stay. For a second. I mean, if you want," she said, stopping and starting, not managing to get anything out right.

"What do *you* want?" Cal's voice was low and perfectly even, giving no hint as to which option he preferred.

She took a deep breath. "Stay. Please stay."

The weight of her words surprised her, but Cal simply nodded, giving nothing away.

Cynthia bit her lip as another quiet moment ticked by. Why ask him to stay if she didn't have anything to say?

Because he doesn't need to hear anything, her dragon murmured. *Because it feels good just to have him here.*

It did, and she was too tired to be alarmed by the idea. Too tired, in fact, to think about why she went to the kitchen and returned a moment later with two glasses and a bottle of wine. Then she paused, looking between a nearby chair and the top stair where Cal sat.

Don't be such a prude, her dragon muttered.

She sank down on the top stair, not too close, but not too far from Cal, and held out one of the wineglasses.

"I'm guessing you can use some of this too."

The corner of his mouth curled up. "Does it show?"

She tilted her head. "Does what show?"

His smile stretched as he took the glass, muttering a single word. "Good."

She filled the glass slowly. Was Cal as emotionally drained by the evening — and the past few days — as she was? Or was he just plain old tired after years of wandering the world?

"A nice Spanish burgundy," she noted as if Cal cared.

He accepted the glass with a noncommittal nod. Cynthia sipped her wine, trying to settle down, but her mind was spinning in circles.

"Stop overthinking," Cal murmured, right on cue.

She sighed. "If only I could."

He let a few seconds tick by before gesturing toward the glittering ocean. "Just look."

She tried. She really did. But she couldn't.

"Look at what?"

"At how the light ripples over the water. How it sparkles — like there are stars mixed in with the waves."

The man was a poet, and he didn't even know it. She sighed and watched the light skip over miles of inky water.

"Now close your eyes and listen to the leaves in the trees."

That didn't sound promising, but strangely enough, it worked, and she found herself tuning in to the sound of leaves rustling in the wind, each one setting another off. And slowly — ever so slowly — a sliver of peace wiggled into her soul, pushing away some of the turmoil.

She swirled the wine in her glass and took another sip, then another. The glass was empty before she knew it, and she reached for the bottle. She offered it to Cal first, but he shook his head. His wine consumption correlated to the words he uttered — only a few and far between. She, on the other hand, refilled her glass and drank. It gave her just enough of a buzz to soften the hard edges of exhaustion. When she put the bottle down, her arm brushed Cal's leg, and little tingles ran through her nerves.

"How have you been?" she ventured. Then she tensed. What if he told her how many relationships he'd tried his luck at since they'd broken up?

But Cal didn't share much. Just a single "Okay" that could have meant anything.

"Where have you been?" she tried after another minute ticked past.

He motioned vaguely. "Here and there."

Cynthia studied her hands. Had he remained in the Northeast, or had he toured the entire continent on his bike? Had he been through a string of rocky relationships, or had he stuck with Sheila?

Wherever he'd been and whatever he'd done, it had left his mark on him. His face was a little more weathered, his arms a lot more scarred, his eyes warier than ever.

"What are you really here for, Cal?" she finally asked, waving her glass at the view as if the ocean had swept him in.

Cal seemed mesmerized by the burgundy shadow the moonlight cast through her glass, but she wasn't fooled. The man was thinking. Considering. Deciding how close to keep his cards to his vest.

Close, it seemed, because his face didn't change, and his voice remained perfectly even.

"I'm here to protect you."

She frowned. "From what?"

He shrugged. "Not sure yet. Nothing good, I know that much."

His words weren't the least bit comforting, but the warmth of his leg against hers was. He was still leaning against the banister, which meant she must have encroached on his space. She cast her wineglass a suspicious glance, then shrugged. Back in the day, the two of them had gotten a lot closer than that, right?

Her dragon heaved a dreamy sigh as memories flashed through her mind. *Much closer.*

She could practically see her hands clutch at his bare back and sense the heat of their bodies rise. She could feel the snug fit of her legs around his waist, and best of all, the hard, hot slide of him inside.

Cal downed a mouthful of wine with an audible gulp, setting off another memory. One of his motorcycle swerving and him muttering, *Jesus, lady. Don't do that to me.*

Cynthia coughed, doing her best to push the sensual images away. "I have all the protection I need."

Cal pursed his lips. "Do you?"

She snorted. "You've met Silas, Connor, and the others. . . ."

Cal nodded curtly. "I have, and they're good. Very good."

"But?"

He didn't say a word, so she answered for him. "But no one is as good as you. Is that what you're saying?"

For a split second, his eyes danced, and she could imagine his young, cocky self drawling something like, *You're the one saying it, sweetheart.*

Her blood raced, and she caught herself wishing he would say exactly that. Wishing they could turn back the clock and be the carefree lovers they'd once been.

But Cal's face grew inscrutable again. "I'm just saying, the more, the better. For Joey's sake."

Her brow furrowed. "You're just saying that because you know I'm a sucker for Joey."

"He is your son."

The thought made her tense all over and blurt, "Do you have kids?"

He laughed, though there wasn't a note of humor in the sound. "No."

She felt guilty for feeling relieved — and guilty to realize how Cal must feel that she had a son with someone else. If he loved her as much as she loved him, that had to cut deep.

He loves us. Believe me, he does, her dragon swore.

The grim resolution in Cal's eyes confirmed it, making her feel worse. Without thinking, she cupped Cal's cheek.

"I'm sorry. So sorry." Her throat was so dry, her voice cracked when she spoke.

"For what?"

"For everything."

When he gazed into her eyes, her breath went all shaky, because it was happening again. That warm, fuzzy feeling that possessed her whenever they got close.

Mate, her dragon murmured.

Cal's eyes glowed, and she swore his wolf side was whispering the same thing. *Mate.*

She found herself stroking his rough, stubbly chin like she used to. Leaning closer. Studying the line where the pink of his lips met the weathered bronze of his cheeks.

Cal put his glass behind her and looped an arm over her shoulder. His hand rested gently on her neck as if to guide her closer for a kiss.

"Ask me again," he said in a hoarse whisper.

She barely breathed. "Ask what?"

He shifted slightly, bringing his knee between hers as they sat facing each other on the top step.

"Ask what I've been up to."

Cynthia braced her free hand on the porch, because she was getting all shaky, and that wouldn't do. When she spoke, her words were hushed, almost afraid.

"What have you been up to?"

Cal's eyes glowed the way they did when he was at his most intense. "Missing you. Dreaming of you. Wishing I could go back in time and live it all over again."

She could have hunched over and cried the way she had so many times over the past years. Having two glasses of wine in her system would have helped the tears flow, but she fought the feeling away.

"Ask me what I've been doing all these past years," she whispered.

Cal flashed that sad little half smile. "What have you been doing?"

"Missing you. Dreaming of you. No — dreaming of us. Wishing I could go back in time and live it all over again."

The words tumbled out in a rush, and she found herself frozen in place. Whoa. Had she just said that?

She had, and she meant it. Which she proved by sliding closer and whispering, "Cal..."

If a smile were a cocktail, his would have been two-parts sorrow and one-part regret, poured over enough ice to dull the pain.

"Cynthia..."

His human side formed the word, but she could sense his wolf howling beneath.

She closed her eyes and leaned closer, letting instinct guide her lips. Just when she feared she'd misjudged Cal, their lips met. His were soft in the middle and dry on the edges, like they'd always been. A little chapped from all that time on the bike. He smelled of leather, sandalwood, and just enough wolf to make her heart skip.

More, her dragon begged. *Please, more.*

His lips played over hers, soft and dreamy.

More, she nearly moaned, opening her mouth under his.

And *zoom*! It was like all those times riding Cal's Triumph, when he'd kicked the engine into a higher gear and rocketed around the curve of a country road. Her ears roared, and if she hadn't been hanging on to him, she might have toppled off the porch the way she'd nearly fallen off the back of his bike a few times. She made little whimpering noises as she tasted him for the first time in over a decade, wondering if it was all just a dream. But Cal had never held her that tightly in any dream, and he'd never kissed her with so much need.

"Cal," she groaned, smoothing her hands over his chest and shoulders, reminding herself just how good she'd had it, once upon a time.

We can have it that good again, her dragon insisted.

Could she? She was painfully aware of the alcohol pumping through her veins, not to mention the wave of emotion that had brought this all on. Still, she held Cal, kissing him hard enough to fight those thoughts away. His knee wandered closer, making hers part to let him in. She found herself groping up the inside of his shirt while shaking her head at herself. But it was hard to care with all that pent-up shifter passion blazing inside, and she started guiding Cal's hand to her heart.

A bat skimmed over the rooftop, casting a shadow over the two of them, and Cal looked up. His chest rose and fell, and his eyes glowed.

"Cynthia..."

He pulled away, and the out-of-control bike they'd been riding coasted to a halt. Cynthia wanted to lean over and give the throttle one last desperate twist.

Wait, she wanted to cry. *Please, let me escape reality for a little longer.*

Cal covered her hands with his, then gently guided them from his cheeks to her thighs, anchoring them there.

"Maybe you should check on Joey," he murmured, looking up as if he'd heard something.

That was the jacaranda tree scratching the porch roof, and Cal knew it. Still, Cynthia forced herself to nod and pull herself together. She was alpha of this pack, dammit, and that meant she had to be self-disciplined at all times. She had no business kissing Cal, especially in her current frame of mind. It was totally irresponsible. Irrational. Childish, even.

But it feels so good, her dragon cried.

It did feel good, but she wasn't the young, single woman she used to be. She was a mother and a leader now, and she'd better remember that.

Cal stood slowly, joints creaking as if his wolf was resisting. He pulled her to her feet then reluctantly released her. A moment later, his hands reached for her again, but then he stuck them deep into his pockets and kept them there.

"I'd better go."

"Me too," she admitted, though it took everything she had.

He backed down the porch steps and paused where the shadows hid his expression.

"Good night, Cynthia."

His voice was a low rumble — a sound she would replay in her dreams, if she ever got to sleep.

She plucked the wineglasses and bottle off the porch and straightened, trying to remember what her mother had taught her about pride and manners. An impossible task, given the animal passion raging inside her.

Finally, she forced out two of the most painful words she'd ever uttered. "Good night."

Slowly, Cal turned to go, and she watched, certain she'd spend most of the night touching herself. But Joey mumbled anxiously in his sleep, and she ended up snuggled up beside him.

"Dragons... Bad dragons..." Joey whimpered.

Cynthia held him closer and eyed the sky outside the window. Were his dreams echoes of the past or visions of the future? A gull's shadow glided over the window, and Cal's words echoed in her mind.

I'm here to protect you.

From what?

Not sure yet. Nothing good, I know that much.

She lay stiffly for most of the night, sure she'd never get to sleep. But she must have, because she found herself awakening with the rising sun. After a few minutes, she padded quietly to the balcony, getting there just in time to see Cal cruising out the driveway on his Triumph.

Where was he going? What was he up to?

When he disappeared over the rise, her eyes wandered over the inland slopes, and her ears strained for the smooth sound of the Thruxton long after it faded into the distance. She hugged herself, pretending her arms were his while she whispered into the wind.

"Thank you, my mate."

Chapter Eight

Cal gripped the handlebars as the Triumph rattled up the scrubby track. Hours had passed, and the sun was high overhead, making sweat run down his brow. His ears rang with the sound of creaking shocks and scattering gravel. In part, that was due to the rough surface and steep slope. He'd been out all morning, caching gear in strategic locations above the plantation.

But the rough ride was just one reason for the tension in his body. The other was the way Cynthia's kiss still burned on his lips.

Burns in a good way, his wolf hummed.

Which, he supposed, was true. For the first time in the past twelve years, he remembered what it felt like to be alive. To look to the future with hope rather than despair. But that kiss had also dredged up a lot of pain and fear. Hope was scary as hell. So were dreams, because of the pain that ensued when they crashed and burned.

The bike kicked up enough dust that he had to keep his lips sealed, which was a good thing. It kept him from smacking them together and replaying every microsecond of that kiss.

So, he hadn't accomplished much that morning in terms of processing that kiss. But he had made good progress setting up his gear. One defensive position was ready to go, and two more were on their way. He eyed the sky, wondering how much time he had left before Cynthia's enemies barreled in, darkening Maui's clear blue skies.

I vote for never, his wolf muttered.

Never would be nice, but he doubted Cynthia would get that lucky. Her enemies were closing in, all right, whether he judged by gut instinct or the reports coming in from Silas's informants. Their arrival wasn't so much a question of *if* but *when.*

He looked over the slopes one more time. He'd already made two trips between the plantation and the hills, and he was itching to make a third. But that much activity in one area was sure to draw attention, so he would have to wait a day or two.

His wolf sighed. *Knowing our luck, it will be sooner.*

Cal slowed down at an intersection, dismounted, and kicked some dirt over the tire tracks he'd left. Then he slid back onto his bike and made for the main road. Minutes later, he was cruising over asphalt with the wind whipping his hair and memories racing through his mind. It was all too easy to imagine Cynthia hanging on to him as he slalomed the bike along that idyllic coastal road, and his body warmed. But when he made the turn for the plantation's unobtrusive driveway, his back grew stiff and his palms sweaty at the prospect of seeing her again.

Tim let him through the gate, raising his thick eyebrows in a way that said, *What the hell have you been up to, you rogue?*

Cal coasted by without a word, thankful that Silas had given him free rein to move around as he pleased. Otherwise, he'd have a hell of a lot of explaining to do.

At the crest of the hill, he paused to gaze over the plantation. Most of it was tangled in overgrowth and dotted with relics of the past — a rusting tractor here, a collapsed shed there. Apparently, the place had been abandoned for years. The patches of land Cynthia and the others had wrestled back into use really stood out. One was the perfectly square plot of land lined with neat rows of coffee bushes that Hailey tended. Another was the tidy grass oval around the main house, complete with flowerpots and climbing tiers of bougainvillea. Then there was the winding track down to the tiny handkerchief of private beach, and beyond that—

He held his breath for a moment. *Beyond* was the best part — the ocean. Miles and miles of it, stretching all the way to infinity. As a wolf shifter, he usually felt most at home in the forest. But the ocean was pretty amazing too. The tangy salt air, the sense of space. . .

I could get used to it here, his wolf whispered.

But then his eyes slid to the figure pacing on the porch of the plantation house, and he pursed his lips. Could he, though? Much as the idea appealed, a single kiss couldn't undo a decade of damage.

Reluctantly, he shoved off and cruised down to the barn, feeling Cynthia's eyes on him the whole time. Once he parked the bike, he ran his fingers through his hair, trying to get himself together. Which was hard with his wolf side replaying that kiss over and over in his mind.

He stepped out into the sunshine, determined to play it cool. But the second he spotted Cynthia, he stopped. Why was she pacing? What was wrong?

Instead of swaggering over, pretending he didn't have a care in the world, he ended up rushing over then screeching to a halt at the foot of the stairs. Cynthia gave him a weak smile while she murmured into her phone.

"How long?" She bit a perfectly manicured nail. "You can't come any sooner?"

Cal's eyes narrowed. Who was coming? Why?

"What about Chase?" she asked. A long silence ensued while she waited for a reply. "Isn't there someone else who can cover for you?"

Cal wondered who was on the other end of the line. Tim came up to wait silently beside him, looking concerned. Finally, Cynthia clicked the phone off and looked down.

"What is it?" Cal asked.

She covered her eyes with one hand, rubbing hard. "Nothing, really."

Cal could have snorted. *Nothing, really* was Cynthia code for a huge problem — one she couldn't ask for help with because of her own damn pride.

He stirred the air with his hands, wishing he could say, *Ask. It doesn't hurt to ask.*

But that was Cynthia — always trying to solve problems alone. The very first time he'd met her, she'd been on the side

69

of the road with a broken-down car, insisting everything was fine when it was far from.

She motioned toward the south. "Dell took Joey to town this morning, but the Lucky Devil needs someone to cover the lunch shift, so Dell can't bring Joey home."

Cal waited. That was the big problem?

"Can't Anjali bring Joey home?" Tim asked.

Cynthia shook her head. "Anjali took the car to Kahului, and she won't be back for a while."

"What about Chase or Sophie?"

Cynthia started pacing again. "They're working too, and the other car is over in Hunter's workshop."

Cal looked from Cynthia to Tim and back. "Can't Joey wait a while?"

Cynthia spun on her heel, and holy hell, did she look outraged. "I will not allow my son to hang around a bar."

Tim shot Cal a look that said, *Never get between a mama bear and her cub... especially if she's a dragon.*

"I thought the Lucky Devil was a restaurant," Cal said, very carefully.

Cynthia made a face. "A restaurant with a bar. And *regulars.*" Her voice dripped with disdain.

Cal couldn't help laughing out loud. "You sound like your mother."

Tim stared at him with a look that said, *You know her mother?*

Cal rolled his eyes. He'd met most of that whole fucking family, and they were a bigger mess than his.

Cynthia thrust her hands onto her hips. "I do not."

"You do too."

Cynthia slumped. "God, you're right. I do."

The urge to reach out and hug her came over Cal. To tell her that she wasn't perfect, but he loved her anyway.

Love you, his wolf crooned.

Cal ordered the beast to shut up, but it was too late. Cynthia looked up, staring at him.

You love me? her voice whispered in his mind.

Of course I love you. He sighed and sent the words into her mind. Then he stirred the air with his hands.

"Anyway... Joey?"

Cynthia jolted, turned pink, and started pacing again. "I just don't want him hanging around with... with..."

Cal waited, watching the pink flush of her cheeks turn into an all-out crimson. Cynthia wasn't a snob at heart, but her upbringing came through sometimes. It was kind of fun to see her struggle with those two sides of herself, though.

"... with bad influences, all right?" She crossed her arms, but it was more of a me-hug than a gesture of defiance.

Cal would have loved to tease her with something like, *Bad influences — like me?* But she was so stressed out, he caved in.

"No problem. I'll take you."

Relief washed over her face. Then she blanched. "Wait. You mean, ride the bike? With you?"

Cal took a deep breath, picturing what that meant. Did he really dare get that close to her again?

Absolutely. His wolf wagged its tail. *Just like old times.*

Cal snorted. This was nothing like old times, not with all the baggage he and Cynthia had accumulated in the intervening years.

"Sure. Why not?" he said, working hard to keep the wobble out of his voice.

"How are you going to get Joey back on the bike?" Tim pointed out.

"We'll get the keys from Chase and drive back."

See? his wolf insisted. *Easy.*

But there was nothing easy about hopping on the bike with Cynthia. Not with the rift that had grown between them in the past twelve years. Kissing her the previous night could be forgiven, because they'd both been worked up. Not only that, but the moonlight had been shining directly on them, making their shifter sides lose control. This was totally different.

Tim nodded. "Oh, right. You mean, Chase can ride your bike back later?"

Cal shook his head. No one rode that bike but him. "We'll swap back later."

Whatever, his wolf grumbled, impatient to go.

Cynthia stared at him so intently, her eyes started to glow.

Yeah, he knew how she felt. She was dying to get close again, just like he was. But she was terrified, too. Keeping their distance was safer than wandering into the minefield of the past, and resenting was easier than forgiving. Did he really have what it took? Did she?

When Cynthia finally spoke, her voice was so quiet, Cal almost missed it.

"All right." A moment later, she added, "If you don't mind."

Cal grinned. *That's my girl.*

His reply was a mumble, because he was trying to dampen his own hopes. "I don't mind at all."

∞∞∞

Minutes later, they were zooming down the coastal highway, though Cal had to pinch himself to check if it was real or the dream he'd used so often to remain sane. But those really were Cynthia's arms around his waist, and that really was her chin resting on his shoulder.

For the first mile, she tried to keep some distance between their bodies, exactly as she had after her car had broken down on the side of the road in the Adirondacks. But trying not to touch was hopeless, and they both knew it. For one thing, the angle of the seat made her body slide against his. And old habits were hard to break, even if they pretended not to think about the intimacy they had once shared.

Eventually, Cynthia gave in to the inevitable, and her arms grew ever more comfortable around his waist. Cal wished the ride to town were longer so he could stretch out that glorious feeling. He couldn't see the long, silky strands of her black hair whipping in the wind, but he could sense all that movement back there. All that excitement too. Cynthia felt it. He felt it. And damn, it was almost like they had a third passenger: destiny.

A thousand scents bombarded him as they buzzed along – some exotic, some familiar. The rose-and-willow scent of Cynthia's skin blended with that of giant pink flowers that grew on the side of the road. A green bird flitted by, brighter than any animal Cal had ever seen. The Triumph cruised past two young guys in a beat-up old Toyota with a pair of surfboards sticking out the back. It was as if all of Maui was trying to cheer him up, saying, *Hey, you're in Hawaii now. Hang loose, man.*

Then, out of nowhere, Cynthia motioned to a beach park on the right.

"Pull over."

Cal glanced back, wondering why she had tensed up. But he did as he was told and pulled into the parking lot. Then he turned expectantly.

Cynthia's face was etched with worry lines, and her eyes were downcast when she whispered, "We have to talk."

The surfers cruised their Toyota into the parking lot just as Cynthia said *talk*, and for a moment, Cal had the crazy impulse to pretend he hadn't heard. Talking was scary, because words were tied to emotions, and behind them loomed a mountain of hurt.

But Cynthia motioned him to move the bike a little farther along, stopping under one of those picture-perfect palm trees that featured on postcards. The kind with happy lovers under the swaying fronds, not couples who had been ripped apart then thrown back together by a tempest called fate.

"We have to talk," she said again.

Briefly, Cal considered reminding her about picking up Joey. But that would be a cheap ploy to avoid a talk, and Cynthia was right. They needed this. So when she slid off one side of the bike, he dismounted off the other. That left the bike standing silently between them, representing the wall that had grown up between them over the years.

Her lips quivered, and a single tear rolled down her cheek. He cupped her face, brushing it away with his thumb.

73

"I'm so confused," Cynthia whispered. Then she bit her lip and looked him in the eye. "Why?"

He tilted his head. Why what?

"You said you loved me."

Cal gave a jerk of a nod. "Of course I do."

Oops. He'd meant to say *I did* — past tense.

Cynthia's eyes flashed with dozens of emotions, all mixing and colliding the way his were.

"I can understand why you left. I had to marry Barnaby, and I told you to go. But..." Her voice faltered, and her eyes burned with tears. "But when I heard you went off with Sheila..."

Cal's mind spun. What was she talking about?

"How could you?" Cynthia blurted.

"How could I what?"

Apparently, that wasn't the right thing to say, because Cynthia's eyes sparked in anger.

"I was forced to accept Barnaby. But no one forced you to head straight into the arms of another woman the minute you left me."

Whoa. He stuck a hand on the Triumph's fuel tank while the world around him spun. Cynthia thought he'd gone off with some other woman? Why would he do that?

"I...what?" Anger boiled up in him, and sentiments he'd never meant to utter came bubbling out. "You were the one who married another guy. Do you know what that did to me, knowing you were with someone else? Night after night..." He trailed off because the thought made him sick. Maybe he shouldn't have come to Maui, after all.

"It wasn't night after night." Cynthia glared.

"It was twelve years. Twelve." Cal snorted. "And you're accusing me of going off with someone one time?" He was going to add that he'd done no such thing, but Cynthia cut in.

"Believe me, Barnaby was about as enthusiastic about mating as I was. We had separate bedrooms. Separate lives."

Cal made a face. "And that's how Joey came about, I suppose?"

She glared. "I slept with Barnaby twice, Cal. Twice in nine years. And believe me, it was all business. Business that made me feel sick. Ashamed."

"Right. Like any guy married to you would be fine with just once or twice. There's no need to make Barnaby into a goddamned saint."

"I never said he was a saint."

"Then what are you saying?"

She paused as if on the cusp of some great secret, her eyes darting from side to side. Then she leaned in to whisper.

"Barnaby was gay, Cal. Gay."

The words rang through Cal's mind, but somehow, he couldn't quite grasp their meaning. "What?"

She looked around again as if a member of her nutty family might be eavesdropping. "I said, Barnaby was gay."

"Gay?"

Cal's jaw dropped. He would never, ever have guessed. But suddenly, it made sense. A slightly older dragon who'd put off mating as long as he could, even when it came to a woman as desirable as Cynthia. A man who'd only touched her to do what the family line required.

"It was just as hard for him as it was for me," Cynthia said, choking up again. "But he was good to me. And he was a great father. He loved Joey more than anything." Cynthia looked as if she might cry, but she straightened her shoulders and composed herself. "I hated what I had to do. But no one forced you to take off with another woman. We promised we would always keep our love alive even if we couldn't be together. Why did you break your word?"

Cal nearly yelled in protest. But the past decade had taught him a lot, like when to keep his mouth shut and think.

"I didn't go off with anybody," he said at last. "I don't know what you're talking about."

Cynthia scowled. "You deny it?"

He just looked at her, letting his eyes do the talking. He'd never, ever touched another woman after meeting Cynthia. He'd never been the slightest bit tempted to do so. Why would he? Cynthia was his mate. There was no one else for him, and there never would be.

Cynthia searched his face, and when she spoke, the hard edge of her voice had faded slightly. "Sheila. They told me you went off to Sheila."

Finally, a lightbulb went off in Cal's head. "My aunt? Yeah, I did head down to visit her after you said goodbye. Way down in Georgia, just to get away."

Cynthia gaped. "Your aunt? But... They told me..."

"Who told you?"

Cynthia's eyes wandered over the beach, but he could tell her mind was on the past, grasping at foggy memories. "I asked my cousins to find you and pass on a message. To tell you how much I loved you, one more time. But they came back, saying you'd gone off to a woman named Sheila."

"And you believed them? You jumped to the conclusion that there was someone else?"

For a moment, Cal teetered on the razor's edge of fury and forgiveness. How could Cynthia believe such a thing?

But he finally had a chance to talk to the woman he loved — maybe even a chance to patch things up. So he held his breath and counted to ten before speaking again.

"Who told you that?"

"My cousins." Cynthia tapped her fingers as she thought. "Presley and... Presley and..." Realization flashed over her face as her voice broke off. "Presley and Moira."

The name came out like poison, and Cal recoiled.

"Moira? And you believed that, coming from her?"

Cynthia paled. "I always thought Presley was okay. And Moira..." The fingers tapping on her arm took on the distinctive curve of talons as her dragon side showed. "Moira was different back then." She made a face. "Or maybe she wasn't. Maybe I just hadn't realized how cruel she was at that point."

Cruel didn't begin to describe Moira. The woman was evil – pure evil. But if Cal really thought about Cynthia's story, it made sense. Back then, Moira hadn't started her steep rise to power. No one could have predicted she would become anything more than a nasty third cousin the family tended to ignore.

Cynthia hugged herself tightly, but that didn't hide the tremble in her arms. "At the time, the only thing that stuck in my mind was that you'd gone off to see a woman. I didn't think about who told me that."

"Well, I guess they weren't exactly lying. I did go visit my aunt Sheila."

"The way they said it was a lie. And God, I believed it." Cynthia's shoulders crumpled. "It's my fault. God, it's all my fault."

Cal figured he could agree with Cynthia and make things worse, or he could reach deep down and be a man about it all. He went with the latter, coming around the bike to wrap his arms around Cynthia while she shook and cried. Every muscle in his body worked at it — holding Cynthia tight but not too tight, all the while wishing he could strangle Moira. But there was a time and a place for everything, and this was the time to hold his mate.

My love, his wolf whispered again and again.

For the past decade, he'd lived in a cloud of hurt and hate. Holding Cynthia didn't make the pain go away, but his anger receded, at least for a while. It was a little like when he'd first arrived on Maui – disembarking the plane, feeling all that sunshine. That nice, warm temperature, working its way to his core.

"Cal," Cynthia whispered, stroking his chest.

The surfers had to have been on their fourth or fifth wave by the time Cynthia stopped crying. But, hell. Cal didn't care how long it took. He could stand there holding her all day. But then the reason they'd set out hit him, and he stiffened.

"Joey..."

Cynthia wiped her eyes, still sniffling. "Oh God. I'm such a bad mother."

Cal shook his head. "Don't you say that. I've seen you with him. You're a great mother, Cynthia. All that cuddling, all those bedtime stories..."

He shut up before she caught onto the fact that he had always been nearby, protecting them both. So near, yet so far.

He cleared his throat gruffly and turned to the bike. "Anyway, you're right. We ought to get him."

Cynthia studied him too closely for comfort. But finally, she wiped her face and nodded. "God. I'm a mess."

He tipped her chin up and flashed a weak smile. "You're the most beautiful woman I've ever seen."

Their eyes locked, and a slideshow of every moment he had ever shared with Cynthia, good and bad, flashed through his mind. And not only that, but images of a future he never thought he would have. Dangerous territory, in other words.

Quickly, before he got all mushy on her — or worse, kissed her, because who knew where that might lead — he slid onto the bike and kicked the engine to life. Then he nodded her onto the back, having had all the talking one lone wolf could handle for a while. Thankfully, Cynthia mounted in one practiced move, and a moment later, they were humming down the highway with her hanging on even more snugly than before.

Just like old times, his wolf whispered, tempting him to hope. To dream. To have his heart broken all over again?

Cal took a deep breath and pretended to concentrate on the road.

Chapter Nine

Lahaina wasn't far enough to allow Cal's heart to settle down again but, hell. They would need to cross an entire continent for that.

He slowed, passing the town limits sign, and followed Cynthia's directions when the road forked. Before long, they were cruising down Front Street, the main drag of the historic town. Rows of two-story buildings lined the sidewalks, each painted a different color. Cynthia waved him into a parking space and motioned up at a green building with a balcony along the upper floor. An old-fashioned wooden sign hung over the sidewalk identifying *The Lucky Devil* and pointed upstairs.

The sign was decorated with a skull and crossbones, with a pair of red horns drawn on the skull. Cal raised his eyebrows in a question, but Cynthia just sighed.

"You'll see."

Chase stood at the door, doing a good job of flashing an expression that any man would interpret as *Don't even think about messing around in here* and any woman would read as *You'll be safe with us.* And though his face registered surprise at the sight of Cal and Cynthia, Chase let them both in without a word.

The creaky wooden stairs and malty aroma reminded Cal of one of the more questionable bars he'd brought Cynthia to once upon a time, where they had headed to a room upstairs, giggling and sweaty after an hour of dancing, ready for a little one-on-one.

Cynthia stumbled over the next stair, caught herself, and glanced back at him, blushing deeply. Cal hid a grin. Apparently, she remembered too.

He steadied her, and they continued upstairs. The corridor was dim, but the sunshine flooding in from above beckoned them on, as did the scent of frying bacon.

His wolf licked its lips. *I like it already.*

A bright, bubbly woman met them at the door with a menu. "Welcome to the Lucky Devil." Her voice faltered. "Oh — hi, Cynthia." Then she spotted Cal, and her voice dropped to a low, sultry purr. "And hello to you too."

"Hello, Candy." Cynthia stepped past the hostess, pulling Cal by the hand.

Cal was glad Cynthia's firm grip gave him the excuse to hurry past the hostess — one of those overeager women who was already undressing him with her eyes. He turned his arm slightly, making sure she got a good look at his scars. Unfortunately, Candy didn't seem turned off. On the contrary, she scurried after him.

"Can I get you a table? You've still got half an hour to catch brunch."

"We're just here to pick up Joey." Cynthia's tone said *Go away* in bold and underlined. Then her eyes fixed on someone at the bar, and her gaze softened to one mothers reserved for their offspring.

"Joey. . ."

Cal scanned the funky bar. Colorful signal flags hung from the rafters, and black-and-white photos of Lahaina's frontier days decorated the walls. The pirate/devil theme was everywhere, but not as overdone as it might have been. And the view — well, wow. The Lucky Devil stood right at the edge of the ocean, and all that turquoise water was a sight to behold.

Dell was behind the bar, jabbering a mile a minute and flashing his trademark grin. His hands moved in a blur, juggling five or six glasses while he told a long-winded joke. Joey was perched on one of the stools at the end of the bar, listening to a grizzled fisherman spin a yarn.

Cynthia's breath caught, and Cal saw all the terrible images her mind conjured up. The old man had to be an alcoholic, regaling Joey with all kinds of inappropriate stories, right?

He tightened his grip on her hand, reminding her to keep her composure as she rushed forward.

"Joey," she called in a voice laced with fake calm.

"Mommy!" The little redhead waved.

Cal followed as Cynthia strode up to the pair, crossing her arms to give the old man a clear signal that Mama Bear was there and on high alert. But her steps slowed as she got close, and her expression changed from one of anxiety to surprise.

"Bruce is teaching me checkers," Joey announced.

Warmth crept back into Cynthia's eyes, because Joey was fine. And Bruce, despite haggard features that spoke of a few too many drinking binges over the years, appeared to be on his best behavior for the kid.

"He's a quick learner, this one." Bruce patted Joey on the back. "Beat me twice already."

Cynthia's eyes scanned the area, no doubt searching for evidence of gambling or some other sin. But it truly was just checkers. A perfectly harmless, innocent game. And hey, Joey seemed to be having a good time.

"Hiya, Cynth," Dell called, making her cringe.

"Cynthia," she sighed, drawing out each of the syllables.

Dell went on without taking notice. "Nice to see you. We've been having a great time. Right, Joey?"

Joey jerked his head up and down like one of those wobbly toys people kept in their cars, making Cal's heart melt. Such a good kid. If only he could have a little more freedom.

Kill Moira, his wolf snarled. *Fulfill the prophecy. Give the boy the freedom he needs.*

Cynthia glanced over as if she sensed the dark cloud that slid over his mind.

Forget that stupid prophecy, he told his wolf.

Just because an old woman had seen a vision when he was born didn't mean it was the real thing. Him, ridding the world of some great evil? He'd be happy just to keep Cynthia and Joey safe.

Dell pointed around. "Look. Joey's got his checkers, his orange juice — vitamin-enriched and everything. We're doing great."

81

Cal hid a snort. The lion shifter could be annoying but charming as hell, and he had a way of calming Cynthia down. Lord knew the woman needed that, she was so high-strung.

His wolf grumbled. *Keeping her calm is our job.*

Yeah, he liked to think so, but he hadn't been able to do that for the past too-many years. He should be grateful somebody had stepped in to help in his place.

Temporarily, his wolf snarled, giving Dell the evil eye.

"Well, that's great. Thank you both," Cynthia said, sounding truly grateful. "But we have to get going now."

"Oh, come on, Cynth," Dell groaned.

Joey cried at exactly the same time, "So soon?"

Cal tugged on Cynthia's hand. Joey was having a good time. Why rush him back home?

"Last half hour to catch brunch," Dell hinted.

Cynthia looked up with a blank expression that said, *Brunch? I don't do brunch. Certainly not in a place like this.*

Cal squeezed her hand a little tighter, and if Dell caught the motion, who cared? Cynthia was his woman.

"We have a special offer," Candy announced in her shrill, *look-at-me* voice. Cal watched as the hostess waved toward the dart board hanging on one wall. "Hit the bull's-eye, and brunch is on the house."

Dell flashed an amused grin. "Yeah. From behind that line."

Cal snorted. Regulation distance to a board ought to be seven or eight feet, depending on the darts you used. But the line Dell indicated — a faded pirate sword painted on the floor — was at least twenty feet from the board.

Joey bounced up and down in his seat. "Cal can do it."

A glint crept into Dell's eyes. "I'd love to see him try."

Cal swung his jaw until it cracked, trying to resist the temptation. But Candy was already bounding to the board and back, bringing him a dart.

"Oh, I bet he could," she cooed, fondling the tip of the dart.

"That won't be necessary," Cynthia snipped.

Cal knew she was about to call Joey and head for the door, but heck. This was one of those *It's good for you* moments he used to treat Cynthia to in more innocent times. The woman needed to get out more. To mingle with the lower classes — like him. To loosen up, have fun, and let her kid do the same.

So he took the dart, checked that the flights weren't warped, and lined up his shot.

"No pressure," Dell announced as more and more people fell silent and looked on.

Cal allowed himself the slightest smile. A dozen tourists and fishermen? That wasn't pressure. Pressure was a dragon coming at you with its mouth wide open, about to smother you with fire.

"You could balance an apple on your head and stand in front of the board," Cal said, keeping his voice smooth.

Everyone laughed — as did Dell, to his credit. "Nah. I'll stand over here on the side. Just in case."

Cal fingered the dart, getting a feel for its weight and balance. It was light — much lighter than the objects he was used to hurling, but the principle was the same. Another four or five people turned to watch, and Bruce cackled.

"Good luck, mister. Your odds are about as good as me catching Moby Dick."

Cynthia pursed her lips in one of those *Is this really necessary?* looks, and Cal hid a smile. This could turn out to be more fun than he'd thought.

Someone chimed in with a snarky comment about the one that got away, and a guy at the bar started taking bets. Cal kept his eyes on the dart board, letting everything around it fade away. Dell's shit-eating grin. Joey's all-too-hopeful gaze. Candy's ever-fluttering eyelids. He even let Cynthia fade out for a moment, zeroing in on the board instead.

A deep, grizzled voice boomed in his head. A memory that said, *You're mine.*

His lips curled upward. Those were the last words of a dragon who'd made the fatal error of underestimating him.

No, you're mine, Cal nearly whispered, letting his mind turn the bull's-eye into an enemy. Like that dragon — one of several Cal had hunted down and killed in retribution for attacking Barnaby's place.

And, *zip!* With a flick of his wrist, he released the dart, hurtling it directly at the—

"Bull's-eye!" everyone cheered.

Cal blinked and looked around, reminding himself he was in a quirky Maui bar, not on a battlefield. And whoa — Candy was coming at him with what looked like a kiss for the lucky winner.

"Ahem," Cynthia fake-coughed, stepping between them just in time.

"I knew you could do it," Joey cheered.

Cal shot him a grin.

"I knew it too," Candy echoed, sidestepping Cynthia.

Cynthia countered by sticking her elbows out, and luckily, a customer called Candy away for a drink. Cal exhaled. Maybe fate didn't have it in for him as badly as it sometimes seemed.

Dell brought his hands together quietly and mouthed a silent *Bravo*, then tipped his head toward a table. "Congratulations. You're the first winner of the Lucky Devil's Dart Challenge. Brunch is on the house."

"But we were just..." Cynthia started, then slowly trailed off.

It was funny, how an idea could grow on a man. Cal hadn't cared much about brunch a minute before, but when he pictured himself and Cynthia sitting across from each other, gazing into each other's eyes...

"Sounds good to me," he murmured, wondering what she would say.

"Come on, Cynth." Cal was surprised to hear Dell call. "One of our best tables just opened up. You can enjoy the view." Dell narrowed his eyes on Cal, giving him a look that said, *Yes, she needs this. And as for you — you make sure you behave, you got me?*

Cynthia stared at the seaside table. She didn't sit down for long meals, let alone take in views. She was the high-powered, *I have another thirty items to check off my list today* kind of gal.

She sure looked tempted, though.

"Brunch," Cal said. Slowly, carefully. Letting her form her own picture of how nice it could be. "Okay with you?"

She bit her lip, studying him. Then, with the slightest bob of her head, she nodded. "I suppose we could eat. Quickly, of course."

"Of course."

He grinned and started pulling her along before she changed her mind. Candy jumped in front of him, letting the strap of her body-hugging tank top slip down one shoulder as she showed them to the table. When they sat down, Candy slapped a menu in front of Cynthia. For Cal, she leaned way over and opened another menu to the centerfold, positioning it just so. The crease in the middle had a way of drawing the eye straight to her cleavage, but Cal kept his eyes firmly on Cynthia.

"Give us a minute," he muttered, trying to keep the bark out of his voice.

When Candy sulked off, Cal pretended to study the menu. He didn't actually care what he was having. Just sitting there with Cynthia was special enough. Out in public and everything, with no fear of someone coming along and saying, *Aren't you the Baird girl? How dare you be seen with this scum?*

The memory must have shown, because Cynthia squeezed his hand, making him look up.

"Look at us," she whispered.

He sighed. "Yeah. Look at us."

For a long minute, they gazed into each other's eyes, letting the past mix with the present, washing in and out like the waves on the shore below. Ebbing in and out in a calm, steady rhythm.

So many years had gone by. So much time had been lost. But somehow, they'd found their way back to each other. His heart rate settled, and his mind did too. The mess of his life wouldn't be resolved in one afternoon. But he could make a new memory – a good one – now.

So, they ordered — a Big Kahuna for him, whatever that was, and a Sunshine Special for Cynthia. He laughed when the meals were served. His was a huge platter covered with bacon, hash browns, the brightest orange cantaloupe he'd ever seen, and something that looked like fried fish wrapped in leaves. Cynthia, meanwhile, got a yogurt, fresh fruit, and a smoothie. She raised her glass for a toast, then hesitated.

"To..."

Cal held up his water and waited.

"To brunch," Cynthia finished a little lamely, though her eyes hinted at something else. Something she didn't dare utter, and neither did he.

He clinked his glass against hers and echoed, "To brunch."

For wolf shifters, meals were more of a destination, not a journey. A means of chasing away hunger rather than a process in themselves. But for once in his life, Cal slowed down and let every flavor dissipate over his tongue. The dark, smoky flavor of the bacon. The crisp contrast of fresh cantaloupe. The surprisingly succulent fish that just about melted on his tongue once he'd picked the meat out of the banana leaf it had been steamed in. He had to hand it to Maui — or to the Lucky Devil. It was the best damn meal he'd had in a long time.

Cynthia ate in small, dainty bites, torturing him with the way her lips closed over her fork, then slowly slid off. Every few minutes, her eyes strayed to Joey. Whenever Cal glanced that way, he caught Dell checking on him and Cynthia in the same way. Appraising. Judging. Sending a clear message that the person he cared for was not to be misused.

But Joey was having a good time, and Cynthia was too. Slowly, she relaxed, and so did Cal. Even Candy cantering over with unnecessary water refills didn't faze them. When the meal was cleared away, they remained sitting, looking at each other or the view. Cal nearly reached for Cynthia's hand, but he settled for resting a leg against hers.

You know, we were good together, he wanted to say.

Cynthia pursed her lips, and he heard her answer in his mind.

Yes, we were. Her eyes took on a soft shifter glow.

He hated the past tense, but okay. He would take what he could get.

The sun glinted off her pearls, and Cal smiled without knowing exactly why. He hadn't forgotten how beautiful Cynthia was, but he had forgotten what it was like to kick back and have a nice time.

Feels good, his wolf sighed.

A boisterous party of four emerged at the top of the stairs, making Cynthia look over. Then she jerked her hand up, checked her watch, and jolted. "Oh, look at the time. We should go."

Already? he nearly protested.

But she was right. Joey had played enough rounds of checkers, and they probably ought to vacate their table to someone likely to tip more generously than he was inclined to do, given the peep show Candy had kept up despite hints he wasn't the least bit interested.

Still, he found it in his heart to round the drinks tip up from fifteen percent — after he finished arguing with Cynthia over who would pay, that was. When they stood to leave, Cynthia paused, looking out at the view, and he swore her chest rose and fell in a deep sigh.

He didn't want to leave either. He never wanted that quiet, uncomplicated time to end.

"Hey, Mandy," a young guy called to his woman.

Honeymooners, judging by the dopey look on the man's face and the *Isn't he amazing* expression on the woman's face.

The groom pointed to the old-fashioned jukebox with a grin. "They have our song."

Cal decided it really was time to go, because they looked like the Cyndi Lauper type, and he wasn't ready for that peppy a song. But the creak of the jukebox's mechanical arm was followed by the scratch of the needle over the LP, and when the first notes of a jazzy trumpet played...

Cynthia stopped in her tracks, and Cal did too.

"Dream a little dream of me." The groom beamed at his bride as the timeless voice of Ella Fitzgerald filled the room.

Cal didn't budge through the first few lines of the song. It was daylight, so the stars weren't shining above him, and there was no bird in a sycamore tree. But damn. The breeze really did seem to whisper, *I love you.*

I love you, he echoed, gazing into Cynthia's eyes.

"Dream a Little Dream of Me" was their song. Or it would be if he had to name just one. They'd slow-danced to it on their second night together. Cynthia had snuck him over to her father's boathouse in the Adirondacks, a rustic little place right on a lake. The band at the fancy club on the opposite shore had played a lot of classics, and music drifted over the water in a magical way. Cal and Cynthia had taken a break from making love long enough to dance a few times. Him and her, holding each other close, their footsteps creaking softly on the wooden slats of the boathouse balcony. Autumn leaves fluttered in the woods, and moonlight rippled over the calm waters of the lake.

Cynthia turned to him with wide, vulnerable eyes, and he gulped. Yeah, she remembered too.

They'd danced to that song dozens of times, and the only part that didn't ring true was the word *little*. *Little* didn't begin to describe his dreams over the past twelve years.

Hold her tight? Tell her he missed her? Hell, where would he begin?

Another few lines went by without either of them making a move, but by the time Louis Armstrong kicked in with his low, gravelly, *craving* lines, Cal found his feet moving. His arms too, pulling Cynthia close. Behind her, the honeymooners started dancing as well, and the other customers turned to watch. Not that Cal cared. His whole world narrowed to the tune in his ears and the woman in his arms.

Just like old times. His wolf grinned.

It was, right down to the smallest details. Like her hand on his arm and the silky brush of her hair over his shoulder as their bodies began to sway. He leaned in, closed his eyes, and inhaled her scent.

Dancing was a funny thing, really. You only took a few steps, but it was like traveling to a different world. A place where only the present existed, along with a sense of calm. A lot like the calm he'd always felt holding Cynthia after they made love. Feeling spent and tired of taking on the world, but relieved at the same time because he didn't have to be a warrior for a while. He could just hold his true love and enjoy.

Dancing had a way of dividing his senses too, keeping part of him aware of the whirling overhead fans, the clatter of silverware, and the sensation of eyes on their backs as people looked on. But that was all detached and distant, and he stayed in his private world as long as he could, relishing every step, every touch, every glance they exchanged.

Far too soon, the song reached its final chords, and before he knew it, the jukebox needle was scratching over silence again. But Cynthia was looking up at him with an expression he couldn't decipher, and her heart beat steadily against his. A smattering of applause made her blush, but she kept her eyes on his.

Just like old times, Cal couldn't help thinking.

Just like old times, Cynthia's eyes agreed.

Chapter Ten

Cynthia sat on the rocking chair on her private wing of the porch, gripping the armrests, trying not to let her hands shake. She closed her eyes, telling herself to clear her mind. It would be dinnertime soon, and there was no way she could appear in such a state.

Still, her fingers tingled, and her blood raced. Cal's heady scent still filled her nose, and her cheeks warmed.

Our mate is back, her dragon sighed. *He really is back, and he really does love us.*

It had been a silent drive home from Lahaina — well, silent between her and Cal, though she could feel sparks fly the entire time. Joey, on the other hand, kept up an excited conversation for the short ride home in the borrowed pickup. It was amazing how her baby had gone from *little boy* to... well, *big boy* — one more curious than ever about the world.

"Bruce said his boat has two engines. Two! And Dell said he catches fish bigger than me! There was a storm once, and Bruce said..."

Her mind had wandered while Joey enthused about everything he'd done, seen, and heard. Cal was back, and he loved her. He hadn't betrayed their promise as she'd been led to believe. And now that she was a widow...

She cleared her throat and rocked faster.

When Cal dropped off her and Joey at home, he'd left the engine running, ready to turn around and head back to town for his Triumph. Cynthia had stepped out of the pickup, intending to utter a quick thanks and walk briskly to the house, because she'd already let down her guard too far. But the moment her

91

eyes met Cal's, her feet refused to move. His deep, smoky eyes sparkled as he took her in.

"Thank you," she'd whispered, hanging on to the door like a woman at the edge of a cliff.

"Thank you!" Joey chirped, making Cal flash one of his rare smiles. Then he went all serious again, with eyes for no one but her.

"Sure thing."

His lips hadn't closed all the way when he finished, and she'd been hit by the urge to clamber across the front seat and kiss him.

Motorcycles are much more convenient, her dragon grumbled.

It had taken everything she had to shut the door and let Cal drive away. Even when he did, she'd stood watching the driveway a long time after the pickup disappeared.

She gave the rocking chair a push and looked out over the sea, trying to distract herself. But instead of the rainbow of blues in the tropical water, all she saw was the worn leather of Cal's jacket. Instead of watching palm trees sway along the edge of the beach, she pictured the thick strands of Cal's hair, curling around his ears.

What's really keeping us apart? her dragon whispered.

Cynthia closed her eyes. Pride. Nothing but damn pride — hers as well as his — not to mention that gaping chasm filled with all the pain of the past. A whole river of regret she was afraid to wade into, lest she get swept away. That, and a mountain of guilt. She hadn't chosen to be mated to Barnaby, but she had agreed in the end, and he'd sacrificed his life for her. Didn't she owe it to him to remain true?

"Look, Mommy. I drew a picture of Bruce on his boat." Joey was sprawled on the floor not far from her feet, and he twisted around to show off his latest artwork.

Cynthia snapped her eyes open to look. "That's great, honey."

Her son's smile was a thing of joy. She took a deep breath and looked around. Joey's crayons scratched across paper, and the corner of his sketchbook lifted and fell in the light breeze. Outside, a myna chattered, busying itself with its day.

Her gaze lifted to the mountains that Cal had roared off to shortly after he'd returned from Lahaina on his Triumph. What exactly was he doing up there? Was he thinking about the future, or was he just as stuck in the past as she?

Every time an engine sounded at the top of the driveway, she jumped to her feet, but the others returned before Cal did. Sometime that afternoon, Anjali and Dell came cruising down in their new minivan — a vehicle that hinted at plans to expand their family, no doubt. Not long after, Sophie and Chase coasted down the driveway in the pickup, met by a happy chorus of barking dogs. The others — Tim, Hailey, Connor, and Jenna — had been out and about, but everyone had promised to meet for dinner. Everyone but Cal.

Joey added some splashes around the hull of the boat he'd drawn. "Maybe someday I can go fishing with Bruce."

She nearly said, *Certainly not,* but she caught herself just in time.

"Maybe you can someday," she whispered.

The sun glinted off his red hair just like it once had Barnaby's, and sorrow sliced through her soul. She'd grown to love Barnaby over time. As a friend, if not a lover. He'd been good to her, a great father to Joey, and he had made the ultimate sacrifice for them both. Was it selfish of her to dream of Cal instead of honoring Barnaby's memory?

She frowned as her mind replayed the last day she'd spent with Barnaby, in what seemed like a different life. She'd woken in her bedroom, showered, and met him in the gleaming kitchen downstairs. Barnaby had given her his usual peck on the cheek, and when Joey came down in his Star Wars pajamas, Barnaby had lifted him high and spun him around.

There's my boy. His rich tenor mingled with the squeak of Joey's laughter and rang through the house.

Cynthia closed her eyes, feeling guiltier than ever.

"I wish..." she whispered, without knowing what she really wished for.

Much as she resented the sharp turns her life had taken, they had each led to something better. Being with Barnaby had given her Joey, and nothing would ever make her undo that. In the aftermath of the dragon attack launched by Moira and Drax, she'd lost everything, but that had also led to her starting a whole new life on Maui. A good life, even though she never would have believed it at the time.

So what exactly did she wish for now?

Cal, her dragon said without hesitation. *Cal. Stop wallowing in the past. Live in the present, and look to the future.*

She would love to. But she was out of practice when it came to that — and not as ready to risk her heart as she had been, once upon a time.

Know this, Barnaby had told her years ago — that evening they'd had a heart-to-heart, when he had revealed all. *I may not be the mate you dreamed of, but I love you, and I want you to be happy. If it were in my power to set either of us free, believe me, I would.*

Freedom. She sighed. She'd only ever tasted it with Cal.

"Hey," someone called from the point where the porch took a ninety-degree turn, giving her privacy from the front of the house.

Cynthia turned to find Dell there, and she didn't know whether to laugh or groan. But the lion shifter wasn't wearing his usual cocky grin, and his eyes weren't full of mischief.

"Just checking," he said, sounding uncharacteristically reserved. Even concerned, if that were possible. "How many places to set for dinner tonight?"

Cynthia tilted her head. Back when they'd all just arrived on the plantation as strangers, she had designed a strict duty schedule, working on her parents' example. Dragons took charge, and it was important to run a tight ship. It had annoyed her to no end when the men had swapped tasks. Contrary to her fears, however, the guys had proven themselves reliable, with each falling into the role he did best. Soon, everything was running smoothly, almost by itself.

Funny how that had all worked out — and how many lessons she had learned along the way. Cooking was a prime example. That had pretty much become Dell's domain, and everyone was happy not to intrude. So why was Dell asking her about such details now?

"I mean, do I set for eleven or twelve?" he asked.

Eleven was on the tip of her tongue, but then she realized what Dell meant. There were eleven residents on the plantation: Connor and Jenna, the dragon shifters; Tim and Hailey, the bears; and Anjali and Dell, the lion shifters, plus their baby, Quinn. Then there were Chase and Sophie, the wolves, and Cynthia and Joey brought the total of their eclectic little group to eleven. So, who was number twelve?

Dell's gaze remained expressionless, but she could have sworn he was holding his breath.

Cal, she realized. Dell was asking about Cal. So far, Cal had taken his meals alone or gone over to report to Silas at dinnertime. But now...

Her lip quivered. Dell was offering to include Cal?

She closed her eyes. How long had she yearned for something as simple as seeing her mate in small, ordinary ways? But now that she had the chance to, the old barriers still loomed in her way.

"Twelve," her dragon made her say.

Hey, she blurted.

Don't overthink things, the beast snipped.

And dammit, the next words out of her mouth were an affirmation of the first — her dragon taking charge once again.

"Twelve would be fine."

Dell nodded, but he didn't move. He just stood there, studying her. Finally, he stuck on an oversized smile and turned to her son. "Heya, Joey. Whatcha drawing?"

Joey held up his stick-figure Bruce and boat, then beamed when Dell lavished him with praise.

"Wow. That is amazing. Will you show it to Anjali and Quinn? Can we put it on the fridge when you're done?"

"Sure." Joey jumped to his feet, grabbed his crayons, and ran toward the kitchen.

"Just make sure Quinn doesn't eat them," Dell called after him. "She's just a baby, you know. Not a big kid like you."

When Joey disappeared around the corner, Dell turned back to Cynthia, and his smile faded.

What? she wanted to scream. Why was he looking at her that way?

"You okay?" Dell finally asked, in a tone softer than he'd ever used with her. No laughing, no teasing, no jokes.

"I'm fine."

Dell rubbed his golden beard. "Really fine? Seriously, Cynthia..."

She did a double take. Dell never called her by her full name. God, was she that pitiful?

"Please don't be nice to me just because... because..." She choked up before getting as far as, *Because my life is a mess.*

Dell cocked his head. "You want me to be mean?"

"No. Just... Call me Cynth."

Dell stared until she banged a fist on the armrest of the chair. "Pretend everything is normal, okay?"

He arched an eyebrow. "Pretend?"

She grimaced. "I'm better at it than you know."

The lion shifter broke into a grin. "And here I was thinking you were all cold and heartless."

She stuck a finger in his direction and turned on her fiercest alpha glare. "Don't you dare tell anyone otherwise."

He crossed his heart. "It'll be our secret. Scout's honor."

Cynthia nodded quickly, fighting the urge to bury her face in her hands. What other secrets had Dell guessed at? She blanched. God, it would kill her if any of the men of Koakea knew she had dirty dreams about Cal.

"Anyway..." She covered her string of pearls, ordering herself not to blush. But if her chest felt that hot, surely her cheeks were about to show it too. "Twelve is fine."

Dell scratched this jaw. Finally, he sighed, turned a chair backward, and straddled it. "Look, I hate to ask..."

So, don't, she nearly said.

"But I will," Dell finished before she had a chance to protest.

The crazy thing was, Cynthia caught herself celebrating that. As if she needed to get everything off her chest at last.

Which was crazy. Dragons didn't confide in anyone. And certainly not in a man-child like Dell.

She pushed the rocking chair back into motion but couldn't quite bring herself to send him away.

"About Cal..." he ventured.

Cynthia rocked harder.

"One minute, I get the feeling you hate him. The next, you act like you love him."

She waved away the notion. "Don't be ridiculous."

Dell tilted his head to one side, then the other, considering. "Is it? I've seen the way he looks at you — and the way you look at him."

The porch creaked under the motion of the rocking chair. "I don't look at him," she insisted.

"Right. And Cal doesn't look at you like a man staring out from a cage."

Cynthia's mouth cracked open. Was it really true?

"If you do hate him, I'd be happy to run him off Maui," Dell offered. "Everyone would pitch in, no matter what Silas says."

Her chest warmed. God. How lucky was she to have friends like Dell? True friends — not acquaintances or hired hands, as her parents had insisted relationships with lesser shifter species should be. Lions could be just as insightful as dragons. Wolves could be just as noble, and bears just as self-sacrificing. She knew firsthand.

"But if you do love him..." Dell whispered.

Her eyes slid closed. *Love.* If only the word slipped as smoothly off her tongue as Dell's. Other than loving Joey, she'd never openly admitted to loving anyone.

Finally, she sighed and whispered back, "I don't hate Cal. I hate myself."

Dell looked bewildered. Clearly, self-loathing was a new concept to the sunny-hearted lion.

Cynthia kneaded her hands, holding back the truth. There was no way she was confiding in Dell. And yet, a moment later, she found herself speaking in halting, nervous spurts.

"My parents had my future all set up. They didn't even tell me they were negotiating a betrothal with Barnaby's family."

Dell's eyebrows shot up. "Negotiating?"

Her shoulders slumped. Dell would never understand. But now that she'd started. . .

"It was a done deal before Barnaby or I even knew about it. We had no choice."

"How could you not have a choice? How could they do that to you?"

Cynthia sucked in a long breath and let it out just as slowly, buying time. "I did have a choice," she said, thinking back to the half-dozen potential suitors her parents had introduced her to. All old, crusty dragons who, like her, were the last of their lines. When she'd finally worked up the nerve to admit to her parents she was already in love, her mother had clapped in delight.

That's wonderful! Who is the lucky man?

The lucky man was a wolf shifter, and when she'd admitted as much — boy, had the shit hit the fan.

What? her mother had screeched.

Who? her father had hollered. Within minutes, he'd called in his dragon allies to drag Cal's undeserving wolf hide in.

Of course, Cal was too crafty to be hunted down by anyone. She'd sent word to him, urging him to flee. Instead, he'd come marching right into her parents' parlor, holding his head high.

And who might you be? her father had demanded.

The man who loves your daughter.

She'd never loved Cal more than in that gallant moment, but even that couldn't change the way things had worked out. Not with twenty generations of dragon ghosts peering over her shoulder, demanding the Baird clan wouldn't die out with her. In the end, she'd been the one to beg Cal to go. She'd even made up some nonsense about not loving him, insisting it was all just a fling.

Never had a man looked more wounded. Never had she felt so ashamed of herself or so angry at what her parents had forced upon her. But they had both passed away since then, and she had only herself to despise now.

She swallowed hard and glanced at Dell. "Old dragon clans take bloodlines very seriously."

He scowled. "I bet they do. But, hell. You'd have to be a goddamn legend to want to preserve the family line that bad."

She kept her eyes level with Dell's, telling him how right he was. He stared, and she could see the gears turning in his head.

"You come from the Llewellyn clan?" he tried. "No? The Draigs, then? The Rhyddericks?"

"Mr. O'Roarke, you impress me with your knowledge of dragondom."

He made a face. "Can't help overhearing some of the stuff you teach Joey."

She frowned. Honestly, she hadn't ever thought through what she'd been teaching Joey. She'd taught him about the great clans because that was all part of dragon lore. But did she really want her son growing up believing bloodlines mattered more than love?

"My husband — Barnaby — was a Brenner," she said.

Dell's eyes went wide. "That old clan with all that property in the Northeast? The Newport mansion?"

Mansions, she refrained from correcting him. Instead, she dropped the bombshell. Why the heck not?

"My maiden name is Baird. Cynthia Baird."

His jaw dropped, and a moment later, he sputtered. "Holy crap. You mean, *those* Bairds?"

Cynthia sighed. "Yes, those Bairds. I'm the last one."

Dell stared at her, and for a moment, everything was silent. Uncomfortably so. Then he found his voice again and dropped his own bombshell. "How could you be a Baird if Moira is your cousin?"

Cynthia whipped her head around. "How did you know that?"

Del shrugged. "Moira told me."

"She what?" Cynthia screeched. "When?"

"In Chicago." Dell motioned over his shoulder as if the Windy City were right there. "When I went to close Quinn's adoption."

Cynthia gaped. For months, Dell had known one of her deepest, darkest secrets, but he hadn't told a soul.

Mother, she wished she could summon her parents. *Father. You were wrong about other shifters. So utterly wrong. They can be loyal. They can be honorable. They can be trusted.*

Maybe even more than fellow dragons, her inner beast growled, flexing its claws.

"How can you possibly be related to Moira?" Dell motioned at her. "You're all... classy. She's just a bitch."

Cynthia laughed. Either Dell was being generous, calling her *classy* instead of *snobby,* or she'd changed for the better over the past few years. Either way, he was right about Moira.

"Sorry," he muttered in an afterthought.

Cynthia shook her head. "Moira is a third cousin, and not a Baird. But yes, we're related. And yes, she is a bitch. But anyway..."

For once, Dell didn't call out her obvious hint to change the subject. He did, however, go back to the original thread of their conversation.

"So why did you do it? I mean, why agree to mate with Barnaby?"

His words were so gentle, it made her feel worse. Damn it. She was the last in a long, proud line of dragons — one of the mightiest clans in history. Bairds were to be revered and admired, not pitied.

But there she was with a lion shifter looking at her with eyes so mournful, she could have cried.

"Cynthia. Why?"

Funny, she'd asked herself that question a hundred times.

"Because two thousand years of pure dragon bloodlines couldn't end with me," she whispered, feeling defeated all over again.

Dell, to his credit, didn't point out how hopelessly elitist that sounded. He just scratched his chin. "The whole bloodline thing is a little outdated, don't you think?"

She slumped. You had to be a dragon to understand, she supposed.

"Seriously, Cynth. Would you force Joey to take a mate he didn't love?"

Her head snapped up. "Of course not."

"So what makes you different? Don't you deserve happiness?"

She blinked back the sting in her eyes. "But... but..."

Dell waited patiently — infuriatingly so — while Cynthia hemmed, hawed, and finally trailed off.

The sounds of the plantation filled in the uncomfortable silence that ensued. Birds calling, crickets chirping, and the distant hum of the ocean rolling over the shore.

"You know what I think?" Dell finally whispered.

Cynthia rolled her eyes, pretending to be annoyed. "What do you think, Mr. O'Roarke?"

Dell let a heartbeat or two pass, making it clear he wasn't about to crack a joke. "I think you deserve happiness. You deserve love. And, really — what's your biggest obstacle? Other than yourself, I mean."

Cynthia stared at a spot on the floor like it was the bare, naked truth she'd never wanted to face.

Dell's chair creaked as he leaned closer, speaking more earnestly than she'd thought he was capable of.

"If you were Joey, I would tell you to fight for what you want. What you really want."

Cynthia gulped.

"But seeing as you're not Joey..."

She glanced up, wondering what he would say.

Dell let a pregnant pause tick by. Then he stood, wiped his hands on his pants, and flashed a quirky smile that said, *The ball's in your court.*

"Dinner's in twenty minutes," he said, turning to go. "See you then, Cynth."

Chapter Eleven

The longer Cynthia rocked, the more her sorrow turned to anger. There were a lot of things she would love to go back in time to do differently. But could she blame anyone? Her parents only wanted the best for her and for the future of the clan. In the end, she had agreed to the betrothal, putting her family's wishes above her own desires. So, really, everyone had acted in good faith.

Except Moira.

She snorted, emitting a tiny spark of dragon fire.

Moira, her inner dragon seethed.

"Twenty minutes to dinner," Dell hollered over the plantation grounds.

Cynthia stood and started pacing. A she-dragon could do a lot of things in twenty minutes — like taking flight, spitting fire, and picturing her nasty cousin finally getting what she deserved. Or was she just misplacing her frustration by directing it at Moira?

No, her dragon insisted. *Dell is right.*

Moira had always been jealous of Cynthia's privileges as a member of the most illustrious branch of the family. Not that Moira had ever taken a moment to consider that privilege came with a mountain of duties. She was only interested in riches and power. Even as a child, Moira had been nasty. But there was a line between nasty and downright cruel, and Moira had long since crossed it.

Cynthia's blood boiled as she remembered her cousins reporting that Cal had gone off with Sheila. The details of that conversation were shaky in her mind, but one thing was clear — Presley's comforting touch on her arm was sincere, while Moira's was more of a scratch, and her expression barely masked a grin of triumph that Cynthia hadn't fully registered at the time.

The next image her churning memory served up was that of Silas, many years ago, looking absolutely crushed. He'd been betrothed to Moira — a fact Moira had never stopped rubbing in everyone's face. But while he'd offered everything Moira's shallow values could have desired — wealth, stunning good looks, and an impressive family line — Moira had eventually shunned Silas to run off with one of the cruelest, most ruthless dragons of them all.

Drax, Cynthia's inner dragon hissed.

Drax had attacked her home. Drax had murdered Barnaby. Drax—

Moira, her dragon corrected. *It all comes down to Moira.*

The sun had started to set, and the reddish-orange hue grew more intense by the minute. Cynthia narrowed her eyes on a patch the color of blood and thought it all through. Moira was the common denominator. A skilled — and dangerous — manipulator of men. Had she persuaded Drax to attack Barnaby in order to seize control of the Brenner fortune?

Cynthia's dragon snorted. *Do you have to ask?*

The hum of Cal's motorcycle sounded from around the corner, and Cynthia was hit by the urge to run over, hug Cal, and never let go. Moira had taken so much from her, but love couldn't be stolen like a jewel.

"Fifteen minutes," Dell called from the kitchen.

Cynthia considered all the things she could do with that time.

Kill Moira, her dragon begged.

She made a face. For better or worse, Moira wasn't close enough to kill. But it sure would be nice to give the bitch a piece of her mind.

Of course, nice dragons didn't do such things. They shouldn't even *think* such things. Cynthia could hear her mother's admonishments loud and clear in her mind. But another voice was louder — the one declaring, *Enough. I've had enough.*

So, in one of the few impulsive acts of her life, Cynthia jumped to her feet, stomped upstairs, and pulled out the leather-bound phone book her mother had given her long ago. Her hands shook, and she paused. Shouldn't she calm down and think things through?

Enough thinking. Enough hiding, her dragon snarled.

She flipped the phone book open to the M page and stared for a minute. Then she picked up her phone, dialed, and waited as the line rang and rang.

"Hello?"

The shrill voice that came on the line sliced through Cynthia's memories, awakening every nightmare.

Cynthia pursed her lips and counted to ten.

"Hello?" the voice demanded.

She took a deep breath and did her best not to spit her reply into the phone.

"Moira."

The line went absolutely silent, and then a cackle rang out. "Why, it's you, dearest cousin!"

Cynthia held the phone away from her ear, reminding herself to keep cool when what she really wanted to do was growl, *You bet your ass, it's me, bitch.*

For once, she wished she had no manners. No social code that made it impossible to utter what was on her mind.

"It's Cynthia, if that's who you mean," she said.

Moira chuckled. "Not *dear*, you mean? You break my heart."

No, Cynthia wanted to say. *You helped break mine with all the meddling you've done.* But saying that would admit to Moira she had succeeded, and Cynthia wasn't about to do that.

"I wasn't aware you had a heart," Cynthia said, picturing Dell giving her a high five for that one. The man was a pro at snappy comebacks.

Moira laughed. "Of course I do. I was absolutely shattered to hear about the death of your beloved Barnaby."

Cynthia dug her nails into the leather cover of her phone book. Moira had been present the day of the attack. Hovering in the background, keeping a safe distance, letting Drax and his henchmen do the dirty work. Which meant she was lying, as usual. But Cynthia wasn't going to let Moira get the upper hand, so she kept to the script she'd thrown together in her mind.

"The way you were shattered when Silas left you?" A low blow, but Moira deserved it.

Moira's voice turned to pure poison. "I left him."

"Oh, of course," Cynthia said in a syrupy voice. "For Drax. You two really were made for each other."

Yeah, her dragon spat. *A match made in heaven — or more appropriately, in hell.* Drax was cruel, ruthless, and totally self-centered — just like Moira.

"Anyway," Cynthia went on. "I'm not calling to exchange pleasantries. I'm calling to warn you."

Another shrill cackle cut through the phone, and Cynthia winced.

"Warn me? *You* want to warn *me*?"

If that wasn't an admission Moira was planning yet another attack, what was?

"Yes, to warn you." Cynthia's voice dropped an octave, and her words became knives. "You meddle in my life one more time, and you're dead. You send another of your mercenaries to Maui, and I will personally come after you. If you so much as imagine launching another attack, I will finish you. Really finish you, Moira. I will strip you of your treasure. Make you a laughingstock before all dragondom. I will watch as the pride and the life drip out of you, one pathetic drop at a time. You will be gone, forgotten. If anyone ever mentions your name again, it will only be to smirk at the disaster you brought upon yourself. Do I make myself clear?"

Cynthia was nearly panting with rage by the time she finished, but it felt good. And it must have worked, because for one blissful moment, the line was quiet. Clearly, Moira hadn't expected her to speak from the heart.

No more playing nice, her inner dragon growled.

"Well, well. Sweet little Cynthia, full of such spite. What would your mother say?"

"She'd say not to waste my time with trash like you."

Moira made a choking sound, and Cynthia knew she'd struck a chord. But it would take more than a few sharp words to silence her cousin for good.

"Maybe I'm the one who's not finished with you," Moira hissed.

Cynthia was treading on thin ice, and she knew it, because Moira had the means — and motivation — to act on her words. But she was tired of letting Moira bully her and the rest of the world.

"When will you have enough, Moira? When does it end? Was killing Barnaby not enough?"

Moira snorted. "Of course it wasn't. I need you dead too." Then she laughed and spoke, sweet as pie. "Don't take it personally, cousin dear. It's just that I can't inherit everything as long as you're around." Then her voice dropped back to a menacing threat in one of those crazed personality switches Moira was capable of. "You would already be dead, if it wasn't for that damn wolf."

Cynthia froze. "What?"

Moira made a clucking sound. "That tramp of yours. What was his name? You know, the one with no manners. No family name. No money."

Cynthia's gut lurched. Cal? God, she'd been so young and stupid to have confided in Moira way back when.

Moira sighed dreamily. "He did have a great ass, though. Too bad his loyalties couldn't be bought."

Cynthia felt sick. Had Moira made a move on the man she loved?

"What have you done, Moira?"

Moira chuckled. "Oh, don't worry, cousin dear. That tramp of a wolf was loyal to you. So loyal, he even made a pact with Barnaby."

Cynthia froze. How on earth could Cal have been in contact with Barnaby? Why?

A dozen questions jammed her mind, but all she could get out was a hoarse whisper. "What kind of pact?"

"To protect you, of course. My God, woman. How blind can you be?"

Cynthia blinked into the distance, wondering the same thing.

"Two men, both so in love with you they'd give up everything." Moira's voice grew bitter. "I mean everything — even their lives. Pathetic, really, if you ask me."

It figured that Moira would find loyalty pathetic. Cynthia, however, knew self-sacrifice all too well. For years, she had endured the cutting pain and wept bitter tears.

She squeezed her eyes shut and wrapped one arm around her waist. Was there more to what had happened than she ever imagined? But why would Cal and Barnaby have worked together? Cal had ridden off, swearing never to return.

Then it hit her. All those secret meetings Barnaby had gone off to, insisting she stay home. All those times she'd felt watched over, even when there was no one in sight. All the close calls she and Joey had been lucky to escape.

Maybe it wasn't luck. Maybe there was more to her survival than she'd ever considered.

Cal, her dragon whispered.

She gulped. What had it cost Cal's pride to work with Barnaby — and to protect Barnaby's son?

At first, sorrow washed over her, but that was followed by a tsunami of rage, making her fingers flex into talon shape. If Moira were nearby, Cynthia really would have ripped her to bits.

"I've had it, Moira."

Moira laughed. "And I haven't even started having fun."

"If you so much as—"

"What? What will you do? Shun me from high society? Freeze my accounts?" She cackled. "Last I checked, you're the one hiding out in the jungle. The one everyone believes to be dead."

Maui was hardly a jungle but, yes. The long-abandoned plantation Cynthia managed was a long way away from the mansions and penthouses she'd grown up in.

Moira went on, gaining momentum. "Be careful how far you push me, cousin dear. I might just be tempted to make you suffer a little more. Do you have another lover I ought to cut out of your life before I kill you? Have you been sleeping around with that stable of shifters you keep at your little place? They are something, I'll give you that. That lion especially..." Her voice drifted into a sultry tone. "Or that tiger from next door. Or one of your dear dragons, perhaps. I guarantee I could make them howl in bed."

Cynthia nearly hung up the phone. Her cousin was a monster in more ways than one.

"Or, wait," Moira went on. "Maybe we could approach this like a couple of civilized dragons and strike a deal."

Over my dead body, Cynthia wanted to say, but she was still reeling from the low blows, and Moira went on.

"Perhaps I should strike where it hurts most. Joey. What is his safety worth to you? Say, your entire inheritance?"

The blood drained from Cynthia's cheeks. Would Moira really stoop that low?

"Sign everything over to me," Moira said as if the solution were obvious. "Make the Brenner and Baird fortunes mine, and I'll let the little brat live."

It was amazing how hard a woman's heart could pound without actually breaking out of her rib cage.

"Never. And you will not touch Joey," she warned in a voice closer to the rough contralto of her dragon's than her normal human tone. "If you ever—"

Moira cut in. "Enjoy that little seaside farm of yours while you can, dear cousin. You never know when you might lose it too."

Cynthia nearly hissed a reply, but she composed herself quickly, unwilling to give Moira the satisfaction of hearing her all riled up.

"If you come near my son, it will be the last thing you do," she said in a low, clear, and frighteningly cold tone. "I will end you, Moira. And I don't mean financially, cousin dear. I will kill you and avenge all the lives you've destroyed. Do you understand?"

She spelled out the last word in syllables, then waited for a reply. Apparently, Moira was too shocked to respond, so Cynthia went on.

"Good," she finished before clicking the phone off.

For the next minute, her pulse raced, and she felt triumphant. Finally, she'd given her cousin a piece of her mind.

But Moira's threats had been real. Specific. Insane, but thought through. Which meant she really was planning something. Something a simple phone call couldn't halt.

I haven't even started having fun.

Moira's words replayed in Cynthia's mind, and her threat hung in the crisp evening air.

Chapter Twelve

The minute Cal cruised back onto the plantation grounds, he could tell something was up. For one thing, Dell came down the porch steps and waved him over, which was strange enough. Then there was the fact that Cynthia was distraught about something. He could sense it even if she was nowhere to be seen.

He parked the Triumph and walked to Dell, while his wolf went on red alert.

"Hey," he grunted, resisting the urge to shove his hands into his pockets. There was no telling what Dell might do.

"Hey," Dell replied in a tone that was impossible to read. The lion shifter studied him for a full minute before speaking again. "Dinner will be ready in fifteen minutes."

Well, that's what Dell said out loud. But his eyes added a lot more. Something like, *Yes, you're actually invited. And yes, I will be watching you closely, wolf.*

Cal stuck his hands up, showing he meant no harm. Dinner? Wow. For the past week, he'd been scarfing down meals alone because it was clear he wasn't welcome at the pack's family-style dinners. And honestly, he had been glad to keep his distance. But now...

Cal tilted his head, studying Dell for some sign of a trap. But there was no ill vibe, just a weary resignation on the lion shifter's part. When Cal glanced up at Cynthia's balcony, Dell gave a slight nod and let enough of his thoughts slip out for Cal to read.

Yes, she's the one who invited you. And no, I don't know what's up. But whatever you do, you make sure you treat her well.

Cal hid a scowl. He'd always treated his mate well, and he always would.

But getting himself uninvited wouldn't help anyone, so he nodded. "Fifteen minutes. See you then."

Dell fixed him with another look of warning before heading back into the kitchen. Cal watched him go, not quite sure what to make of it all. Part of him rejoiced because, hell — even a lone wolf appreciated being included from time to time. And any chance he had to be close to Cynthia was a prize. But something had upset her, and he prayed it wasn't him.

He strode off to the washroom, cleaned up quickly, and stared into the mirror for a while. Barely a decade had passed since he'd first met Cynthia, but somehow, he looked – and felt – thirty years older. That many more lines on his brow, so many more scars. He stared into his own eyes, wondering when they had gotten so wary, so dull. A tiny spark of hope remained, but he wasn't sure if that was a good or a bad thing.

Then he shoved away from the sink and marched back to the main house. He was invited to dinner, damn it. No way was he going to pass that up.

"Can I help with something?" he offered, peeking in the kitchen.

The contrasting scents of lemongrass, ginger, and coconut milk hit his nose, one sharp, the other earthy, and the latter sweet. Dell stood at the stove, tending to two steaming pots, a wok, and what looked like a fresh loaf of bread. His daughter, Quinn, was in a baby recliner nearby, waving a wooden serving spoon and squeaking in glee. Joey was there too, bustling between the cupboard and the porch table.

Dell jerked his chin toward the little redhead. "You can help Joey set the table."

Joey nodded earnestly. "Mommy says everyone has to help."

Dell tousled his hair. "You got that right."

"We have to set it for twelve people," Joey said like he had the most serious task in the world. "Not just eleven."

Cal shadowed the kid, wondering how awkward the evening would feel. But as the others appeared, one by one, everything went surprisingly smoothly. Their eyes might have widened at the sight of him setting the table, and he did get side glances that reminded him he'd better behave, or else. But otherwise, everyone seemed okay with him there.

"Hey," Connor grunted, sitting at the head of the table.

"Hi, Cal," Jenna called brightly, taking the seat to Connor's right.

The others filled in around them while Dell set out the food, but no one touched anything, and the minutes quietly ticked by.

"Is your mom coming?" Anjali finally asked Joey.

He barely looked up from the picture he was coloring to pass time. "She said soon."

Everyone exchanged concerned glances, a few of which ended accusingly on Cal, but no one said a word. Slowly, haltingly, conversation started up, growing smoother as time went on. Anjali talked about her trip to Kahului, Connor raved about Jenna's latest surfboard design, and Sophie and Hailey exchanged notes on their latest crops.

"The coffee beans are just starting to bud..." Hailey said.

"The children's shop had the cutest onesies..." Anjali smiled.

"Her best board yet," Connor announced, touching Jenna's shoulder with pride.

She laughed. "Says the guy who's been out surfing... twice?"

"Three times."

Before long, conversation was in full swing, with everyone chatting away. Everyone but Cynthia, and even Dell shot a pointed look at the clock. Cynthia was never late. She was always early – obsessively so.

"Hi, Mommy!" Joey called when she appeared at last.

Cal's head whipped around, and he held his breath, steeling himself for the jolt he always got from seeing his mate.

And, wow. She was gorgeous as ever, but stressed too. More stressed than usual, which was saying a lot. Still, she flashed a smile at Joey and nodded to the others in that regal way of hers.

"Sorry I'm late."

"I knew you'd finally come around to island time," Dell cracked.

Cynthia stooped to kiss Joey and slipped into her seat at the opposite end of the table from Connor, which put her kitty-corner to Cal. Her face was flushed, and the light tone of her voice was forced. "I just had to—" She broke off and covered her mouth, looking at the unserved meal. "I'm so sorry. You shouldn't have waited."

"You're right." Dell grinned and started filling Cynthia's plate. "But there's this thing called etiquette. And apparently, it's rubbed off on me." He faked an exasperated sigh. "Promise me you'll never tell my friends."

Connor cleared his throat in a sharp hint, but Dell just shrugged. "I mean, besides these yo-yos."

"You actually have other friends?" Tim asked.

"Let's say I pretend."

Everyone laughed, and Cynthia shot Dell a grateful look. Still, her brow remained deeply furrowed, and she barely glanced at her food. Cal let his gaze wander in the direction of the stairs Cynthia had come down. Earlier that day, she had been so much more relaxed. Now she was as tight as a bowstring. Who — or what — had done that to her?

At least it didn't seem to be his fault, as he concluded when Cynthia flashed him a genuine smile.

"Okay, everybody. Dig in." Dell waved, taking his seat.

Silverware clattered, and dishes were passed back and forth, with seconds and thirds served. Cal had no idea what the main course was — some kind of Thai-style chicken, maybe? It was good, but he was too tuned in to Cynthia to really taste the food. She kept eyeing the horizon, and when she did remember her food, she stabbed at her plate as if picturing an enemy.

Conversation went on all around them, but Cal tuned out, trying to think of something that would cheer Cynthia up.

Adirondacks. Nighttime. Boathouse, his wolf hummed.

Bittersweet memories washed over him as he thought back to his very first night with Cynthia. A night he'd replayed countless times over the past years whenever he found himself losing hope.

He closed his eyes and let his senses fill in the details. The scent of fall leaves carpeting the ground. The silver lines of moonlight rippling over a long, narrow lake. The sound of music drifting across the water and the warmth of Cynthia in his arms.

And just like that, he drifted away from Maui and into that perfect Adirondack night. A thrilling, once-in-a-lifetime kind of night, because it had been his first with Cynthia. The first of what he'd hoped would extend over a lifetime...

He caught that thought and reeled it back. That wouldn't help Cynthia unwind. Only the good parts would, so he concentrated on those. The haunting call of a loon, the wingbeats of geese heading south. The brilliant fall colors of the forest, mesmerizing even when viewed as shades of gray in the dark. And above all, the enduring sense of peace.

Cynthia sighed quietly, so Cal kept it up, carefully shielding his thoughts from the others and aiming them all toward her. He imagined the creak of the steps as they climbed to the second floor of her father's boathouse. The squeak of rusty door hinges letting them into the loft. The soft heaven of the mattress he and Cynthia sank into. The tangy goodness of her lips, opening under his.

Cal took a deep breath, trying not to let things get too X-rated. But it was hard, what with Cynthia so close. A good thing the others didn't seem to notice.

"...too much acidity in the soil..." Sophie was saying. Or was that Hailey?

"...but I still need to adjust the curve of the rails..." someone else said. Jenna? Cal couldn't tell, because half his mind was on Cynthia, and the other half was in the past.

Kiss me... Cynthia's eager whisper echoed in his mind.

Cal's fingers twitched as he relived the silky feel of her skin under layers of clothing he helped her out of, one by one. His hand cupped her breast — at least, in his head, it did — and he could feel her heart race.

115

Something moved beside him, and he opened his eyes long enough to see Cynthia take a hasty gulp of wine. Then he let his eyelids slide down again and dove back into the memories.

Please, please don't make me beg. Her voice was a whisper on the wind.

His hands slid over the swell of her hips and held her body against his.

Nothing's off-limits, he'd replied.

The memory was so vivid, he almost believed that too. That nothing was off-limits, and not even a decade of cruel destiny could stand between them. Nothing. No one. Never again.

"Hey, Joey," Dell said, ripping Cal out of the fantasy. "Are you ready?"

Cal's head snapped up, and Cynthia's did too. Dell couldn't have picked a more poignant reminder of everything that still divided them.

"Ready for what?" Cynthia asked.

"For camping!" Joey squeaked in glee before running inside.

"Anjali and I promised to show Joey how to pitch a tent and sleep out. Remember?" Dell cocked his head.

"Oh. Right," Cynthia bluffed. "Tonight?"

Tim laughed. "It's Dell's way of getting out of washing the dishes."

"Me and Quinn are the cowboys, and Dell and Anjali are the Indians," Joey explained, clearly thrilled.

Anjali let out a wry grin. "Yep. Real Indians. You get it?"

Dell laughed, though the comment seemed to go over Joey's head.

"Camping out?" Cynthia murmured, still looking a little lost.

Cal couldn't blame her. Part of his mind — and all of his heart — was still in the Adirondacks.

For the next few minutes, the porch was a flurry of activity as the last bit of food was scraped off the plates. Joey bounded upstairs and back, appearing with a backpack of supplies that

Cynthia fussed over as if he were leaving for months instead of one night.

"Your flashlight... Your teddy..."

"I've got everything," Joey insisted as Anjali, Dell, and Quinn waited at the edge of the porch.

Cal could see *mommy* vibes fluttering around Cynthia like angels' wings.

"If you need anything..."

"Good night, Mommy." Joey reached up for a hug.

Cal sighed. It would have been nice to have a childhood like that.

"Good night, sweetie." Cynthia knelt and enveloped her son in a huge hug, rocking him back and forth.

Cal could see Cynthia force herself away before she — or the kid — got second thoughts. Then she motioned out into the night. "Have a good time."

"You too," Anjali called with a mischievous wink.

Dell shot Cal a frown that said, *Don't read into that.*

When they all turned and disappeared down a footpath, Cynthia watched for a long time, clutching a column of the porch.

"Well, I guess we'll get going too," Jenna announced, pulling Connor up.

"We are?" He looked up from his second helping of dessert.

"Yes, we are." The she-dragon's voice was firm as she dragged her mate toward the stairs.

"We'll do the dishes," Tim said, heading to the kitchen.

Hailey shot out an arm and redirected him toward the stairs while nodding to Cal behind Tim's back in some kind of hint he didn't understand. Then it hit him.

"I'll do the dishes," Cal rushed to say. "It's the least I can do."

"We're happy to help," Chase added.

Tim growled under his breath and pinned Cal with yet another look of warning. *Yeah. We'll help — and keep an eye on you, wolf.*

"We would love to help," Hailey agreed, pulling Tim toward the stairs. "But sadly, we can't. Remember that project you said you'd help me with tonight?"

"What project?" Cal heard Tim ask as they disappeared into the night.

Hailey's answer was lost as another two chairs scraped across the porch.

"We have to get back to the dogs." Sophie gave Cynthia an apologetic smile and steered Chase gently in the direction of their house.

"But the dishes. . ." Chase started.

"Like I said," Cal murmured. "It's the least I can do."

Chase didn't look so sure, but Sophie's demure smile made his eyes glaze over slightly, and he followed her down the porch stairs. Clearly, the woman had more on her agenda for the evening than just walking the dogs.

Plus another agenda, Cal suspected when he found himself alone with Cynthia. She was still gazing off in the direction Joey had gone, her hand tight around the banister.

Cal sighed and collected the dishes as silently as he could. The women of Koakea were stars to give him this one-on-one time, and even if it only amounted to washing dishes in Cynthia's company, he'd take what he could get.

He made three trips, carrying plates and platters to the kitchen, then filled the sink with warm water, squirted it with soap, and rolled up his sleeves.

"Hey," Cynthia whispered.

He glanced up to see her leaning against the doorway, watching him.

"Hey." He nodded back.

He stirred the water in the sink until the soap sudded up, then circled the sponge over a dish.

Cynthia sighed and gestured over her shoulder. "Sorry. They guys can be a little. . . overprotective."

"Good," Cal grunted, and he meant it.

For the next few minutes, neither of them spoke, and the only sound was the quiet swish of water or the muted clink of silverware. Well, that was the only sound in the house.

Outside, Maui was more alive than ever, with chirping crickets and the distant crash of surf.

Cynthia stepped forward, and they fell into a system without so much as a word. He pre-washed the dishes, and she loaded them into the dishwasher while he scrubbed the pots and pans. Then she stood beside him, drying each of the remaining items as he placed them in the rack. Once again, she was so near yet so far, and he ached to pull her close.

"Everything okay?" he murmured, keeping his eyes on the frying pan he washed next.

"Sure," Cynthia said, a little too breezily.

If she'd left it at that, he'd have figured it meant, *I don't want to talk right now.* But a moment later, she added, "Why do you ask?"

Which was about as clear a signal a woman could send that she wanted to talk.

So he replied, trying to keep his voice light. "You came to dinner looking like you were ready to murder someone, and you're still a little tense."

He left out the part in between when she'd started slipping over toward *sensual,* as he had.

Cynthia straightened her shoulders. "I am perfectly relaxed."

Cal's inner wolf stole close enough to the surface to growl, *I'd like to show her relaxed.*

Another flurry of heated images rushed through his mind, and he shuffled slightly, fighting the tightness in his groin.

Beside him, Cynthia stiffened and cleared her throat.

Cal hid a smile. "My mistake, then."

Not a mistake, his wolf growled, sniffing the air. *She remembers too.*

When he reached his mind toward hers, her thoughts were a jumble. But images of the two of them wrapped around each other that night in the Adirondacks definitely occupied one corner of her mind.

Cynthia whisked the dish towel over a pan then hung it on a hook with a sharp clang. A moment later, she spoke in a tight voice.

"I made a phone call. One I've been meaning to make for a long time. I just wish I could have talked in person instead."

Cal frowned. "Talked to who?"

Cynthia let half a second go by before muttering, "Moira."

The pot Cal was washing slipped out of his hands and disappeared with a splash that splattered suds as far as his chin. "Moira?"

Cynthia shushed him and shot a pointed look toward the porch. Everyone had gone, but if anyone caught wind of Moira's name, they would come rushing back.

"Yes, Moira," she growled.

He stared. "You called her? Why?"

Cynthia set the pot down with a firm thump. "Oh, you know," she said, forcing a casual tone. "I just wanted to get a few things off my chest."

It was all Cal could do to finish the dishes instead of grabbing Cynthia's shoulders and demanding to know more.

"But she might—" he started quietly.

"Find out where I am?" Cynthia snorted. "She's known for a while."

"How do you know?"

"She admitted as much to Dell."

His jaw dropped. "Dell?"

Cynthia nodded without showing any emotion, and Cal had no choice but to wait for her to say more. He pulled the plug, draining the sink, and scooped the scraps out of the strainer before rinsing his hands.

"Moira had quite a few things to say," Cynthia went on.

Cal froze, then hurriedly dried his hands. "And you believed her?"

Cynthia made a face. "Some things, yes. Others, no. Believe me, I can tell the difference now."

Cal understood the bitterness in her tone. If he could have gone back in time and given Cynthia that ability a decade ago. . .

She hung the last pot on the pegboard and stood facing it rather than him.

"So..." Cal finally prompted, edging around to watch her eyes.

Cynthia made a face. "It was the usual delightful conversation. Including her saying, 'Don't get too comfortable on that farm of yours.'"

Her eyes blazed, and he could hear her inner dragon growl something like, *It's a plantation, it's home, and we'll get as comfortable as we damn well please.*

His hackles rose. Typical Moira — posing veiled threats.

"You think she's planning something?"

Cynthia made a face. "I know she is. The question is when. How. Where."

Her eyes drifted out the door. The kitchen faced the central hallway, and the view opened all the way across the porch and into the darkness of night. A firefly flickered, and the tiki torches that lined the walkway danced in the night. Cal gazed out, balling his fists.

"Anyway..." Cynthia murmured, then trailed off, looking into his eyes.

Another quiet minute ticked by, and Cal had the distinct feeling she was brimming with more. A huge, oppressive *something* she simply had to share. But when she opened her mouth—

Something flickered through her eyes, and her lips sealed again. When she finally spoke, it was with a note of defeat.

"Well, it's getting late."

He nodded dumbly.

"Better get to bed," she added, in a voice that begged him not to let her go.

Cal stood still, not sure what to do. Then, idiot he was, he echoed her words. "Better get to bed."

It was as if destiny was in the kitchen, determined to fuck up his one last chance by making him say the opposite of what he really meant.

Don't go, Cynthia. Stay. Let me touch you. Hold you. Kiss you.

Cynthia stepped toward the stairs — the demarcation line to her private turf that no one ever crossed. Her movements were mechanical, as if she were a marionette controlled by a cruel puppeteer. She paused with one foot on the bottom step and looked back at him with huge, hopeful eyes.

"Good night," she whispered.

His heart pounded. His fingers twitched. His wolf howled.

No! Don't let her go!

But pride was a funny thing. It could keep a man from reaching out and grabbing his wildest dreams. It could parade the past before the windows of your mind, making damn sure the pain and betrayal sank deep. Deep enough to form a chasm you could never, ever cross, even if it meant losing your mate.

"Good night," he heard himself echo.

Still, neither of them budged. They just stood there, eyes locked, chests rising and falling, brows sweaty despite the cool evening breeze.

Cal would have sworn that another *almost* encounter was about to slip out of his grasp, when fury swept through him. Was he really fool enough to let the woman he loved go?

His blood rushed. His cheeks heated, and his back itched the way it did when his wolf threatened to take over.

No, his inner beast barked.

And just like that, he was striding across the floor. Purposefully. Intently. His eyes never left Cynthia's lips, and the moment he got close—

The imaginary barrier that had been looming between them crumbled, and they fell into a huge, hungry kiss. Their bodies collided. Their tongues tangled. Their hands bumped. Like they had to make up for a decade of abstinence in a single, fiery moment.

Heart pounding, he laced his fingers through Cynthia's, raised her hands over her head, and crushed his lips against hers. She opened her mouth eagerly as he pinned her against the wall.

"Yes," she whispered. "Yes, please."

Chapter Thirteen

For a few breathless moments, all Cynthia could do was wrap her fingers around Cal's and hang on. Her body was on fire, and her blood rushed.

Yes! Yes! We have our mate back again! her inner dragon cried.

Technically, he had her, nice and tight against his hard body. But that was fine too.

She panted, trying to touch Cal everywhere at once. His chest. His shoulders. His face. A sound escaped her lips that was right on the border of a laugh and a sob, and she had no idea which. Either was perfectly possible, given the way she felt.

"I missed you so much..." she whimpered between kisses.

"Missed you too much," Cal murmured back, and she could feel the pain coded into his words. The world didn't often summon something that was *too much* for Cal, and for him to admit as much...

She imagined all her pain, all her loneliness, and all her regrets, then turned around and imagined them all from his point of view. How much had it pained Cal to see her come and go with Barnaby? Worse, to see her pregnant and then cuddling that other man's child?

A sob racked her, but Cal's insistent kiss pulled her back from the brink.

"Cynthia..."

He smoothed her hair back with one hand while tangling it with the other. The two sides of her lover showing again.

Then he let out a low, rumbly growl, pressed her even harder against the wall, and went to work on her in earnest.

Locking her hands in place, raking his free hand over her body, pressing his hips against hers. She felt weightless, as if floating on a cloud, but at the same time, she felt every inch of his hard, unyielding weight. It took a few seconds to realize he'd lifted her clear off the ground and that she'd wrapped her legs around his waist.

"Okay with you?" Cal growled.

She barely managed a nod. Hell yes.

Cal chuckled, regaining a little control. "You mean, right here by the front door?"

She blinked, looking over his shoulder. They were well inside the house, but yes — anyone walking past would be treated to a side of their co-alpha they'd never seen before.

Not that she cared much. All she wanted was him. In her. Over her. Around her.

On the other hand... She glanced up the stairs. There was a perfectly good wall up in her bedroom, and they could use the trip up to strip.

"Good idea," Cal muttered, reading her mind. He lowered her in a rush and pulled her up the stairs.

She kept one hand on the banister and one on his shirt, yanking it up to touch the checkerboard of his abs. Cal, meanwhile, got to work opening the top buttons of her dress. Halfway up, they stopped and went back to rushed, anxious kisses, as if they might never get the chance again. Then Cal motioned her onward, and the idea of a bed spurred her on. But at the top stair, Cal groaned.

"Forget it," he muttered, wrapping his arms around her waist and lowering her to the floor right there at the top of the stairs.

She lay back, tingling with anticipation. "What about the wall?"

"Oh, that's coming. I swear it is. But first..." His glowing wolf eyes prowled over her body, and his fingers hooked over the bodice of her dress. "You like this dress?"

She held her breath, then lied.

"No."

His eyes sparkled, and in one sweeping gesture, he tore down the front of her dress. Buttons popped into the air, and several bounced down the stairs with gleeful little taps. One landed in the hallway and spun there for a while. Spinning, wheeling, just like Cynthia felt when Cal unclasped her bra and lowered his head to her chest.

She gasped and bucked at the searing touch of his lips. Cal kneaded and teased the soft flesh until her nipples hardened. For the first time in over a decade, she felt desired. Worshiped. Coveted, like a goddess.

"So beautiful," he groaned.

His stubble scraped her sensitive flesh, and he rolled his fingers, coaxing her nipples into high peaks.

More... More... She wanted to beg.

She didn't have to finish the thought, because Cal was already there, wrapping his lips around her tight pink beads. Sucking hard, then smoothing over them with his tongue, blinding her with desire.

When her hips jerked against his in a sudden reflex, Cal glanced up with a pirate's grin.

"Exactly what I was thinking..." he murmured, sliding down her body.

His hands were everywhere, his lips moving steadily downward, and his tongue—

Oh, yes. She barely bit back a moan when she caught a glimpse of what he had in mind. The man was going straight for her core, and she couldn't wait.

His tongue teased her navel while his hands pushed away the rest of her dress and panties, leaving her bare. Not asking for permission, but not needing to — not with the way she guided his head down. He slowed just long enough to spread her legs, trace one thick finger through her folds, and take a deep breath.

Mine, his eyes blazed.

Then he dipped his head and put his mouth against her, making her jolt. Soon, she was writhing in unbridled pleasure as he brought her to ever higher heights.

Vaguely, Cynthia realized that might not take much. She'd been living the life of a nun—

Her dragon cackled. *A nun?*

Well, maybe not a nun, given the number of nights she'd dreamed of Cal and touched herself. But that only had a marginal effect, and she knew he was about to blow her mind.

"You make me feel like a virgin again," she groaned.

Cal lifted his head, though he kept circling one finger inside. "Again, again?" He flashed a wolfish grin.

She would have laughed — because, yes, he'd been her very first lover — but the only sound she could produce was a moan.

"You want me to take it easy?" he teased.

"Don't you dare."

If her hands were free, she would have shaken a finger at him. But they were too busy guiding his head back to where she needed him most.

Cal readily complied, and before long, she had to cover her mouth to suppress her own cries.

Yes... yes... She wanted to howl out loud.

Lying sprawled over the top stair shouldn't have felt so wickedly good, but Cal was a master when it came to pleasuring her. Plus, the front door was ajar, lending the air a sense of danger.

One sound, and everyone will come running...

She was naked but for the pearls around her neck and splayed out for anyone to see. But a freight train was speeding through her veins, and when it hit exactly the right spot—

Cal plunged his fingers deeper, triggering a colossal orgasm, and she groaned. Cal helped her muffle the sound even as he coaxed shudder after shudder out of her.

I want to hear you, his voice boomed in her mind. *Me, and no one else. Let me hear you. I want it. I need it.*

His body was tight as steel, telling her he wasn't kidding about the *needing* part. So she let the fingers over her mouth open slightly, releasing just enough of her moan to fill the space around them.

"So good," she sang. "So, so good..."

In her mind, she rose and fell like a ship in stormy waters. Eventually, the waves receded, leaving her high and dry. Panting wildly, she threaded her fingers through his thick hair and lay limp.

Cal ghosted kisses over every inch of her body until he reached her mouth. There, he laid his lips over hers, matching every curve, every seam. Then he swept his tongue over hers in a slow, sultry dance.

Her eyes went wide, and she nearly broke out of the kiss. She'd forgotten the sweet taste of her own pleasure mixed with the deeper flavor of Cal.

She laughed, and the sound rang down the stairs.

Cal cocked his head. "What?"

She touched her pearls. The middle one felt warm, which just went to show how much Cal turned her on.

"Something tells me my mother never felt that kind of pleasure."

Cal made a face. "Please don't make me think of your mother at a time like this."

She laughed and pulled him into a hug. And Cal, bless him, managed that without crushing her, even though they were teetering at the top of the stairs. He let her keep him there for a full minute before gently easing away.

"Now about that wall..." he murmured, making her nipples peak all over again.

His voice was deep and needy, and the sound vibrated like a drum. When he stood and offered her a hand, he made her feel like a lady instead of the depraved wild woman who'd just let him strip her naked on the stairs.

Speaking of naked... Her dragon growled, admiring the rear view of his jeans.

Almost a shame to take them off, she joked.

Almost, but not quite, her dragon shot back.

She stopped Cal with a quick tug. "My turn..."

Smoothing her hands over the hard planes of his chest, she rolled his shirt up and over his head. She paused, ready to admire his body one more time. Then she froze and covered her mouth with one hand.

"Oh, Cal..."

Burn marks covered most of the upper right side of his body, running from the solid block of his shoulder all the way down his thick, muscled arm and ribs.

Slowly, Cal pulled her hand away from her mouth and held it in between them. Then he grunted, and his shoulders drooped slightly.

"Not what you wanted to see, huh?"

She clasped his hand with both of hers and kissed it, making his eyes go wide. Then she took a deep breath. "It's all I want to see. You. Me." She motioned between them. "Like we are now, not like we used to be."

His eyes shone with hope as she went back to touching him, caressing every inch of his chest. The puckered burns, the unscarred fields of bronze. He'd always been a warrior in her eyes, and now more than ever, it showed.

"Now, about those jeans," she said, trying to joke away the last bit of tension.

He smiled and raised his arms out of the way. "All yours, m'lady."

She grinned so broadly, it hurt. He'd used the term a few times in the past, and it had always made her blush. Now, it just made her laugh. If her mother could only see her now. She wasn't much of a lady any more.

Cal groaned. "Enough with your mother. Please."

Oops. She'd have to watch her thoughts more closely. Or rather, make sure only certain ones got through. Like the image that popped into her mind a moment later — one of her kneeling before him, cupping his cock in both hands, and...

Cal made a choked sound. "Haven't you tortured me enough?"

He was joking, but a stab of guilt consumed her when she considered everything she'd put him through. So she sidled closer, slipping her hands into the waistband of his jeans. Once she'd helped him out of them, she ran her hands under his boxers, almost as timidly as she had so many years earlier.

"No scar tissue there," he said in a low, rumbly growl that went right to her core.

"Not what I was worried about."

He raised an eyebrow. "No? What then?"

She palmed him. "Just worried about an old maid like me ever fitting a man like you in, that's all."

It was only half a joke, because it truly felt like her heart wasn't the only organ to have shriveled in the past years.

Cal cupped her face in both hands. "Not an old maid. You've only aged in good ways."

She snorted. "Like a fine wine?"

He shook his head. "In experience. And believe me, it's like riding a bike. You never forget how. At least, so I'm told."

His words hit her hard, and she gulped. Cal had been celibate for years, and all for her.

So, fix that already, her dragon said.

She worked up the nerve to run her hand down the front of his boxers. Then she pressed close, letting her breasts squeeze against his chest. Slowly, she wrapped her fingers around his shaft and worked her hand up and down.

"All those nights I was alone..." she whispered, then let her thoughts fill in the rest.

Cal's eyes glassed over as he processed the image in her mind. An image of her, naked and dreamy-eyed in her solitary bed, sweeping her hands over her own skin. Delving deeper, pleasuring herself as best she could.

"Did you ever..." she started, then cleared her throat.

Cal's mind opened to hers, sharing an image of him leaning against a wall in a place she didn't recognize. Someplace dark, dingy, and nowhere near as finely appointed as her private suite had been, but just as lonely.

"Did I ever what?" he murmured, placing his hand over hers to set the perfect pace.

She cleared her throat, fighting the prim princess away. "Did you ever... I mean, did you..."

The act seemed so private, so secret, she couldn't bring herself to say it.

"Did I ever jack off, wishing it was you?" He tightened his fingers over hers as his shaft swelled. "Only about a thousand times."

129

Coming from anyone else or in any other situation, his words might have sounded crude. But Cynthia's blood heated. Maybe he'd done it at the same time she had. Maybe the link she'd always felt had kept them bonded even when they were miles apart.

She'd never been so tempted to drop to her knees and suck him in as then, but something made her pause. *Really* pause until Cal slowed too, quietly studying her eyes.

"Anything you want, Cynthia. Anything."

Cynthia glanced at the bed, then at him. "Can I take a rain check on the wall? I mean, just for a little while?"

"Tell me what you want, even if it's to tell me to leave."

She shook her head. "I do *not* want you to leave. But. . . "

He followed her eyes to the bed, then glanced up with a knowing grin. "As you wish, m'lady. As you wish."

He started backing toward the bed as if he'd peeked into her mind and discovered exactly what she wanted. If he had, he seemed to be all in. Because the second his calves hit the mattress, he lay back, tugging on her hands.

Cynthia crawled over him, kissing and nudging him higher up the bed until they had plenty of space. Then she straddled him — too high, but damn, fireworks were already going off in her mind. She dragged her body against his, conscious of how wet her core was — and how hard Cal was. He gripped her hips and guided her lower until they were lined up.

"Perfect," he murmured, looking up into her eyes.

With a deep breath, Cynthia slid down until the head of his shaft settled into exactly the right place. Then she started rocking, taking him in one burning inch at a time.

Cal's eyes went to half-mast. His hips moved slightly, coaxing her on.

Yes, her dragon hummed, relishing the tendrils of heat that curled throughout her body.

It did burn, and that *virgin* feeling was never far away, but Cal was right. It was like riding a bicycle.

More like riding a cowboy, her dragon cackled, making her draw him deeper. Deeper. . .

Cal's hands snuck from her hips to her breasts, making her gyrate and moan. Was it even possible to feel so good? Was she really with her lover, or was it all a dream?

Dreams don't hurt so good, her dragon murmured. *Dreams don't make you want to breathe fire.*

Breathe what? Cal broke in, alarmed.

She dipped lower, kissing the notion away. Then she sat back, and wow, was that angle good.

"So good..."

Her head and shoulders were thrust back, her hips rolling, her mouth forming silent cries of pleasure. It was a damn good thing the guys couldn't see her now and discover she wasn't as prim and proper as they imagined.

"Promise me the guys will never see you like this," Cal groaned.

She crouched over him, grinning wickedly. "Believe me, I promise. Especially not like this..."

She dipped one shoulder, tempting him with her breast. Cal puckered up, caught the nipple, and swirled his lips around it.

"Or like this," she murmured, offering him the other side.

He lapped at it, then nipped, making her squeak. Then he drew his hand along the crease of her leg until his thumb touched her clit.

She shuddered against him. She was going to come soon, and come hard. Still, she managed to toss her hair back and tease him one more time.

"Or like this..." she said, leaning back and rocking harder, letting her breasts bounce.

But the more she moved, the more desperately she needed release. She ground harder, biting her lip against the exquisite pleasure building inside.

Faster, her dragon urged. *Deeper.*

Cal gripped her hips tightly, jerking up but leaving her in the dominant position. She rocked harder, feeling power course through her veins. For years, her life had been out of her control. But now, she was finally able to take the reins. To call the shots. To release her wild side.

Yes, her dragon hissed as her body danced faster.

Cal's eyes glowed — not just with passion but with wonder.

You will command armies someday, he'd said to her once. And for the first time in years, it didn't feel impossible. She could do anything. Go anywhere. Claim her life back for herself.

Claim your mate, too, her dragon cried.

Her jaw ached from the pressure of her canines trying to extend, but she fought them back. Maybe someday, she would be able to give Cal the mating bite and seal their bond forever. But for now...

She leaned back, propping her hands on his thighs. As the angle increased, so did the inner burn, and Cal groaned.

"Right there..."

She pressed harder, surrendering to raw need instead of fighting it as she'd been taught.

Nice girls don't get involved in that kind of thing.

Nice girls don't lose control.

Nice girls don't feel this good, her dragon growled.

Sweat beaded on her brow, and her pace quickened.

So close... Cal groaned in her mind.

In the past, she'd been happy to lie back and let him do most of the work in bed. And honestly, she'd be happy to do a lot of that in the future. But at that moment, it was all up to her.

All up to you, her dragon echoed.

So Cynthia did what she'd never done. She closed her eyes and let go of her self-control. Every single strand of it until she barely knew where she was. All she sensed was the need to take herself and her lover into the deep void of pleasure for a while.

"Yes..." Cal groaned, going stiff all over.

Cynthia took him even deeper, clamping down with her inner muscles at the same time. Light exploded in her mind, zipping around in little spirals. Cal shuddered, groaning with his release. A moist, hot flash filled her, and she whimpered, cherishing every drop. Then she went limp and dropped to his chest. How long she lay there panting, she had no clue. Only that she felt more fulfilled — and more emotionally drained — than ever before.

Cal's chest heaved too, and for a while, they lay splayed against each other, a complete, wonderful mess. Then he guided her to his side and spooned around her, making her feel complete.

"Whoa," he half whispered, half laughed. "Where did that come from?"

She kissed the thick arms encircling her. Her warrior was protecting her again. Loving her. Making her feel complete.

She turned, looped her arms around his neck, and gazed deep into his eyes. There was only one answer to that, and she knew it.

"From the heart, my mate. From the heart."

Then she kissed him, feeling warm, loose, and totally serene.

Chapter Fourteen

Cal closed his eyes and held Cynthia tightly. Her body was already spooned against his, but still — it felt as if he could never hold her close enough. His arms crossed over her chest, and he could count her every heartbeat. Which he did, just to assure himself he was in reality and not another dream.

"Mmm," Cynthia sighed, running her hands over his arms. Then she chuckled. "Are you marking me?"

He froze in the act of dragging his chin across her shoulder in slow, side-to-side movements.

"Um... I might be. Got a problem with that, miss?"

She wiggled, prompting another long scrape of stubble against skin. "Don't stop, and you won't have a problem, mister."

He grinned. There were so many sides to Cynthia. Classy and reserved. Cool and commanding. Warm and nurturing, though she rarely revealed that to anyone but Joey. She also had an elusive, saucy side, not to mention that take-charge-in-bed side that only came out once in a blue moon, like tonight.

I like, his wolf hummed. *I like.*

He went back to rubbing his chin over her skin, basking in the moment. One round of sex might not wipe away a decade of pain and sorrow. But, hell. It was a good start.

He thought back, trying to pinpoint what had finally made Cynthia flip that inner switch and allow him to get intimate again. Was it the song in the restaurant earlier that day? The subtle encouragement of the women in her pack?

Cynthia smoothed the hair of his forearms in one direction then the other, whispering, "No."

He held still. Had he done something wrong?

"Neither of those things," she said.

He exhaled. Apparently, she'd been reading his mind, and his train of thought had disturbed her sense of peace.

He brought his knees higher, snuggling her rear with his body, and all but growled in her ear. If destiny thought it could mess with him and his woman again, it had another thing coming.

"Forget it. Not important," he insisted.

A minute passed, and Cynthia relaxed, though not quite as much as before. Then she sighed, turned in his arms, and cupped his face.

"It is important," she said, looking far sadder than a woman ought to after sex as amazing as that. "I've been so blind. It kills me to think how much I put you through."

Cal shrugged. All that mattered was holding her again.

But Cynthia shook her head and held him tighter. "Like I said, I spoke to Moira before dinner."

He frowned. "I swear, that woman is at the root of all evil in this world."

Cynthia stroked his cheek, looking more sorrowful than ever. "She told me, Cal."

Her words were heavy with significance, and he immediately went on guard. "It's better not to listen to the lies she spins."

"True, but one comment sort of slipped out, and I believe it."

"That's the tricky thing with her kind. They use a kernel of truth to sell their lies."

"She told me about Barnaby's meetings with a certain wolf." Cynthia's voice was slow, careful.

Cal lay perfectly still. How the hell had Moira found out about that?

He tried bluffing it away. "Why would Barnaby do such a thing?"

"You tell me."

He took a deep breath, taking his time. In his dreams, he'd lived this moment a thousand times. His chance to finally tell her everything. All the sacrifices he'd made, all the battles he'd fought — all for her, his one true love. But as much as it killed him, he couldn't reveal a thing.

He closed his eyes. "I can't tell you. I promised."

She stroked his cheek softly. "You promised Barnaby?"

Damn it. Had Moira told Cynthia everything?

He nodded the teensiest, tiniest bit.

"What did you promise Barnaby?"

God, was he sick of the past. Sick of it flashing before his eyes, even when he had them closed. What the hell had he been thinking when he'd made that dumb promise?

We were thinking, anything for her, his wolf recalled.

"Cal..." Cynthia's voice was soft, sweet. Honest, because she didn't know any other way. "What did you promise Barnaby?"

He inhaled and exhaled slowly. Surely, Cynthia could understand why he wouldn't mess with a promise.

"All right, then let me guess, and you just nod or shake your head," she said. "That doesn't break the promise, does it?"

"Kind of pushing the boundaries, don't you think?"

She flashed a bittersweet smile, then grew serious again. "Barnaby called you in..."

Cal considered. Technically, no, but he wasn't keen to get into the details of how he'd snuck in to kill Barnaby.

"And you got to talking..." Cynthia continued.

He grimaced. Barnaby had done most of the talking.

"He offered you money..."

Cal looked up, feeling his eyes heat. Did Cynthia think so little of Barnaby — or him?

She nodded curtly. "I didn't think so. So damn honorable. Both of you," she muttered, though she didn't really sound angry. "Anyway, he asked you to stick around. To protect me."

Her eyes bored into him, and Cal had no choice but to nod slightly.

"To protect Joey, too?"

Cal's gut roiled as hard as it had the day he'd discovered she was pregnant, but he nodded. "Joey, too."

ANNA LOWE

"You did that? For me?" Cynthia's voice trembled.

"I love you. I will always love you," he whispered. "I would do anything for you."

"I love you too. More than anything else in the world. And yet..."

Her eyes grew blurry, and his wolf snapped to attention. *Whoa. Is she crying?*

She was shaking a little, that was for sure. Cal rubbed his thumbs over the back of her hands. "Cynthia..."

She turned away, burying her face in the pillow. "I loved you so much, but I didn't love you enough. God, Cal. I was so selfish. So stupid..." She broke into sobs.

Slowly, gently, he pried her away from the pillow and gathered her into his arms. They'd both experienced enough sorrow to last a dozen lifetimes. Why entertain more?

"You had no choice. They forced you." He smoothed a hand over her cheek, trying to find the right words. "I would have done the same thing, just to stay sane."

"But you didn't," she insisted, shaking in his arms. "You didn't try to forget me. You didn't pretend."

"I pretended lots, believe me."

Words didn't help, though, and he gave up after a while, holding her instead. Fighting the burn in his own eyes, not that he would admit as much.

Finally, Cynthia's tears eased, and she looked at him through huge, vulnerable eyes. Cal stroked her cheek. God, were they birds of a feather. Driven by the instinct to appear tough, even around each other.

"It doesn't matter any more," he whispered, guiding her hands to lie nice and flat against his chest instead of clutching at the sheets.

She started to shake her head, but he spoke first. "The past doesn't matter. Well, except maybe the good parts."

Her lips curled upward slightly.

"And Moira doesn't matter." He hated bringing up that bitch, but it had to be done. Once and for all, they had to agree on that one thing. "She won't mess with us again."

Cynthia shook her head. "She'll try. I guarantee it."

"Okay, she will. But she won't succeed. And you know why?"

Cynthia searched his eyes.

"Because love wins." He said it loudly, firmly, in case destiny was listening in. Destiny needed to hear that as much as Moira did. So he said it one more time for good measure. "Love wins."

Cynthia's smile grew, and she echoed his words. "Love wins."

Cal nodded. Then he kissed her, chasing away her doubts. Love would win, dammit, because he would fight for his mate to the very end.

"Mmm," Cynthia breathed into the kiss.

Slowly, their bodies cozied up in a whole different way. Not so much clutching each other but cuddling. Playing. Calling to one another. Cal moved his kiss from her lips to her shoulder because, hell. Every part of Cynthia needed to know he meant what he said.

When she settled into the mattress, he scooched lower, following her collarbone... her sternum... her breast...

Cynthia arched sharply, and her nipple begged for his lips. He popped it in and out of his mouth, suckling gently. Yeah, her nipples definitely needed to feel the love too.

"Cal..." Cynthia breathed, guiding his head to the other side.

"As you wish..."

The longer he touched her, the harder his cock grew, and before long, her wandering fingers homed in on that aching part of his body. When she grasped him, he hissed in raw desire.

"And what do you wish for, Mr. Zydler?" she breathed.

He grinned against the soft flesh of her breast, letting her figure that out on her own.

And sure enough, Cynthia started sliding her grip up and down his cock. Delicately, like he was made of her mother's goddamn china.

Not the mother again. Please, his wolf begged.

He snuck a hand down between her legs, marveling at every inch. All that smooth skin, free for him to enjoy. A fantasy come true in every possible way.

Cynthia arched as his fingers zeroed in on her core, but he didn't look up. He went right on kissing — licking — suckling her nipples, unable to get enough. Everything else faded away until it was just him and her. Her intoxicating scent. The silk of her skin. The heat of her body, calling to him.

"Cal. . ." she panted, hooking her legs around his waist.

He gritted his teeth, telling himself he could draw out this pleasure a little longer. But within seconds, he reared up and repositioned himself. Anchoring his hands on either side of her head, he lined up their bodies.

Cynthia looked up with those dark, dancing eyes that had seduced him from day one. Her raven-black hair was fanned out over the pillow, and her mouth opened a crack.

"I need you so much. . ." she whispered.

She raised her knees along his sides, which meant the only thing left for him to do was—

"Yes. . ." she groaned as he thrust in.

Cal closed his eyes, hanging on to the sweet burn. When the edge wore off, he withdrew then slammed forward.

Cynthia cried out, abandoning her inhibitions yet again. Handing the reins over and settling back as if to say, *Please make me feel good enough to chase the past away.*

Cal would have loved to utter another *As you wish,* but he was too busy losing his mind to sheer bliss. Having Cynthia ride him earlier had been incredible, and he'd loved every second. But this was different — even more intimate, somehow, because their bodies were wrapped around each other, creating a sensual cocoon. Her arms played over his back, her knees cradled his sides, and her hips rocked in time with his.

"Yes. . ." she moaned, extending her arms over her head.

He gripped them, pinning her in place against the force of his thrusts.

So good. . . Her voice echoed through his mind.

Faster. Harder, his wolf growled.

As the momentum built, so did the pressure in his body, until he was desperate for physical and emotional release.

Just a little longer, his wolf urged.

How he kept moving, he had no clue. His cock ached, and his knees felt like they were about to give out. Cynthia clenched her inner muscles around him, making him groan. Finally, he gathered every scrap of longing that had accumulated over the years, withdrew, and took a deep breath.

"Cal—"

Cynthia's voice cut off as he plunged deeper.

His vision dimmed. His shoulders stiffened, and every muscle in his body went rock hard. It was heaven. It was every forbidden dream come true. The impossible made possible, at least for one night.

Yes, his wolf hummed. *Yes...*

Cynthia went limp before he did, but a moment later, she cried out and shuddered a second time. Her nails dug into his shoulders, giving him the edge he needed to pump into her one more time.

Then they both collapsed into the sheets, panting. Cal used his last ounce of energy to pull her close. Then he shut his eyes and concentrated on breathing for a little while. Not that he'd mind dying from sheer ecstasy, but he'd rather spend more time with his true love first.

He cracked open an eye, then let it shut again. Okay, so the bed was a mess. The room was strewn with clothes they'd eventually have to reclaim. The night wouldn't last forever, and in a few short hours, Joey would come skipping home. But for now...

Let go, Cynthia whispered in his mind.

Funny, that was supposed to be his line.

But, hell. He'd never felt wearier or so utterly satisfied. Maybe they really could ignore the outside world a little longer.

Let go, Cynthia said, caressing his back.

Cal inhaled... exhaled... and slowly, comfortably, eased into a deep, contented sleep.

Chapter Fifteen

For the first part of the night, Cynthia slept like a baby, bliss-fully unaware of anything other than Cal's arms around her. Later, she woke briefly, smiled at her sleeping lover, and ran a hand along his cheek. Then she closed her eyes and let her-self drift in and out of dreams. The best dreams ever, because they focused on the present instead of a past she'd never get to relive. Peppered into those nice dreams were glimpses of a future that looked brighter and more joyful than she'd ever dared to imagine.

But something dark and foreboding crept along the edges of her dreams, and she awoke with a jolt, looking around. Cal was still spooned up against her, his arms wrapped around her exactly as before. His deep, steady breaths indicated he was sound asleep, though Cynthia felt wide awake. She lay still, piquing her senses.

The nighttime sounds of the plantation were as peaceful as they'd ever been, with leaves rustling gently in the breeze. The scent of night-blooming cereus drifted past billowing curtains that danced before the balcony door. Moonlight streamed in with the scent, beckoning her outside.

She slipped out of bed, feeling unsettled yet silly at the same time. Dell and the other guys were right about her being too uptight. What kind of person couldn't sleep through a night as perfect as this?

Still, something gnawed at her nerves, so she stepped out-side and rested her hands on the balcony railing. Moonlight rippled over the ocean, and palm trees waved to her from the shoreline.

Go to sleep, they seemed to yawn. *Go to sleep.*

A glance in the direction of Dell and Anjali's house drew a faint smile to her lips. That was probably it — she was unsettled because Joey wasn't home. She closed her eyes, picturing how excited he'd be to rush home in the morning and tell her all about camping out. Dell would have told him funny stories and probably cast shapes on the tent walls with his hands and a flashlight. A grand adventure in Joey's eyes.

She smiled into the moonlight, letting her gaze wander over the plantation grounds. Such a peaceful night. So perfect. So—

Her head jerked to the right, and she squinted. What was that, moving in the distance?

She searched the sky just above the horizon. That had to be Kilauea, spewing more ash over on the Big Island, right? Or had that been lightning, flashing beyond the clouds?

Just as she was beginning to relax again, that faint, distant *something* moved again, and a chill went down her spine. Should she wake Cal — or better yet, Connor, who was responsible for security? She grimaced, wondering what exactly she would report.

I saw something.

Connor would rub a hand over his sleepy eyes and ask, *What? What did you see?*

I'm not sure. But something moved way out there.

It would sound ridiculous. Worse, she'd sound paranoid, and everyone already considered her far too wound up. Besides, she was covered in Cal's scent, and she wasn't ready to make the others aware of that.

But something had moved out there, dammit. She glanced at Cal. He was as close to baby-faced with slumber as his grizzled features were capable of, and there was no way she would disturb that. *The sleep of the just*, as her grandmother used to say.

Instead, she took a deep breath and extended her arms, tuning in to the wind. Her fingers stretched, and her nostrils flared.

Yes, her dragon hummed. *Let me out...*

The skin around her nostrils burned, as it always did when she was seized with the urge to shift. She hurried to fasten her necklace around her ankle first. She wore it everywhere — around her neck as a human and around her ankle as a dragon. Yes, it was silly, but she'd promised her mother to always keep the pearls close, and that was the best way.

She pushed open the swinging railing Tim had installed on the balcony, took a deep breath, and jumped, letting her dragon take over. Dive shifts were always exhilarating since they began with a free fall. But the moment her wings snapped open, the plunge turned into a graceful upward arc. With a sharp flick of her tail, she climbed into the sky, then beat her wings to gain altitude. As she flew, she flexed her claws, thrilling in her own power.

Feels so good, her dragon hummed, banking left and right to warm up.

It did feel good. A different kind of *good* than sleeping with Cal—

That wasn't good, her dragon insisted. *That was amazing.*

She grinned. *Amazing* was right, and she'd hated leaving him. Still, if she was lucky, they could squeeze in one more round of sex before the sun rose. But right now...

Beating her wings steadily, she headed out over the sea. All she had to do was fly out for a few minutes to assure herself nothing was moving in the darkness. Then she could head home to sleep off the remainder of the night.

But a few minutes turned into fifteen and then thirty as she flew on, chasing the elusive sight. It was like climbing a mountain — just when she thought the end was near, another bend would appear, making the journey stretch on.

The longer she flew, the more the feeling of dread grew. She studied the waves below, imagining sea dragons staging an attack. But there was no indication of any such thing. Just a flickering motion straight ahead and a strange pounding in the air. Faint yet foreboding, like a set of drums warning her...

She frowned into the night. Warning her of what?

The sound grew louder, and alarms clanged in her head. She banked sharply, then climbed.

Whoa, her dragon muttered at the shape hurtling along a trajectory opposite the one she'd just been on. Something with wings, a tail, and long legs, like a giant bug.

No, wait. Not a bug, she realized as it shot past. A helicopter.

She whirled, following it with her eyes. What helicopter flew without lights at night, keeping barely above the wave tops?

One that doesn't want to be spotted, her dragon said. *One headed straight for—*

Her heart stopped. That helicopter was heading straight for Koakea Plantation.

She whipped around, ready to chase down the helicopter and incinerate it. But a cackling sound filled her mind, and she slowed, drawn in the direction of the Big Island.

Feeling a little conflicted, cousin dear? a voice burst into her mind.

Cynthia's mouth burned as she let out a burst of fire. *Moira.*

She hovered in place, trying to think over the distraction of her cousin's nasty laugh. But it was hard, what with panic threatening to engulf her.

Whatever will you do? Moira goaded, bullying her way right into Cynthia's mind.

Cynthia took a deep breath and partitioned her mind. She couldn't lock Moira out, because she had to find out what her cousin was up to. But she'd be damned if she'd let Moira overhear her call to the others.

Cal! Connor! Silas! she screamed, using the mental connection they shared.

Groggy whispers ghosted through her mind, and finally, one voice called out. *Cynthia?*

Her heart ached. It was Cal, and she could sense his confusion.

Moira is here, she said, wishing she had time to explain why she'd flown off without waking him. *Or rather, she's near. She's sent a helicopter, and it's headed straight for Maui.*

Moira? Silas's voice cut in.

One by one, the members of her pack awoke, filling her mind with a babble of concerned shouts. *Who? What? Where?*

I'll track down Moira, she barked. *You take care of that helicopter.* Her gut lurched, and she slipped sideways, losing her grip on the thermal she'd been riding. *Joey. Watch Joey. Keep him safe.*

Wait, Silas called, but she concentrated on Cal.

Cal, I beg you. Protect Joey. Keep him safe. Please.

Cynthia— he called, but Silas cut in sharply.

Wait for Connor and Jenna. They're on their way. Wait for backup. I repeat, wait for backup. Do you copy?

She snorted and flapped her wings, racing for the Big Island. No, she did not copy. She wasn't a member of Silas's Special Forces team, and she was through with letting other people fight her battles. Moira was out there somewhere. And though it went against every motherly instinct to fly away from Joey rather than racing home, she knew she had to hunt her cousin down.

Moira was the source of so much evil in the world, not to mention so much of the sorrow in her life. Moira had tricked her into believing Cal had betrayed their bond, and Moira had tried to kill Joey in the attack Barnaby had barely staved off, sacrificing his life. Moira had harassed and targeted the shifters Cynthia loved, again and again.

Not any more, her dragon vowed, speeding into the night. *Not any more.

∞∞∞∞

*

The air rattled with an explosion, and a towering cloud of ash and steam rose before Cynthia. Her heart pounded, conflicted by so many emotions. Like rage, directed at Moira. Anxiety for Joey's sake, and for her friends. Concern for the citizens threatened by the volcano. But she couldn't afford to face Moira without being fully focused, so she forced herself to concentrate on the map in her mind. As long as she followed the northeast shore of the Big Island — easy enough, given the

147

row of lights along the coastal road — no one would spot her. Moira had to be hiding at the edge of the erupting volcano, as she had done months earlier when she and Drax had come to Hawaii to confront Silas and his mate, Cassandra.

Not hiding. Waiting, Moira spoke dryly into her mind. *You won't be late, will you, cousin dear?*

It pained Cynthia to listen to Moira's chatter, but she forced herself to home in on her enemy and to think things through at the same time.

Don't get too comfortable on that farm of yours...

Moira hadn't been lounging on a couch in a penthouse when she'd said that. She'd been plotting an attack.

Cynthia raked the sky with another long blast of fire, and her dragon snarled. *When I get a hold of that bitch...*

She wanted nothing more than to race in, tear Moira apart, and head back to the people she loved — Joey, Cal, and the shifters who'd become a second family to her. But Moira was a cunning enemy, and an expert in laying traps, so Cynthia proceeded as cautiously as a furious mother could.

Another blast split the air as Kilauea spat more heat and ash. The clouds to Cynthia's right billowed against the dark backdrop of night. The mighty volcano had been sputtering and coughing for months, forcing hundreds to evacuate their homes in fear of lava and poison gases. The land below looked like a war zone with ash-covered ground, charred trees, and the ravaged foundations of houses.

One thing was for sure — Kilauea did provide the perfect cover for a dragon fight. Cynthia had to give Moira that much. What the darkness of night didn't conceal, the volcanic activity would.

There, her dragon grunted as the long, bony finger of a peninsula appeared ahead.

She slowed to reconnoiter before landing. An ancient lava flow had formed a long tongue of land ringed by steep slopes. The hills were dotted with flashing red lights, like runway markers blown into disarray. A closer look revealed those to be crevices in the brittle surface where bubbling magma showed.

Cynthia sucked in a long, steadying breath. Moira loved overdoing things, but this had to be her most audacious staging ever. And sure enough, she made her usual grand entrance. Moira stood in the midst of that fiery landscape, wearing a red gown that billowed in the wind.

Cynthia scowled. Moira had chosen that outfit to heighten the effect, no doubt — trying to impart the impression that she could control the volcano along with the financial empire she'd amassed. Well, Cynthia knew better than that.

Still, her gut twisted when she counted four...five...six more dragons perched on the surrounding cliffs. Each held his wings out in a sinister salute to their mistress.

A gas vent erupted, and Cynthia squinted against the heat.

Ah, Cynthia. Do come down where we can talk, Moira called.

Cynthia made another pass along the shoreline, debating what to do. She'd expected a few mercenaries, but she'd been entertaining the fantasy that she could take them on thanks to her recent training. But facing six big male dragons at one time?

Stall, her dragon said firmly. *Connor and Jenna are on their way. They can take care of the others while we kill Moira.*

Cynthia hated the idea, but what choice did she have? Moira had to be stopped, once and for all. As for herself — well, she didn't have to be a hero. She just had to get the job done.

Curving the edge of her left wing, she lined up for a landing. Jagged lava loomed wherever she looked, so she braked with her wings rather than attempting the usual jogged-in landing. Reaching out with her claws, she held her breath. A one-touch landing was the hardest kind, and if she didn't judge the wind just right...

Hot air blasted from a vent in the earth. Cynthia gritted her teeth, reached with her talons, and—

She exhaled and folded her wings primly, faking a look of nonchalance.

Aced that landing, her dragon crowed.

Even Moira looked impressed — for about five seconds, at least. Then she grinned and cackled. "My, my. You have been hanging around those toy boy soldiers for too long, my dear Cynthia. Whatever would your mother say?"

"My mother would ask how much lower you could stoop, Moira. Sneaking around at night? Hiring mercenaries?"

Moira snorted. "You're the low one, Cynthia. Hiding on a farm in the middle of nowhere. Using a false name. Letting your son grow up among those heathens. . . "

Cynthia showed her fangs. The men of Koakea were not heathens. They might not have the polished manners of the dragons she'd been raised among, but they showed more heart, loyalty, and courage than the mightiest dragons she'd known.

A twinge of sorrow went through her. Barnaby had possessed all those qualities too. Barnaby had been a good man and a great father. A loving partner, in his own way.

She steeled herself. One more reason to rid the world of Moira right now.

When Cynthia stalked forward, Moira shrank back. But the dragons on the surrounding ridgeline leaned in, extinguishing the little rush of power Cynthia felt. In dragon form, she was four times Moira's human size, and her golden scales glittered in the glow of the lava. Golden dragons were rare, and Cynthia's markings were the rarest of all, thanks to the solid black ring around the crown of her head. A sign of the noblest dragon lineage, descended from the royalty of old. Moira, on the other hand, was a dull, grayish-brown in dragon form.

Look at me, her dragon nearly hissed at Moira. *Do you really dare take me on?*

Once upon a time, Cynthia might have been guilty of a little too much pride in her dragon looks. But she'd learned the hard way that nobility came from one's actions rather than an accident of birth. Connor had proven that, as had the other men and women of Koakea. Still, she could feel the power of her ancestors swirling in her veins, giving her courage. Courage she would need, she was sure.

"What exactly would you like to talk about, Moira?" she asked, speaking out loud in her low, growly dragon voice. Her throat burned when she did so, but it was intimidating as hell, and the flash of worry in Moira's eyes was worth it.

However, Moira recovered as quickly as ever and thrust her hands onto her hips. "What do I want to talk about? Well, my fortune, for starters."

Cynthia laughed, letting the rough rattle frighten Moira into another backward step.

"Of course. Your favorite subject. Money." Cynthia narrowed her eyes, letting her fury show. "Are you referring to the fortune you stole from unsuspecting dragon families?"

She didn't say *my family*, because most of her own wealth had been carefully hidden away. But Moira had seized as much of Barnaby's holdings as she could, plus whatever she had managed to grab from the estate of her dearly departed lover, Drax, and a dozen other dragons Moira had used, abused, and eventually disposed of.

"It's all a matter of perspective." Moira flapped a hand, unconcerned. "Right now, I prefer to focus on the fortune I am about to expand."

"And how do you intend to do that?" Cynthia clawed the ground.

One of the surrounding dragons launched into the air and circled high above in a silent reminder of what Cynthia was up against.

Moira smiled and leaned closer. "By killing you, of course."

Cynthia thrust her wings wide and opened her mouth, daring Moira. But her cousin went on, unimpressed.

"Oh, I *will* kill you, dearest Cynthia. It's inevitable, you know. It's your sweet little boy we're here to talk about."

Rage like nothing Cynthia had ever experienced coursed through her veins, and she lunged forward. But Moira's guards launched into the air, halting her in her tracks.

"You will not utter his name," Cynthia hissed. "You will not touch him."

Moira's eyes glowed as she flung her arms wide, preparing to shift. "Oh, but I will."

Her fingers elongated, as did the webbing between them, forming wings. Her toothy grin made the horrifying transition

ANNA LOWE

into a set of fangs, and when scales broke out over her body, the remaining scraps of her red dress billowed in the wind.

Moira laughed and motioned toward Maui, speaking in her raspy dragon's voice. "And who knows? I might just claim him for my own."

Bile rose in Cynthia's throat. It was bad enough imagining Joey threatened. But for Moira to steal her son and brainwash his innocent mind...

She could picture it all too well. *Your father was a coward,* Moira would say, patting the poor, confused boy's head as servants scurried around in muted fear. *Your mother was pure evil. If it weren't for me...*

Moira grinned. "Why, Cynthia. You read my mind. That's exactly what I have planned."

A thunderous roar escaped Cynthia's throat, and she launched herself at Moira, bellowing, "Never. Never!"

Chapter Sixteen

Cal had been sleeping so well — possibly the best sleep of his life — until something tapped at the edge of his mind. He rolled and extended an arm, searching for Cynthia. The bed was warm, but she wasn't there, and the feeling of doom intensified. Moments later, her voice sounded in his mind, and he jumped out of bed. Rushing to the balcony, he reached for the shadow racing toward the horizon.

"Cynthia!"

But she was gone, and worse — she had shut him out of her mind. He knew all too well how necessary that was in a fight, but damn. It still hurt.

He hurried to the door, grabbing his clothes as he went. Then he raced outside with Cynthia's words echoing in his mind.

I beg you. Protect Joey. Keep him safe. Please.

Damn it! He was supposed to be the one rushing into battle, not her. Moira was bound to have an army of mercenaries with her. What was Cynthia thinking?

She was thinking revenge, his wolf pointed out.

That, he could understand. But being left behind while the battle raged elsewhere was new.

Not for long, his wolf said, sniffing the air.

He pulled up in mid-sprint, staring at the horizon. Cynthia was too far to make out, but another shape formed in the darkness.

Incoming, a voice growled into his mind.

He spun to find Connor running up, barefoot, bare-chested, wearing nothing but a pair of cargo pants.

"Damn it," the dragon shifter said, staring at the helicopter hurtling toward them.

"You got a contingency plan for this?" Cal demanded, balling his fists.

Connor nodded curtly as he jogged to the north. "We have a plan for everything. Including—"

He pulled up short and stared at Cal, nostrils wide.

Shit. Cal was dressed, but Cynthia's scent still clung to his skin.

"You smell like sex," Connor snapped.

"So do you," Cal retorted. He didn't have time for the dragon's bullshit.

Connor's eyes glowed, and his canines extended. "Yeah, well, Jenna happens to be my mate."

"And Cynthia happens to be mine," Cal barked just as several more people ran up.

Silas, Tim, Dell, and Chase froze in their tracks and stared. Cal glared back, bristling. He was sick of men who could parade their mates around for all the world to see, with nothing and no one coming between them. He appreciated their instinct to protect Cynthia, but when were they going to accept that she didn't need protection from him?

He pointed out to the horizon. "That's our enemy, damn it. Focus on that."

For one iffy moment, the air crackled as they stared each other down.

"I said, focus. If you care about Cynthia — or your own sorry hides — you'll focus. Now."

Chase, Tim, and Dell glanced at Connor, who looked ready to explode. He stepped forward, scowling furiously. Silas opened his mouth and stepped toward the dragon shifter, but Connor slowly lowered his hands.

"You're right." Connor didn't quit glaring, but he did back down. Then he turned to Silas. "Plan Zulu?"

Silas nodded once. "Zulu."

And just like that, everyone turned and rushed off to whatever task Plan Zulu assigned to them. Clearly, they'd practiced the scenario.

"You and Jenna go back up Cynthia," Silas ordered Connor. "Kai, Cassandra, and I will cover for you here."

For the first time ever, Cal wished he were a dragon and not a wolf. Or a griffon, or even a goddamn pegasus — anything that would let him fly to his mate's side.

"And Tessa, you mean," Connor said.

Silas gave a curt shake of the head. "Not tonight. Not for the next six to nine months, from what I gather."

Connor's eyes went wide, and Dell grinned. "Son of a gun. Kai and Tessa—"

Cal stirred the air with his hands. Now was not the time to get all misty-eyed about whoever was expecting the next baby born on Koa Point.

"Move it, soldier," he barked.

Connor jolted into action, and Dell looked about to as well, but Anjali came running up with baby Quinn.

Dell motioned toward Hailey. "You need to meet up with Boone and Nina to keep the kids safe."

Anjali nodded, then looked around. "Where's Joey?"

The clearing had been a hive of activity for the past minutes, but everyone froze at her words.

"I sent him into the house," Dell said. "I thought he was with you."

Anjali turned white. "I thought he was with you. Oh God..."

Everyone appeared ready to scour the countryside for the boy, but Silas clapped for their attention. "Hang on. Anjali, get over to Boone and Nina. Keep Quinn safe. Hailey, Dell, and Cal — search for Joey. The minute you find him, bring him to Boone's, then hustle over to your posts."

Cal could have torn out his hair. He had his own plan, and he needed to get into position — pronto. But Silas was right. They had to find Joey first.

"Everyone else, to your posts," Silas barked.

With one last, concerned look at each other, everyone fanned out.

"Joey!" Hailey called, running toward Dell's house.

"Joey!" The lion shifter's voice cracked with worry.

155

"I'll check the main house," Cal said, splitting off to the left. It made sense for the kid to have headed there if he got wind of the emergency, right?

But the house was eerily empty, with curtains billowing and the rooms devoid of life. Cal stared around, aching inside. Hours ago, the place had been bustling with activity. Now, the emptiness carried a sense of foreboding he just couldn't shake.

For one gut-wrenching moment, Cal wondered whether Moira's forces could have snuck in and kidnapped Joey. But there wasn't a trace of a stranger's scent, and the helicopter hadn't landed yet.

He spun and strode to the porch, thinking it through. All the comings and goings had eaten up a good ten minutes. Plenty of time for a kid to wander off somewhere and hide. But a scared kid didn't hide — he'd run to his mom, right?

Joey wouldn't be scared, his wolf growled with a strange sense of pride. As if that were his kid or something. Jesus, was his mind fucked up.

But it was true. Joey idolized the men and women of his pack. He wanted to be a hero just like them. Which meant...

Cal stepped down the stairs, wondering what the hell Plan Zulu was and what role Joey would want to fill. Then it hit him.

Not Plan Zulu? his wolf asked.

He turned to the mountain slopes rising from the upper edge of the plantation, remembering his own words.

See that ledge? That would be the perfect place to position your defenses, don't you think?

His jaw dropped. The kid wouldn't have run off the grounds, would he? Surely, he was too much like Barnaby to do any such thing. Ponderous. Cautious. Taught from birth not to act without thinking.

But, damn. The kid also shared Cynthia's stubborn streak, and Cal had seen fire burn in Joey's eyes once or twice.

One quick leap took Cal flying over the last few stairs, and soon, he was churning up the ground, sprinting for his Triumph. A minute later, he was roaring down the road.

"Hey," Tim yelled, flagging down the bike at the front gate. Apparently, Plan Zulu called for a bear at the upper entrance.

Cal motioned furiously at the gate. "It's a long shot, but I think I know where Joey went."

Tim's face fell. "Off the plantation?"

Cal revved the engine in a not-too-subtle hint. It was possible, yes. The grounds were hemmed in by sections of wall and fence, but Joey could probably find a place to wiggle through.

"Open the damn gate."

Tim hesitated a moment longer, then obeyed, and Cal roared off into the night.

∞∞∞

Technically, Cal didn't need the bike to chase the kid down, but it would speed up the process. Especially on the steep uphill slope, and especially in the middle of the night. His mind spun as the Triumph's engine strained. If he was wrong about Joey...

He pushed the thought from his mind. If he was wrong, Joey was probably back at Dell's place and already being bustled into the pack's safe house. That would free up Cal to man his own battle stations. Either way, he was headed in the right direction.

But Christ, did his heart pound, and damn, did his palms sweat.

He crossed the main road — not another vehicle in sight at this hour of night — and gunned the bike up the steep trail on the opposite side. Following instinct, he headed to the very end of one branch, then ditched the bike, sprinting before he hit the ground. His weapons cache was only a few yards away, and—

"Joey," he breathed, stopping in his tracks.

It was dark, but there was no mistaking the little redhead. He was up on tippy toes, straining to lift a spear into the frame Cal had built.

"Joey," he called.

157

Joey turned, looking more earnest than ever. "I think I know how it works. The spear goes here, right? But I can't lift it..."

Cal stared. Did the kid really think he could protect his home from a pack of mercenaries?

The fierce set of the little boy's jaw answered that one loud and clear.

Cal held back from screaming, *Are you nuts? Everyone is searching for you, feeling scared to death.* Instead, he spoke as calmly as he could.

"Dell needs you back at home, Joey."

Joey shook his head. "Mommy says everyone has to help."

A helicopter thundered overhead, and Cal dove for Joey, hoping they hadn't been spotted. He rolled and held Joey flat along the ground then brought a finger to his lips.

Quiet. Okay? he let his eyes say.

The kid nodded once and stayed still.

Good kid, Cal's wolf murmured.

Cal rolled his eyes. He wasn't sure whether he wanted to hug or kill the kid. But he had bigger problems now, because the helicopter was touching down not too far away. Cal belly-crawled to the edge of the rise and watched as four men and two tigers leaped from the helicopter and fanned out. When an engine revved on the main road, he whipped his head around and saw at least a dozen more men — and animals — leap out of a van and scatter into the vegetation surrounding the plantation grounds.

Jesus, this was it. The attack they'd all been preparing for. Somehow, Moira had managed to sneak her forces in from the mainland — or more likely, stage them over from the Big Island. Silas had informants all over the islands, but if Moira chartered a private plane to the Big Island and moved fast, anything was possible.

It's more than possible, his wolf grunted. *It's happening.*

His heart pounded, partly in elation, because this was the battle he'd spent a lifetime preparing for. But part of that was in fear, because this wasn't how it was all supposed to unfold. Instead of hiding in safety, Cynthia had raced into battle. And instead of being able to arm the defensive positions he'd prepared, Cal had a kid to think of.

Shuffling backward, he grabbed Joey and rolled into a hollow, hoping the boy wouldn't yelp. But the kid was a trooper and remained quiet, though he did tremble in Cal's arms.

"Don't move," Cal whispered.

The bushes before them rustled. Something big was on the move.

Joey's chin dipped the slightest bit, and Cal could feel the kid hold his breath.

A huge, plate-sized paw came into view, along with the lower edge of a furry leg. One of the tigers was stalking along, blending into the landscape.

Cal clenched his teeth. If the breeze wavered the slightest bit. . .

But it didn't, thank goodness, and the tiger disappeared a moment later, intent on the property below. The lights were all out on the plantation, but Cal knew it was there.

So did the tiger, it seemed. Not good.

Moments later, another striped shadow slunk past, and even the crickets stopped chirping at that. Cal didn't exhale until what felt like a good minute later, when the shifter had passed.

Joey's eyes were wide as saucers, and his face was pale.

Not knowing what else to do, Cal patted his shoulder.

"Don't worry," he whispered. "Dell and the others will be ready."

When Joey turned those huge green eyes on him, Cal swallowed hard.

"Are you sure?"

Cal pursed his lips. Hell, he sure hoped so. Then he nodded. "Hang on. I'll make sure they know."

He gazed over toward the property and half closed his eyes, concentrating hard. *Dell. . . Silas. . .*

It was one thing to communicate mind-to-mind with another shifter up close. But to make that mental link over a distance, with shifters he'd only barely gotten to know — and with everyone scrambling in preparation for a fight — was hard.

Finally, he homed in on Silas's powerful aura and traced it over to the right.

Two tigers coming in from the mountains. Four other shifters not far behind.

Joey... Silas grunted in a voice tight with concern.

I have him. Tell the others. And watch out for—

Footfalls sounded in the darkness to his right, and two shadows swooped overhead. Cal swore under his breath, then concentrated on Silas again.

Two tigers, plus two wolves and two dragons moving in.

Four dragons, Silas corrected a moment later when two additional winged shadows swooped in from the south.

Cal remembered the van, then turned away. Silas, Dell, and the others had been warned. He had to get moving if he was going to enact his secret plan.

Gently, he pushed Joey uphill. "Come on. Help me over here." Three steps later, they reached the earthwork he'd dug days ago, along with the equipment he'd concealed. "Can you grab that end?"

Joey had followed instantly, but the moment Cal threw back the camo netting covering his construction, the boy stared. "Wow."

Cal nodded to himself. Yeah, *wow* fit that weapon, all right.

"It's called a *ballista*. Kind of like a slingshot, but bigger," he explained while stepping behind the firing mechanism.

And deadlier, his wolf snarled.

"Ballista?" Joey breathed, looking absolutely rapt.

Cal allowed himself a microsecond to admire the device. While it was fairly simple, it was also fail-proof. All he had to do was crank the launcher arm back, sling the spear into position, and... Enemy dragons, watch out.

"Get that end, will you?" He motioned. Not that he actually needed Joey's help, but he figured it would keep the boy distracted enough to avoid panic.

Together, they maneuvered a ten-foot spear into place and cocked the mechanism that would release it.

"See how it works?" He pointed along the moving parts. "You sight along here, then pull this..."

"Wow," Joey mumbled. "I thought wolves fought with their teeth and claws."

Cal made a face. He wished.

"That works with other four-footed shifters, but not against dragons. So I came up with this."

Actually, the idea was Barnaby's, but that would take too much explaining right now.

Would rather fight, his wolf grumbled.

As usual, the beast ached to face his enemy on four feet. But Cal had learned the hard way that only brains — and the element of surprise — would allow a wolf to vanquish a dragon.

He sighted down the shaft of the spear then gave a curt nod. Weapon One, armed. It was time to set up the second launcher he'd hidden in the undergrowth. The motions were all familiar, but one thing was not. How was he going to keep Joey safe while he fought? Another shifter might prowl out of the undergrowth at any time, and—

A huge shadow rose from somewhere behind him, and his blood went cold.

"Down," he hissed, taking Joey with him a second time.

The hairs on the back of his neck tingled as his nose registered a familiar dragon scent.

Kravik, his wolf snarled.

Slowly, Cal turned his head, watching the dragon rise higher into the sky. The blood in his ears pounded so hard, he worried that Kravik might hear.

That bastard. Here? his wolf growled. *Now?*

They'd tangled twice over the past three years, but Kravik was a slippery bastard, and nearly impossible to kill.

His wolf growled as he looked up into the darkness, tracing Kravik's outline against the backdrop of night. The bastard was magnificent — Cal had to give him that, with black-on-black scales that glittered in the moonlight. He was also considerably bigger than the average dragon — a yard extra in snout-to-tail length. His eyes glowed red in the night — red, snobby, and fucking entitled.

Cal swallowed away the bitterness in his mouth. It figured that Kravik and his gang of European dragons would eventually become entangled in one of Moira's schemes. But Cal had never anticipated everything coming to a head now. Not when the woman he loved had set out to fight a battle on her own. Not with her son entrusted to his care. And not with what looked like an entire shifter battalion poised to batter down the gates of Koa Point.

And yet there he was — Kravik, the massive black dragon, hovering overhead while eyeing the ground. Searching for him?

A low, throaty sound yanked Kravik's attention around. Another two dragons appeared, reporting to their leader. The three of them swooped in slow circles, watching the fight unfold from a distance.

Cal did a quick count. Four dragons were already flying over the estate and plantation grounds, engaging with Silas, Kai, and Cassandra. Countless other shifters stole through the shadows on the ground, met by a fierce shifter pack determined to protect their home. Kravik and his two cronies remained overhead, hanging back for the time being. Apparently, they were waiting for their frontmen to weaken Silas and the others before they moved in for a final assault. Meanwhile, Moira and her personal bodyguards had to be over on the Big Island facing Cynthia, Connor, and Jenna. All in all, enough to make a wolf's mind spin.

What it really came down to, though, was Moira and Kravik. Two of the most ruthless, evil dragons the world had ever known. The only real question was which of them was the other's pawn?

Cal dug his fingers into the ground. The details didn't matter. He'd come to Maui ready to slay a few dragons, right? Having Kravik there gave him the opportunity to kill two birds with one stone.

Or three, or four... his wolf snarled.

He looked right, judging the distance between his first launcher and a cache of spears he'd stashed earlier. Then he tapped Joey on the shoulder and motioned to the right.

"Time to mobilize, kid. You ready?"

It was unfair to ask the kid as much. But Joey was a Brenner and a Baird. And, hell, maybe there really was something about classy old bloodlines. Because the little guy, though pale and trembling, nodded immediately.

"Yes, sir. Are you?"

Cal nearly laughed at the way the kid mimicked the Special Forces men he'd spent so much time among. A moment later, Cal's smile faded, replaced by a grim frown as his wolf vowed to bring hell and damnation on the dragons overhead.

"Ready. Let's go."

Chapter Seventeen

Cynthia lunged for Moira with her teeth bared, screaming to herself.

Kill her. Kill Moira, once and for all.

But Moira was shockingly fast and managed to heave Cynthia aside. Cynthia barely had a chance to fold her wings before crash-rolling over the ground. At the sound of a hiss, she rolled again — just in time to avoid the scalding blast of a volcanic vent. Then she scrambled to her feet and launched herself into the air.

Moira did the same, and her guards swooped in, all converging on Cynthia at the same time. Licks of flame nicked her wings, tail, and ears. She spun in midair, releasing a burst of flames bigger than anything she'd ever produced before.

Back! her dragon screamed, spraying a circle of fire.

A moment later, she hovered, blinking at the tails of six retreating dragons and reeling from the echo of her own roar. Had that really been her?

Bet your ass, it was, her dragon murmured, borrowing a line from Silas's mate, Cassandra.

Even Moira looked a little stunned, but she covered up quickly. *My, my. And I always thought you were all proper and ladylike.*

Watch me, Cynthia grunted back.

Curling her wings, she circled Moira, looking for an opening. Moira's guards quickly regrouped and started swooping around both of them, moving in the opposite direction. All that motion was enough to make her mind spin, especially with the volcano belching toxic gas and blistering heat.

Damn it, she muttered, looking for a clear flight path through that gauntlet.

Did I hit a nerve, dear cousin? Moira taunted.

Cynthia didn't bother answering. Instead, she darted toward Moira, nipping at her long, brown tail. But one of the surrounding dragons dove at her, aiming to shred Cynthia's wings with its razor-sharp talons.

Quick, she yelped at herself.

She folded her right wing while tipping the left and barrel-rolled. Then, with a snap of her tail, she twisted in midair and spat fire.

Her attacker screamed and beat its wings, trying to escape, but Cynthia exhaled long and hard, maintaining her fire until it chased the enemy right into the ground. The dragon crashed, making the earth shake, and a primal cry escaped Cynthia's throat. A victory cry that wasn't so much her voice as the voices of her ancestors.

You shall not best us. We are Clan Baird.

Energy like nothing she'd ever felt coursed through her, and she took a deep breath. Maybe there were advantages to being the last in her line.

She glared at Moira. *I will not back down. I will fight until you are gone.*

Without thinking, she gained altitude, making sure she didn't offer Moira any advantage. The power of her ancestors might be fueling her, but Connor's military-style training had taught her when to attack and when to observe.

Observe, a little voice said in her mind.

She glanced around. One of Moira's henchmen lay dead on the ground, but the other five were circling with a sharp new look in their eyes. They wouldn't underestimate her again, that was for sure.

Moira stared at the limp form of the dragon below. Apparently, she'd underestimated Cynthia, as well. But in typical Moira fashion, she just laughed.

Oh, you're making this so much more fun.

Cynthia spat flames in her direction. What kind of person found death and destruction fun?

Moira, her inner dragon grunted in reply.

You remind me of Barnaby, Moira sighed into her mind. *Playing the brave, selfless dragon.*

Cynthia roared. *Barnaby wasn't playing, and neither am I. Not that you'd understand anything about bravery.*

Moira turned, tracking her movements. *What do you know about bravery? Or are you mixing up bravery with that laughable thing called pride? Barnaby wasn't so interested in protecting you as protecting his own name.*

Cynthia knew better than to answer. But then again, she had to buy time, so she hissed a comeback into her cousin's mind.

He was protecting the people he loved. Love, Moira. A concept you'll never understand.

Another vent blasted below, and even from fifty feet up, Cynthia could feel the air rush. She backed away quickly, as did Moira, just in time to avoid the column of scalding steam that rose between them.

Oh, I know all about love, Moira murmured smugly. *I love power. I love revenge.*

Cynthia had never been much of a revenge gal. But, heck — she was starting to see the appeal. On the other hand, her father had been right in teaching her the dangers of that path.

Revenge starts but never ends, he used to say. *It will only eat you up.*

Love was like that too, but in a good way, she mused. Like her love for Joey. Her love for Cal that had held up over so many years. Her love of her packmates — yes, her packmates, right down to the infuriating Dell.

She found herself smiling, but it faded quickly as she thought things through. Any of her packmates would die for her or Joey. Was she prepared to do the same for them?

Her heart twisted at the thought of leaving Joey an orphan. He'd been through so much already. But even if it came to the worst, he would have the others. He would have love... and memories.

For the space of a few heartbeats, sorrow consumed her. But then she bared her teeth and focused on the she-dragon who'd orchestrated so many attacks on the people Cynthia loved.

Her cousin cackled. *Oh, Cynthia. You're a princess, not a warrior. Don't even try.*

Cynthia inhaled, letting her anger form a bubble inside. *Princess* might fit her upbringing, but fate had long since re-shaped her path. As for being a warrior — well, she might not have the Special Forces training of her friends, but she was a mother, and that gave her a whole different kind of power.

Moira has destroyed so much, and she will destroy more if she isn't stopped, a little voice whispered in her mind.

Cynthia shot a long lick of fire at her cousin.

She fooled you into letting Cal go, the voice continued.

She flapped her wings, gaining altitude.

She wants to take your child away from you.

She roared and dove at Moira. *No, she won't.*

Moira's guards all dive-bombed at her, but Cynthia focused on the embers that burned deep within her dragon soul. Her blood rushed as she summoned threads of fire from every part of her body until they formed a huge, swirling ball in her lungs. Then, with the mightiest breath of her life, she released it all.

Moira screamed and rolled. Cynthia followed relentlessly, blasting Moira with flames. But the guards were right on her tail, about to catch her in a pentagram of fire, so Cynthia twisted in midair and aimed at them instead.

The next few minutes went by in a blur of ear-splitting roars and thunderous wingbeats. Cynthia had the vague sensation of an ache in her right wing and the sting of sweat in her eyes. Blood dripped from her talons, and she wasn't sure whose it was. She didn't care either. She raged on, channeling her inner power. Power that came from the heart, from the life-force of her ancestors, and from some strange sensation she traced to... Her ankle? It was tingling intensely. Was something wrong with her pearls or had she been burned there? In the heat of the fight, she didn't have time to check.

The dives, rolls, and twists she'd learned from Connor kept her a hairbreadth ahead of the enemy. When a dragon ap-peared out of nowhere, spitting fire at her wings, she rolled out of the way. Another evaded her raking claws only to stray into her line of fire, and it plummeted toward the ground. How she found the energy to fight them all, Cynthia didn't know. Only that it had something to do with the heat building around her ankle.

When she glanced down, she was startled to see a glowing ring of bluish-white light coming from her pearls. Which seemed significant, but she didn't have time to process the notion just then. Not with another dragon approaching from the side, blasting fire.

She rolled, turned, and returned fire until it all became a blur. In the throes of that wild aerial dogfight, she lost track of Moira. Heat vents blasted from below, adding to the confusion. Somewhere to the right, Cynthia noticed a long line of fire — a river of lava flowing crimson in the darkness of night.

Watch out! a voice roared in her mind.

She spun just in time to fend off an oncoming dragon, then whipped around to face the next one, opening her jaws wide to release another burst of fire.

Stop! a familiar voice cried.

She blinked at the hazel eyes before her. *Connor?*

Whoa, he sputtered, backing away. *Yes, it's me. And that's Jenna over there.* He jerked his head up and to the right. *Try not to kill us, will you? Just the bad guys.*

Cynthia nodded and rolled back to face the others. But the tight phalanx of dragons had divided into two groups. One of Moira's mercenaries had turned tail to flee, chased by Jenna. Another two lay scorched and lifeless on the ravaged terrain below. One swooped in from overhead, attacking her.

I've got this bastard, Connor barked into her mind. *You get Moira.*

Cynthia broke away, searching the darkness intently. Sure enough, Moira was slinking away, protected from the rear by the last of her guards. Cynthia beat her wings, racing after them.

Don't let her go, the voice called to her.

Not Connor's voice, nor her dragon's. She faltered slightly when she realized who that was.

Barnaby, she whispered.

A lump filled her throat, blocking the flow of fire. She flew on, consumed by grief. There'd been too many losses, too much suffering. Too much pain caused to the people she loved.

So, end it, Barnaby's spirit whispered. *Avenge me, and live on. You and the man you deserve.*

She could have crumpled to the ground and sobbed. Barnaby was a good man, yet she'd never loved him as much as he deserved.

All that matters is you. Joey. The future, he assured her. Then his voice dropped into a near growl. *And Moira. End her, once and for all. End her!*

Cynthia took a deep breath, unsheathed her talons, and sprinted after Moira.

The mercenary guarding Moira turned as Cynthia approached, but she steamrolled him in a relentless flood of fire. He tumbled through the air then plummeted. Cynthia didn't pause to watch him crash, but she heard the hiss of a heat vent and an ensuing cry. An instant later, her nostrils filled with the scent of singed leather. Another enemy was dead.

You bitch! Moira screamed, circling back the way they'd come.

Cynthia didn't waste a breath to reply. Beating her wings hard, she dashed after Moira.

You can't! Moira cried, hurtling to one side. Fueled by desperation, she managed to elude Cynthia's next three attacks. Moira's eyes darted all over, looking for reinforcements that didn't come.

No one will come for her, Cynthia's dragon growled.

The contrast was striking, because Cynthia had an entire pack on her side. Connor and Jenna had raced all the way over to the Big Island to help her, and the rest of the pack was on Maui, protecting Joey. Cal was with them, and even Barnaby's spirit was at her side.

She closed her eyes briefly, counting her blessings. All that love. All that loyalty. She almost felt sorry for Moira.

Not sorry enough, her dragon snipped, speeding after Moira.

The first flame she spat singed her cousin's tail. The second made Moira turn right, and the third—

Moira twisted in a shockingly fast move and snapped at Cynthia's wingtip. Cynthia almost veered right, but an echo of the past sounded in her head.

There's an even better move, Connor had once said.

Without thinking, she folded her wing against her body and rolled. An instant later, she dropped directly beneath Moira, flicked her wings open, and shot upward, spitting fire.

No! Moira screamed. She turned away, only to expose her left wing to the blast of fire. She half fell, half fluttered to the ground, just missing the river of lava. Cynthia followed, landing on the jagged earth two body lengths away. She panted, amazed at the move she'd just executed.

Execute, her dragon murmured. *Good word.*

Moira dragged her wounded wing, backing away in haste. Her eyes were wide, and her tail lashed from side to side.

Cynthia watched closely, but the only tricks Moira had left relied on words.

You can't. Leave me alone.

Cynthia showed her teeth. *The way you've left me alone?*

I'll make it up to you, Moira cried, glancing at the molten lava that cut off her escape.

Cynthia roared. *You can never make up for what you've done, whom you've killed, or the pain you've inflicted. Never.*

Moira shifted to human form and held up her arms to plead. Well — she held up her right arm. The left lay singed and useless at her side. But if she thought she could appeal to Cynthia's mercy, she had another thing coming.

"You can't. You can't kill me," Moira tried.

"Watch me," Cynthia growled aloud, stalking closer.

"But I'm hurt. See?" Moira gestured meekly.

Wings flapped overhead, and Cynthia looked up. It was Connor, thank goodness, along with Jenna, who was—

Watch out! Jenna screamed.

Cynthia scuttled backward as Moira made a lightning-fast shift back into dragon form.

Die, Moira cried, blasting Cynthia with a well-aimed burst of fire.

Cynthia scrambled back, barely avoiding a vent. Then rage bubbled through her soul, and the heat around her ankle intensified. Roaring, she counterattacked. Their flames collided, making them both stagger. A moment later, each she-dragon renewed the force behind her flames. Cynthia found herself inching forward, driving Moira backward across the ground. Slowly at first, then faster, until Moira teetered on the very edge of the molten lava.

No! Moira screamed, flapping her wings desperately.

But it was too late, and a moment later—

Cynthia forced herself to watch as Moira plummeted into the lava. An ungodly scream pierced the air when she hit the molten river, and the sickening smell of burning leather filled the air. Within seconds, all that remained visible was the ashy tip of a dragon's wing. Then it, too, it sank out of view. The lava bubbled, then smoothed over and flowed toward the sea.

Cynthia's pulse hammered away, and the only sound was the hiss of red-hot lava vaporizing against the ocean. Was that it? Was Moira really gone?

Cynthia slumped, unable to rejoice. She'd just killed another living being — her cousin, no less. Slowly, she rose into the air, joining Connor and Jenna as they rushed to her side. No one said a word. They just glided in weary circles, studying the river of lava below. Surely, this was another of Moira's tricks. She had to be down there somewhere, hiding among the rocks, right?

Connor swept down to search more closely, and he returned with a grim look.

She's gone, all right. You did it, Cynthia.

Still, she circled, not quite ready to accept that. Shouldn't she feel terrible about killing her own cousin? Could there have been a better way?

But the answers were *no* and *no*, and she knew it. Slowly, she cut away from the lava fields to follow Connor and Jenna, who were already flying toward Maui. Her mouth was ashy, her throat scorched. Her body so, so tired. When she glanced back to make sure no one followed, her gaze caught on a flash of light at her ankle. At first, she just blinked uncomprehendingly. Her pearls?

She remembered fastening her pearl necklace there before shifting, but they'd been their usual eggshell color at the time. Now, the one in the middle was glowing with a bright bluish-white light, sending heat through her body in waves. A good form of heat that gave her the energy to go on when she had every right to crumple to the ground in exhaustion.

Jenna circled back. *Are you doing okay? We could—*

The words cut off as she spotted the pearl.

Your pearls. . . Jenna breathed. *They're glowing.*

Cynthia nodded slowly. Not all of them, no. But the middle one sure was.

Connor circled back, and his eyes lit up too. When he spoke, his voice was a hush in her mind. *Is that what I think it is?*

She nearly scoffed. What did Connor mean? Those were just her pearls, right?

Then it hit her that maybe the power that had fueled her throughout the battle wasn't simply the power of an enraged mother. Maybe it had been the pearl. But what kind of pearl pulsed with energy and light, filling its bearer with supernatural power?

A pearl of desire, she remembered Jenna whispering once upon a time, cupping the pearl she'd discovered off the shore at Koakea beach.

Hailey had worn the same look of utter wonder when she'd discovered her pearl, as had Anjali and Sophie when their times came.

Now, your time has come, a deep, unearthly voice whispered in her mind.

But how could she possibly possess a pearl of desire? She blinked in sheer exhaustion. Maybe she was just imagining things.

But Connor and Jenna really were staring, and the pearl shone so brightly, she swore it was winking at her.

Cynthia tucked her leg up under her body, moving the pearls out of sight. Right now, she was unable to process anything but the thought of getting home. She eyed the distance, dreading the trip already.

Get yourself home, Barnaby said gently. *To Joey. To your mate.*

Cynthia forced her mouth into a straight line because otherwise, she might cry.

You were always so good to me, she whispered, hoping that really was Barnaby's spirit and not just another illusion in her poor, exhausted mind.

You deserve no less, he said. Then he sighed, and she felt him slip into the distance. *Now, go home. Start over. Find the man destiny intended for you all along.*

She swallowed hard and flapped her wings, heading home. Connor and Jenna flanked her, but they kept edging forward, then hanging back for her.

Um. . . I think I'll go ahead, Connor murmured. He glanced at Jenna, and a silent conversation passed between them. *Just in case.*

Sure, Jenna replied. Her normally upbeat tone was tight, though.

Cynthia frowned as Connor shot off. In case of what?

Tentatively, she reached her mind toward Cal and Joey, ready to break the good news that Moira was gone.

But the moment she made the mental connection, she cried in alarm. Cal was fighting fiercely, though she couldn't identify his foe. Joey was crouched nearby with fear and determination swirling through his mind. Fire burst through the air, and the ground shook.

"Cal. . . Joey. . . " She couldn't risk the distraction of calling to them directly, but she did croak their names into the wind.

Jenna glanced over, and her eyes said it all. The battle wasn't over. It had only begun.

Chapter Eighteen

"Down," Cal grunted as a trio of dragons hurtled at him.

Joey hit the dirt, and Cal lay over him, covering them both with a cloak. In the darkness of that cover, he strained for every sound. The air whistled as three huge dragons raced by, roaring and spurting fire in long, deadly flames. Then came the whipping sound of tails and the heavy beat of wings, signaling that the dragons had flown past, having failed to locate their prey.

Cal counted three of Joey's shallow breaths, then threw the cloak back and grabbed for the trigger of his ballista.

"Stay down," he muttered.

Joey, thank goodness, did as he was told. He clutched the cloak, looking at it with huge, innocent eyes.

My dad gave this to you? Joey had asked moments earlier, looking on in horror when Cal sliced it in two.

Cal swung the ballista, following the dragons with the tip of the spear as the past rushed through his mind. Not only had Barnaby given him that fireproof cloak — one of many items from his huge, glittering treasure hoard — he'd trusted Cal with secrets too. Like where a dragon's most vulnerable point lay.

Oh, you mean here? Cal had grunted in reply, grabbing a silver sword and swinging it directly against Barnaby's chest.

Yes, right there, Barnaby had replied without blinking an eye.

The stare-off that ensued was as epic a battle of wills as any physical fight Cal had ever been in. He couldn't believe Barnaby's nerve. Was the dragon really trusting him — a lone wolf with every reason to despise the man who'd stolen his mate — not to plunge that sword deep and go for the kill?

Yes. Yes, I am trusting you, Barnaby's eyes had said.

In the end, Cal had no choice but to lower his weapon and give in. There would be no honor in killing Barnaby and no happy end for himself and Cynthia. All Cal could do was accept the cloak along with Barnaby's challenge to do the right thing.

He followed the dragons' movements with steely eyes, forcing himself to focus. All the threads spun by fate were coming together after twelve long, lonely years. Him. Cynthia. Barnaby.

"Kravik," Cal added, muttering under his breath.

That bastard was responsible for so much evil in the world — evil that Kravik was intent on spreading over a new continent after being shunned by the shifter establishment in Europe. Cal had already hated the dragon, but now, he hated Kravik more for forcing him to slice his most prized possession — the cloak — in half.

"Bastard," he grunted.

The evil dragon couldn't have heard him, but he might have sensed the challenge in Cal's words, because he spun around for another pass, flanked by his henchmen. The trio swooped over the bowl etched into the mountainside, keeping low to the ground. The perfect target for a ballista, really, except for one thing.

Cal cursed as the dragon on the left nosed ahead of Kravik, blocking a clear shot. Still, he yanked on the trigger, letting the spear fly.

It was amazing, how much force could be generated with a few levers and some torsion springs. The hardwood spear ripped through the air and then through the dragon's scales. The beast screamed and lurched, slamming into his master.

Cal would have loved to watch as that dragon crashed to his death against the ground, while the other two tumbled through the air, wondering what had hit them. Instead, he grabbed Joey and ran, deliberately making a bush sway. Then he dove behind a rock and covered himself and Joey with both pieces of the cloak just in time.

Whoosh! A burst of fire incinerated the bush, and a dragon screamed in fury. Heat buffeted them, but Cal held on to the cloak, keeping one arm curled around Joey. Crackles filled the air as vegetation burned, and it was hard to breathe. But as long as he and Joey remained covered, they were safe.

Cal strained for the heavier crack of burning wood, but there was none. Which meant the dragons hadn't noticed the launcher under its camouflage net.

Three... two... one...

He counted down, then peeked at Joey.

"You remember what I told you, partner?"

Joey nodded quickly.

Cal checked to make sure the dragons hadn't spotted them yet. Then he turned back to Joey, making sure his face conveyed total confidence even if he felt anything but.

"Ready, kid?"

"Ready." Joey's voice trembled, but his nod was firm. Damn, had Cynthia raised a good kid.

Cal checked the sky one more time, then thrust the cloak at Joey. "Okay. Go."

Joey paused one last time. "You promise you won't go far?"

Cal nodded. "I promise. We're partners, right? Now, go!"

He pushed Joey toward a hiding place higher up the slope, then sprinted toward his cache of spears. The smaller piece of cloak flapped in his hands, but that was fine with him. Anything to draw attention away from Joey.

It worked, and both dragons trained their beady eyes on Cal. One released that throaty roar dragons used when locking on to a target. The air swirled, then rushed ahead of the advancing dragons. Cal waited for the last possible second before diving and covering himself with the cloak.

He braced himself just in time for the flames to hit — something he'd learned the hard way. The heat of dragon fire was one danger; the sheer force of it was another, akin to being hit by a massive wave. So he tucked his chin and hung on to the scrap of cloak his life depended on.

A moment later, the punching force swept away, and Cal rolled to his feet. Within a few steps, he'd reached his cache, grabbed a spear, and turned.

"Over here, you bastard," he yelled.

When both dragons whirled and came at him, he had to fight hard to stay cool. Sooner or later, the dragons would figure out what his cloak did and tear it away from him. The trick would be killing them first.

He was still weighing up whether to throw his spear or duck under the cloak when Kravik broke off his attack with a long, upward curve. With a sharp clack, he ordered the other dragon to follow, and a few thumping heartbeats later, Cal found himself staring down both dragons. They curled their wings and lashed their tails, hovering while they glared.

"Well, well. You again," Kravik called in the low, scratchy voice dragons used to communicate aloud — a voice laced with a rich European accent of some kind.

Cal relaxed his spear ever so slightly and shouted back, "Funny, I was going to say the same thing. Wherever I smell a sneaky coward, I find you."

"How interesting." Kravik jerked his long, scaled neck, ordering the other dragon to stand back.

Cal took a deep breath. He'd crossed paths with Kravik several times — all part of the dragon-slaying mission Barnaby had inspired him to set out on. Kravik hadn't had anything to do with the attack Barnaby had died in, but the newcomer had started to associate with the evil dragons who had nearly killed Cynthia and Joey that day. Cal had held them off long enough for Cynthia to escape, killing two. When he'd set off to hunt the rest down afterward, he'd found Kravik increasingly involved in their dirty deals. Twice, he'd had an outside chance of killing the bastard, but the dragon had always managed to slip away, leaving Cal with the lesser satisfaction of eliminating Kravik's hired hands. But he'd never actually faced the dragon one-on-one.

Now, we do, his inner wolf growled.

He stretched to his full height and waited.

"Interesting, indeed," Kravik mused. "You must be that tiresome dragon slayer I keep hearing about."

Cal knew the stab of pride he felt at that comment was ridiculous, but hey.

Kravik sniffed the air, and a moment later, his eyes flashed.

"Dragon slayer. Wolf shifter. Interesting, indeed."

Cal gripped his spear tighter, eyeing the spot on Kravik's chest where the scales met, forming a notch. He'd show the guy *interesting*, all right.

He shouted back, using the spear to emphasize each point. "And you would be Kravik. Bastard. General lowlife. It figures you and Moira would hook up."

Kravik laughed. "Hook up? Moira is a useful... ally, you might say. But I have far better taste, believe me."

Something in the dragon's cackle made Cal tense. What exactly did that mean?

Behind Kravik, the second dragon swept back and forth, waiting for the signal to attack.

"You new-world shifters are so ignorant," Kravik sighed. "My blood is far too noble to be mixed with the likes of Moira LeGrange. Her cousin, on the other hand..."

Cal's blood ran cold. Kravik wasn't just power hungry. He was after Cynthia, too.

His disgust must have shown, because Kravik burst into deep dragon laughter. "Do you really think I'd travel thousands of miles, putting up with Ms. LeGrange, simply to attain a new property?" He flicked a wing toward the plantation. Then he broke into a grin. "Unless you mean property of a different kind, such as the lovely Ms. Baird. Or should I say, my future bride?"

Cal's hand shook. No way. No one was taking Cynthia away from him again.

"She will never be yours."

Kravik snorted. "Of course she shall be. The woman has royal blood. She's one of the last of her kind, as am I. We're a match made in heaven."

179

Teeth bared, legs braced, Cal shouted back. "She will never have you."

Kravik laughed. "She won't have the choice, you fool. As if it's any business of a lowly wolf like you..."

Cal bristled. Yes, it was his business. And damn, did he hate dragons.

Most dragons, his wolf corrected.

Well, Cynthia was an exception. She'd been special right from the start, seeing past the rougher edges to the real him. Open-minded and adventurous, she was everything most dragons weren't.

Of course she is, his wolf hummed. *She's mine.*

Tensing his arm muscles, he sighted down the length of his spear. But Kravik, the bastard, was just out of range. If only he could get to the ballista...

Kravik's eyes wandered back to the plantation. "And, as for that boy of hers..."

Cal stood perfectly still.

Kravik's gaze swung back. "Ah, now I've placed you. You're that mercenary Barnaby hired."

Cal glared. "The only mercenaries here are the ones you've hired."

The black dragon leaned closer and whipped his tail. "Is that so? Well, poor Cynthia. Won't she feel betrayed when she discovers you killed her son?"

Cal's jaw hung open. What the hell? He would never harm Joey.

Kravik stirred the air with his talons, deep in thought. "Yes, yes. I can picture it now. What a sad tale Ms. Baird will have to endure. Imagine, the jealous wolf from her past, stalking her all these years..."

Stalking? Cal's cheeks burned.

"Pretending to love her..."

Not pretending, his wolf hissed. *Never.*

Cal's mind spun. How did Kravik know about him protecting Cynthia from the shadows for so long? His eyes darted to the horizon, and he cursed. Moira. Of course.

Kravik, meanwhile, went on conjuring up a vision that seemed to amuse him.

"Let's see... You regained her trust, only to betray her in the most heartless way." He sliced the air with a talon, making it all too easy to image Joey there.

No, Cal wanted to shout. *Never.*

"Killing her sole offspring." Kravik sighed. "Yes, a sad story indeed. One that might even compel Ms. Baird to find a shoulder to cry on. You know, once everything she ever loved is gone. Her son. Her friends. The man she thought she loved."

Cal jabbed the spear toward Kravik. "She loves me. Always has, always will."

Kravik shrugged. "Regardless, she shall be mine. The sole inheritor of the entire Baird legacy, under my control. Her royal blood, ready to mix with mine."

Cal shook with rage. He'd always pictured protecting Cynthia against enemy dragons, but Kravik's plan went a step further, and it made him sick.

Fucking dragons. They think they can take anything they want, his wolf snarled.

"Ah, I believe she's coming now," Kravik murmured at a shadow on the horizon.

Cal shook his head as his entire plan threatened to dissolve before his eyes. He needed to keep Kravik close to be able to kill the bastard. If the dragon flew off now...

A rustling sound came from the left, and he couldn't help but glance over. The moment he did, he swore. God, no.

Joey, he hissed into the boy's mind. *No. Get down. Hide.*

But Joey went right on cranking back the ballista's firing mechanism, making the wood frame groan under the pressure. Kravik didn't notice, but when the spear notched into place with a sharp click—

The dragon whirled, and his nostrils flared. "Well, well."

Joey went right on cranking, so intent that his tongue showed between his lips. The sight ought to have warmed Cal's heart, but all he wanted to do was scream. *No, Joey. No...*

181

Kravik's eyes narrowed, and he gestured the second dragon to his side. Together, they nosed forward, eyeing Cal. He couldn't hear them communicate, but he could see it in Kravik's eyes.

Kill the wolf first. We'll get the boy on the second pass.

Cal swung one foot back to brace himself for their on-slaught. But the rock underfoot gave way, and he slipped. That left him with no choice but to drop the spear and duck under the cloak.

Half a second later, flames buffeted the cloak with the force of a fire hose. It was all he could do to hold on as both dragons pounded him with flames. When he gasped for air, his lungs burned. Just when he thought he couldn't hold out a moment longer, the pressure lifted as the dragons swept past.

Cal jumped to his feet, swaying through a haze of pain. His skin wasn't burned, but his body was battered.

Spear, he told himself. *Spear.*

Spear hardly described the charred stick left behind in the dragons' wake, so he stepped toward his cache for another, one aching step at a time.

A high-pitched voice tapped urgently at the edge of his mind. *Hurry.*

That was Joey. It had to be. Cal mustered the strength to get his joints working again. He grabbed a new spear and whirled around. Kravik and the second dragon were looping back. The arc of their turn was graceful, even unrushed. But the moment they faced Cal, their wings swung faster, and their ivory fangs flashed. Four points of red hurtled through the night, marking two pairs of ruthless dragon eyes.

Cal stood his ground, widening his stance. This was it. And hell, the chances were slim. Even if he killed one dragon, the other was likely to get him, and that would be that. But the effort might buy enough time for the others to rush back and protect Joey.

Cal found himself smiling at nothing in particular. It was funny, how a man's goals could change. Twelve years ago, he'd wanted to kill Barnaby. Then he'd shifted over to protecting Cynthia. And yes, he'd even entertained himself with the vague hope of winning her back one day. But now, all he really cared about was Joey. The boy was Cynthia's treasure. Her future. Her everything.

The breeze toyed with Cal's hair in the lull before the dragon's onslaught, and something in him shifted. The pent-up anger and jealousy dulled, leaving. . .

He frowned. What was that feeling, exactly?

Then it hit him. Fate was smiling on him for the first time. A sensation so unfamiliar, he didn't know how to respond.

Focus, his wolf hissed. *For the kid's sake, focus.*

He raised the spear, calculating quickly. Somehow, he had to take out one dragon, avoid the second, and get his hands on another spear.

A creak sounded, drawing his attention to the ballista and the little boy with wide, hopeful eyes.

Ready, sir, a squeaky voice sounded in his mind.

Cal had no choice but to nod, hoping against hope. Hell, maybe the kid could actually spear one of the dragons. And if Cal got the other one. . . Well, hell. Maybe there was a breath of hope, after all.

"Right here," Cal muttered, turning back to Kravik. "Over here."

The dragon's eyes glowed an even brighter shade of red. Yeah, well. Cal's eyes were glowing too. He could tell from the heat.

"Right here," he whispered, tunneling his vision down to Kravik, who opened his jaws wide. A reddish-orange point glowed in his throat, indicating he was about to spit fire.

Cal counted microseconds that dragged as slowly as hours. Displaced air rushed ahead of the dragon, pressing Cal's shirt against his skin. He braced his back leg and gripped the spear tightly.

Die, Kravik's wide jaws said just as Cal's inner countdown hit zero. *Die.*

"No, you die," Cal grunted. With a heave, he threw the spear.

The force made him stumble, then look up. Death had to be watching closely, because everything moved into superslow motion. His spear flew at Kravik, straight and true. At the same time, a thin line of fire extended from the dragon's mouth. Something whistled from the right, but all Cal had eyes for were the spear and the fire, rushing along parallel paths — the spear flying at the dragon's chest while the fire rushed toward Cal's head.

No, wait. The fire was aimed at where his head had been before he'd stumbled, so Kravik had to tilt his chin, redirecting his attack. Too late to incinerate the spear in midair... but not too late to kill Cal?

Cal rolled aside, praying for a miracle. But even if he evaded Kravik's fire, the chances of him grabbing a new spear in time to kill the second dragon were slim. It was flying beside Kravik, ready to finish Cal off.

But suddenly, the second dragon screamed and lurched to one side

Joey! Cal's wolf cheered, spotting the spear stuck deep in the beast's ribs.

The boy had done it! He'd struck the second dragon, making it veer into Kravik. The flame extending from Kravik's mouth broke off as he twisted in anger, distracted just long enough for—

Kravik screamed in agony as Cal's spear buried itself in the dark scales of his chest, and his eyes glittered with pain. An instant later, the second dragon crashed into him, and they both tumbled to the ground.

Cal's heart leaped in hope. They'd done it — he and Joey had done it!

Except for one thing. Kravik was mortally wounded, but now, both dragons were plunging directly at Cal. He yelped and dove to the right, but it was too late.

Pain ripped through his body, and his vision flashed as a force like nothing he'd ever experienced crashed into him like a hurtling train. The world went sideways, and everything became a blur of colliding bodies, flying dirt, and solid rock.

Then everything went still — very still, and the only sound was that of his labored breathing. Cal found himself on his back, trying to blink the stars out of his eyes. A mighty weight was squeezing the life out of him, and no matter how he kicked or clawed, he couldn't get free. The body of the second dragon was crushing him.

If he'd had the lung power, he would have yelled at fate. Jesus. Couldn't it give a guy a break? Both dragons were dead, judging by the hush that set in. But, damn. Cal figured he didn't have long himself.

He tried again, pushing with all his might. But the dragon was huge, and the body refused to budge. Cal dropped his head back to the ground and closed his eyes.

He thought he'd been ready to die. But now that he was actually on death's doorstep... it hurt. Not so much in the body, but in the heart.

Cynthia, his wolf cried.

He'd never touch her... hold her... kiss her ever again. He'd never get his second chance.

Of course, he should have predicted it would end this way. Yet again, he was so close yet so far from the only prize he'd ever coveted. Cynthia.

Well, if nothing else, he'd die her hero. At least there was that, right?

Still, the bitterness remained. He would have loved to swing one more punch at fate. Just one, once.

"Cynthia," he whispered as a slideshow played in his mind.

He saw her eyes smiling at him while they danced. Her hair whipping in the wind as he raced the Triumph over a country road. Her fingers, intertwined with his.

Someone tugged at his shoulders and whispered. "Cal?"

That was Joey, and Cal summoned enough energy to look up. The kid was leaning against the dead dragon, pushing with all his might, but the earth slipped away under his feet.

"Heya, Joey," Cal whispered when the boy dropped to his knees, spent. "It's okay."

"It's not okay," Joey insisted.

Cal wasn't ready to have his heart broken another time, so he pushed the achy feeling away.

"Nah, it's fine," he said, though his voice was more of a gasp.

But, shit. The kid was crying, and he couldn't bear that.

"Shh," he tried.

But Joey just wouldn't listen. Still crying, he stood and stumbled away. "I'll get Dell."

Cal reached out to stop him, but the boy was too far.

"Joey!" he called. There was no telling how many of Moira's shifters might be prowling around out there.

Joey's footsteps crunched over the landscape, then faded into the distance. Cal listened, totally on edge. But everything was quiet, and when he closed his eyes, peace gradually filled in all the achy places in his body and soul.

The ground beneath him was cold, and the dragon's leathery body ought to have made his skin crawl. But the more he thought of Cynthia, the less any of that mattered. Something told him Joey would be okay, so Cal kept his thoughts on Cynthia and savored every memory. Their dance in the Lucky Devil. The calm he'd felt when he'd held her. Her happy sigh after they'd made love. . .

How long he lay there, he had no clue, but it seemed like hours. Night seemed to fade, along with the stars. Or maybe that was his vision, giving up like his lungs.

"Cal. . ." someone called.

He smiled faintly. It was funny how the mind worked. Now he was imagining Cynthia there.

Hands pressed on his shoulders, and he opened his eyes.

"Cynthia. . ." His lips curled. It really was her, looking as beautiful as ever, if a little distraught. Behind her, the first rays of dawn were coloring the sky, pushing the night away.

"Oh, Cal," she whispered.

He smiled. For all the pain, for all the wasted years, for all the regrets — it was good to see her. To be her hero at last.

"Cal," she cried, touching his shoulders.

He closed his eyes, reaching out to her with his mind when he couldn't find the strength to speak.

It's okay. You're okay. That's all that matters.

She didn't seem to get that, but he didn't have the energy to explain. Why try to scratch out a few words when he could concentrate on the warmth of her hands and that amazing rose-and-willow scent? Why move when he had such nice visions dancing through his head?

Slowly, his senses started tuning out, and Cynthia's voice grew faint. He didn't have the strength to fight death any longer, but that was okay. With every fading breath, Cal resigned himself to lie quietly in her arms and slowly, comfortably, drift away.

Chapter Nineteen

"Cal..."

Cynthia called his name so urgently, Cal fluttered his eyes. Vaguely, he felt her shake his shoulder, but he didn't respond. Didn't she get it? Dying was okay, because she was all right. Besides, he was tired. Really, really tired, and drifting away was so much easier than dragging himself back to a world filled with pain.

"Cal..."

Her hand clutched his, and he squeezed the little bit that he could, telling her it was all right. He loved her. And as for death... Well, he might not have lived honorably, but he sure as hell would die honorably. So why couldn't she just let him go?

"Help me push," Cynthia said to someone else.

Pain flashed through Cal's body as the heavy weight rolled over him, and he groaned. Then it was gone, and Cynthia was touching him again.

Nice, his wolf hummed.

But she was talking, too, damn it. Refusing to let him go.

"Cal, stay with me."

Couldn't she tell it was too late?

"Come on, man..." someone else urged. Was that Dell?

Cal felt himself going all stubborn. No one told him what to do, especially not that stupid lion.

"Cal, please," Cynthia begged.

The tears in her voice made him ache, but surely, it was better this way. She could remember all the good times instead of the bad.

Listen to her, a deep, earthy voice said. *You don't need to die to be worthy.*

If his ribs weren't screaming with pain, he might have laughed. Was that destiny, finally rooting for him?

She needs you.

"Please..." Cynthia pleaded.

Something warm and wet dripped on his face, and he panicked, thinking it was blood. Was Cynthia hurt? But that wasn't blood, just tears. Her tears.

"My love..." she whispered.

His heart swelled to about five times its usual size. God, did it feel good to hear that. Which meant it was probably as good a time to die as ever. He relaxed, letting that warm, bright light pull him in like a laser beam.

Cynthia clutched his shoulder, and a moment later, her voice changed.

"No. No. Don't you dare."

Cal tensed, and the laser beam paused. Was she actually ordering him?

"Yes, I am ordering you," she shouted.

"Um, Cynth," the lion murmured, trying to calm her down.

But she went right on tugging on Cal's hand, insisting. "I will never forgive you if you die."

Cal frowned. That wasn't fair. Heroes were supposed to be heroes even if they died.

But then Joey chimed in, making it even harder to slip peacefully away.

"You promised," the little boy said in a teary whisper. "You promised."

Cal wanted to say he'd made no such promise but, damn. He had, hadn't he, when Joey had pleaded with him. *You promise you won't go far?*

I promise, he'd replied. *Now, go!*

"Look at me, Cal," Cynthia ordered, cupping his cheeks.

He wasn't going to, because he knew that would just make it harder — for him and for her. But then fate, the bastard, chimed in too.

Look at her.

So, he did, even though his eyelids felt like cement and didn't want to budge. At first, all he saw was dawn, and it was spectacular. Streaks of orange and pink bursting over the mountains, the whole sky giving him one final show. Then he gradually focused on Cynthia's face, and that was even more spectacular. The dark, deep black of her eyes, brimming with tears, yet burning with fire.

Burning with love, he realized.

A lump formed in his throat. If that was his last time getting to see her... Well, damn. That thought hit him a hell of a lot harder than the notion of a last dawn or a last anything else.

"Don't leave me. Please," she whispered.

Then she kissed him — on the lips and in front of everyone, or at least, anyone who was there. Joey, Dell, and a couple others Cal sensed go totally still. Not that he paid much attention to them, what with that kiss sending little zings of energy through his body. Her rose-and-willow scent made his head feel light. He sniffed deeply, then frowned. Her scent was tinged with smoke, ash, and something else...

Dell. Cal's eyes snapped open the moment he identified that scent, ready to tear the lion shifter apart. Then his eyes caught on the white shirt draped over Cynthia's shoulders, and he growled. A big men's button-down covered her body, if only barely.

Just as he was summoning the strength to get to his feet and attack Dell, the truth hit Cal, and he sank back. Dell hadn't been messing around with Cynthia. He'd just covered her with a shirt after she shifted out of dragon form. Other than that shirt, she was bare all over — unless he counted the strand of pearls she clutched in one hand.

"Whoa," he murmured, squinting at the bright light.

"Cynth..." Dell whispered in awe when he noticed it too.

The middle pearl was shining brightly, as if someone had turned on a bulb inside it. The warm, ivory light seemed to glow brighter with every breath he took.

Cynthia didn't seem to notice, though. She kept her eyes on his and her hands tight on his shoulders. "Cal. Stay with me. Please..."

His eyelids drooped again. God, he was tired. Tired of lots of things, but mostly, tired of resisting. If Cynthia wanted him to live, well, maybe he'd give it one last try.

So he focused on the glow of her pearl instead of the light calling him toward death. He sucked in a little more air with each breath, even if it did hurt. And though his eyes drifted shut again, he listened to Cynthia.

"Stay with me..."

His lips curled a teensy, tiny bit. Was it all a dream?

∞∞∞∞

The next time Cal's eyes opened, he was in a house, and the dawn colors were streaming through the window. Or maybe that was sunset? He wasn't sure, and before long, he drifted away again... and again. He drifted in and out of consciousness for what could have been days or hours. Sometimes, there were people in the room, whispering to each other or to him. Sometimes, it was just him and Cynthia, and that was the best. So good he wondered if he was dreaming again.

But, no. It wasn't a dream. In dreams, pain was sharp and terrifying, whereas the ache in his body was dull, as if an elephant had tap-danced on his chest. His ribs screamed, though the worst was when a couple of the guys had come along and lifted him. His lungs groaned with every breath, and every beat of his heart hurt.

On the other hand, Cynthia was there, and that made up for the rest. She touched him. Kissed him. Whispered to him, giving him something to focus on other than pain.

Like the future. A life together. All the things he'd wished for, plus some things he'd never even considered before. Like the sound of pages turning slowly and the soft voice of a young boy reading aloud.

"*Frog pushed Toad out of bed...*"

It was Joey, sitting on the edge of the bed Cal found himself in, reading to him about a frog and a toad who were friends.

"*Then Frog said to Toad, in the evenings we will sit right here on this front porch and count the stars...*"

Cal had no idea what was up with Frog or Toad, but it was kind of nice to listen, knowing someone cared about him.

He drifted in and out of that story — and a bunch of others, and another few sunrises and sunsets. Until one day, he woke up for good. Well, at least for a few hours at a time. Hours he got to spend with Cynthia, who wouldn't release his hand as she went over everything that had happened — the good and the bad. About Moira and the fight on the Big Island. About rushing back to find him at the edge of death. About Joey, being so brave...

Her voice choked up there, and he held her for a little while. Then she sat up, blew her nose, and started listing his injuries. By the time she was moving on from *broken ribs* to *collapsed lung*, he'd shushed her.

"Good thing we shifters heal fast."

She frowned in disapproval. Yeah, he knew how close it had been. But now that the worst was past, he was ready to look forward, not back.

"Is everyone else okay?" he asked, holding his breath.

If Cynthia's face fell, he'd know one of her friends had died in the battle. In a pack as close as hers, there was nothing as terrible as that kind of loss.

She nodded quickly, thank goodness. "Anjali and Nina kept the kids safe, and the others made sure none of the attackers got close. Silas and Kai killed the dragons they were fighting, and you and Joey..."

Her voice cracked, and Cal's gut sank. Yes, he and Joey had killed the three dragons waiting to launch a surprise attack. But a kid that young shouldn't have been part of such violence, even if it did make him a hero in his own right.

"How is he?" Cal asked quietly.

Cynthia's hand tightened in his, but her eyes shone. "He's more focused on the how than the what, thank goodness. You really impressed him with that bastill... ballis..."

"Ballista," a deep voice said from the doorway.

Cal glanced past Cynthia and spotted Silas leaning against the doorway.

Cal did a double take. Silas was one of those blue-blooded, impeccably brought-up dragon shifters — a lot like Cynthia. Their kind didn't lean casually. Hell, they rarely even smiled. Mostly, they stormed around, stressed, and snorted fire. But there Silas stood, looking happier and more relaxed than ever a dragon had been.

"You've got Joey tearing through my library for books on Roman warfare, you know."

Cal studied him, waiting for more. But that appeared to be it. And, wow. If that was the worst the dragon planned to accuse him of, he'd take it.

Cynthia, on the other hand, sat upright and yelped. "Roman warfare?"

Cal winced, steeling himself for her to flip out about exposing Joey to that kind of thing. But a second later, she sighed. "Maybe I can get him sidetracked on to something like aqueducts."

"Roman warfare. I never would have thought of that." Silas raised his eyebrows at Cal. "Something you learned about... How, exactly?"

Cal shrugged. "You're not the only dragon with a sizable library."

Cynthia's jaw dropped. "Barnaby? But... But..."

Cal gulped. Someday, he'd tell her the story of how he and Barnaby had worked things out. But right now...

"The ballista was Barnaby's idea. He loaned me some books once I realized killing dragons with my bare teeth wasn't going to cut it."

Too late, Cal realized he was rubbing the burn scars on his arm. He stopped abruptly, but Cynthia — and Silas — had noticed. Both studied him with a whole new glint in their eyes. A glint that hinted at respect, maybe even awe. Cal shrugged it off, but inside, he glowed. Yes, he really had taken on his first dragon in wolf form and lived to tell the tale. But no, he really didn't want to talk about it.

Luckily, Joey ran in just then, waving a book. "I found it! I found it!"

He hurried over, plopped on the bed beside Cal, and started leafing through the pages. "Somewhere here. . ."

Cal froze and glanced around out of the corner of his eye. Joey seemed totally fine with Cal being in his mother's bed, and Silas didn't bat an eye either. Even Cynthia didn't seem to mind her son cozying up to him.

His lungs still hurt, but Cal took a deep breath anyway, wondering what Barnaby would have to say about that. But when he pictured the older dragon, the man was standing in his study, holding a glass of brandy, not the least bit angry.

Cynthia loves you. She will always love you, Barnaby's voice whispered in his mind. *And as for Joey. . .* He heaved a deep, sad sigh, and Cal sensed bottomless sorrow. *I can no longer be there for him. But you can. You must be.*

Joey was talking and pointing, but Cal's gaze wandered to the patch of sky outside the balcony door.

Barnaby, he wished he could go back and say. *You are twice the man I gave you credit for.*

The Barnaby in his mind — a ghost? A memory? — smiled and sipped his brandy, then held it up in a toast. *Well, you know how dragons are. Being noble is everything.*

Cal shook his head. *Not all dragons. Just a few.*

Then he bowed his head, considering Barnaby for another minute or two. Someday, he'd have to find himself some brandy and drink to the man. But right now. . .

He dragged his attention back to the there and then. To Cynthia, cuddled up beside him like she would never let him go. To Joey, who seemed fine with the idea of having another surrogate father in his life. To Silas, regarding him with cool, calm acceptance.

He closed his eyes. Injuries, he knew how to handle. But massive strokes of luck, not so much.

Luck has nothing to do with it, Cynthia whispered in his mind. She looped an arm over his shoulders and sat straighter, prouder. Proud of *him.*

195

Cal puffed out his cheeks a little, letting himself feel a little pride too.

"Oh, look," Joey sang out, pointing to a picture. "A ballista on wheels. Cool!"

"*Calliballista*," Silas murmured.

Cal rolled his eyes. Did every blue blood learn that in dragon school?

"Can you help me build one?" Joey begged.

Cal stuck up his hands, then winced at the motion. "Maybe someday."

Cynthia, to her credit, didn't protest. She just helped him settle back against the pillows and fussed with the sheet. "I think Cal needs some rest now, Joey."

Cal wanted to protest that he needed no such thing, but... Well, maybe he did.

Silas held out a hand to Joey. "Connor told me to tell you he was ready for more flying lessons now."

Joey's eyes went wide, and he raced outside after a quick hug from Cynthia. "Bye, Mommy! I have to go."

Cal's eyebrows shot up. *Flying lessons?* he mouthed.

Cynthia sighed. "Only with a kite, thank God. But someday..."

The stairs creaked as both Silas and Joey departed, leaving them alone.

"Someday?" Cal tried — and failed — to strike a casual tone. "You think you might keep me around that long?"

Cynthia threw her arms around him. "Not letting you go ever again, wolf." She sniffled, and her hug was tight enough to hurt, but he didn't mind. Then she pulled back abruptly and looked at him, suddenly worried. "That is, if it's all right with you."

He grinned. "Not letting you go ever again, m'lady."

Her smile was like sunshine pouring out between two clouds, and a little tease snuck back into her voice. "No? You think you can handle a high-strung she-dragon as a mate?"

He laughed. "I know I can."

Her expression grew more serious. "And Joey? And a whole pack of infuriating shifters?"

"Infuriating? You know you love them."

Cynthia bit her lip, and she nodded. "I do. Not the way I love you," she rushed to add. "But, yes. I do. They're like family to me. I feel closer to them than the family I was born into."

He refrained from pointing out how that shouldn't be hard, considering Moira was her cousin. But, yeah. He got it.

Cynthia dropped into another hug. A nice, close one, with her face nestled by his ear and her arms resting lightly on his shoulders. Her body warm and soft in all the right places.

His inner wolf started humming, giving him all kinds of bad ideas.

With every deep breath, her breasts pressed against his chest, and slowly, Cal became aware of all kinds of other body parts. He slid his arms around her waist and turned his head slightly, bringing his lips to her neck.

"Mmm." She sighed, giving him more space.

A little tug was all it took to make her shift closer. Cal let his hands creep higher, teasing the lower edge of her breasts. Her breaths grew heavier, as did his, but this time, it didn't come with pain. Only a shot of warmth and desire.

He was just pulling her into straddling him when she blinked and pulled back. "Oh, my gosh. I'm so sorry. You need to rest."

He tugged her back and growled in her ear. "Need my mate."

"But... but..." Her protests turned into quiet moans when he slid one hand down her backside and the other over her breast.

"But...?" he challenged.

She started rocking over his groin. "I already forgot what. Oh..." She tilted her head back and parted her lips, surrendering to his touch.

He kissed her collarbone, working open the buttons of her blouse. "Too many clothes."

She helped him with the blouse and her shorts, then pulled aside the sheet with a wicked grin. "And you, I see, are conveniently naked."

197

He grinned. "I think this was all part of your diabolical plan. I'm innocent, I swear."

She laughed outright. "There's not an innocent bone in your body, wolf. Now, if it weren't for these injuries..."

"Where there's a will, there's a way. See?" He pulled her back into a straddle. The moment her soft core pressed against his cock, he jerked. That activated all kinds of aches and pains he'd forgotten about, but what did that matter when he could bond with his mate?

"You sure you don't want to wait?" she whispered, easing away.

He shook his head. He'd waited for twelve long years. Enough was enough.

"No more waiting, my mate."

Her eyes shone, and he caught the series of images that flashed through her mind. In them, she was panting and rocking over him. Nipping his neck as he pumped upward into her from his seated position. Biting deep and then—

His breath caught as he realized what she had in mind. The mating bite. He'd dreamed of marking her with his bite for years, and it wasn't the first time he'd caught her thinking of claiming him back. Usually, the male shifter went first, but considering the circumstances...

He gripped her hips harder and leaned back. When he spoke, his voice was gritty with need.

"I like that plan."

"You do, don't you?" she purred as she rocked over his lap, letting their bodies line up.

The moment his cock met exactly the right spot, she hissed. Then, looking more intent than Cal had ever seen her, Cynthia pushed down, taking him deep.

Cal inhaled, savoring the sweet burn. Then he push-pulled on her hips, coaxing her on. Cynthia's eyes glazed over as she started rocking again. Her long, silky hair flowed over her bare shoulders, and her breasts swayed. Cal made mental notes of all the fun he'd treat his mate to when he was fully recovered.

Got to make her our mate first, his wolf pointed out. *For real. Forever.*

Cal gritted his teeth and drove deeper up her slick, tight channel.

Cynthia, his wolf cried dreamily.

The only woman he'd ever loved. The only woman he ever would love, even if he lived to eternity.

"Oh..." she cried out.

He pumped harder, keeping her hips tight against his.

"Yes..."

Her head was tipped way back, and the pulse beat in her neck, tempting him. But a moment later, she folded forward and kissed him hard on the mouth. *Really* hard, whimpering with need. Using one hand, she tipped his head back, ducked down, and—

Cal's pulse spiked as her teeth scraped his skin. Jesus, did that feel good.

She moved a little too far left, then backed up, searching for the right place to bite.

"Right there," he groaned instinctively when she lined up with the groove beside his Adam's apple. "Right there."

Right now, she cried into his mind, rocking her hips hard.

Three more pumps were all he needed to explode inside her, coming with a muffled groan. A groan cut off by the sharp slide of two points into the flesh of his neck. His mind blanked out at the sheer pleasure, and when she exhaled...

He howled, low and hard. A howl of ecstasy at the rush of heat through his veins. Dragon fire was something to avoid — at least, it had been for the last decade of his life. Now, a little lick of it was racing around his body, marking every inch of him as hers. And man, was it good. Amazing. Beyond his wildest, dirtiest dreams.

Mine, Cynthia cried as her body convulsed. *You are mine.*

How long she held on to that bite, Cal had no clue. At some point, she slowly released him, keeping her lips sealed over the bite marks, making sure they healed before a single drop of blood could escape. Then she slumped over him, totally spent. Cal lay back, cradling her against his body, murmuring incoherently. His human side and his wolf were both trying to express how good he felt at the same time, but all that came out was a babble of animal and human sounds.

A tear slipped out of Cynthia's eyes, then another, and in spite of her whisking them away, they wouldn't stop.

Cal wiped their bodies with the sheet, then eased her back until she was lying beside him and snuggled close.

"I know just how you feel," he whispered, letting her cry.

Some things, you just had to let out. Like the sorrow of a long, hard past and the joy of a sunny future.

He kissed her shoulder and concentrated on the *future* part. "Believe me, I know how you feel."

Chapter Twenty

"Are you sure you're ready?" Cynthia asked.

Her dragon hummed as Cal emerged from the shower in a cloud of steam, wrapped in a towel. God, the man was chiseled. Tall. Handsome in that *weary warrior* way. And who could blame him? The past decade had been hell on them both, and the last six days had been a roller coaster of their own.

Was it really over? Was he really all right?

"I'm fine," he assured her for the twentieth time.

He scrubbed a second towel over his chest, and she couldn't help watching. Every muscle — and every scar — on his body told the story of his unwavering devotion. Would she ever be able to repay him for what he'd done?

"Yes, you can," he said, handing her the towel.

She blinked a little, then jolted. Oops. She'd have to be more careful to guard her thoughts from her mate.

"Can you dry my back? I'm still a little too stiff to reach there."

"As if that makes up for everything."

He kissed her knuckles. "Only the present and future count now. The past is the past."

He turned before she could answer, and she rubbed the skin gently, marveling over every inch of her mate. She'd nearly lost him for the second time, and she couldn't quite shake the fear that fate might come along and—

Cal turned and pinned her with a stern look. "Now, repeat after me. Life is one big maybe..."

She made a face. "That's supposed to be comforting?"

He went on without a pause. "...But if you have faith, it will all turn out okay."

She hugged him. Probably too tightly, but Cal didn't seem to mind. A minute later, he eased gently away.

"Believe me, I'd be happy to keep that up, but we have a meeting to get over with."

She took a deep breath. Right, the meeting. The whole reason Cal had dragged himself out of bed.

"It could wait a day, you know."

"I'm ready. Well, ready enough. But I wouldn't mind if you helped me with these clothes."

She helped him into the shirt and pants, then smoothed her hands over her white dress and checked herself in the full-length mirror. Cal hugged her from behind.

"Wow. Look at you," he breathed in her ear.

She smiled so broadly, her cheeks ached. "Look at us."

She refrained from saying *Look at you* because that might make him self-conscious. But, wow. The man looked amazing in that crisp white shirt and black slacks. In truth, he smelled amazing too, what with the lingering aroma of aftershave mixing with his natural sandalwood scent.

He pursed his lips. "Not sure I can get used to looking so. . . respectable."

She laughed. "Maybe just from time to time. The bike's still in the barn, you know, and your jeans are over there." There was no reason to change anything about her mate. She loved him exactly the way he was.

He grinned. "Just wait. When the meeting is over, I might just take you for a ride."

It was ridiculous, how the thought thrilled her. Like she was twenty all over again and a handsome, enigmatic stranger was asking her out for the first time.

"Promise?"

"Promise." His deep, steady rumble hinted at promises that went far, far beyond one ride.

I promise everything, his wolf whispered. *A lifetime.*

She tilted her head against his, then turned to the door and took a deep breath. "Ready?"

Cal nodded firmly. "Ready."

He looked it — fierce, determined, and confident. Still, his tight grip hinted at the resolve that took. After all, he was about to face her entire pack — a group filled with hugely protective alpha males. It would be like meeting a prospective father-in-law — times five.

She fingered her pearl necklace and led him down the stairs.

"Wait a minute." She pulled up short on the porch. Why wasn't the table set? Where was everyone?

A pot lid clanged in the kitchen where Dell was cooking up a storm, while Chase and Joey bustled around, collecting plates and bowls.

"Hi, Mommy!" Joey called. "Hi, Cal."

Cynthia smiled. "Hi, sweetie."

Cal tousled her son's hair. "Heya, Joey."

"Oh, there you are. *Finally.*" Dell made a show of rolling his eyes. "Grab those, will you?"

Cynthia took the platter he indicated. "Where is everyone?"

"Waiting."

She glanced around.

Dell gave an exaggerated sigh. "Just follow Joey. You'll see."

"You know how many places I set?" Joey said as he led her and Cal down the stairs, across the lawn, and toward the barn.

Cynthia glanced at Cal, then at the barn. Why on earth was Joey headed there?

"How many, sweetie?"

He turned the corner of the barn and called out cheerily. "Twenty-four places. A new record."

The moment Cynthia saw what he meant, her jaw dropped, and she pulled up. Cal nearly bumped into her, but Chase dodged them both and went through the wide-open barn doors as if nothing special was going on.

"Oh, hi, Cynthia!" Anjali called and lifted her baby daughter's arm to wave. "Say hi, Quinn."

"Hi," Cynthia whispered, staring.

"Is it Christmas or something?" Cal murmured in her ear.

Cynthia could have sworn December was still months away, but it sure looked festive. The interior of the barn was strung with party lights, and the long row of tables set up was covered with steaming dishes — so many, she could barely see the colorful Hawaiian print of the tablecloths underneath.

Anjali laughed. "Not Christmas. But it is a special occasion." Her eyes danced as she looked them both over.

"It is indeed," Silas said, coming up with a champagne glass in his hand. He kissed Cynthia on both cheeks, then shook Cal's hand. "Good to see you."

"Good to see you," Cynthia managed, still stunned.

Everyone was there — literally, everyone. The whole gang from Koakea Plantation was there, plus their neighbors from Koa Point — the dragon, wolf, tiger, lion, and bear shifters who were her closest friends, and everyone was grinning like a fool.

She gripped Cal's hand. Those friends weren't just smiling at her. They were smiling *for* her, celebrating the happy ending she never thought she would have.

"Come on, Cynth." Dell came up from behind with a basket of steaming coconut milk bread rolls. "Don't just stand there."

"What should I do, Mr. O'Roarke?"

He put the rolls down and turned back to her with a grin. "You should let me congratulate you, for starters. Both of you."

Cynthia looked on, speechless, as Dell shook Cal's hand, then reached for hers to do the same. Then he muttered, "What the hell," and hugged her instead. A brief, brotherly, *Hey, you did it* hug that caught her totally off guard. Then he stepped back and winked. "Also, you should sit down so we can finally eat."

"All right, everyone." Connor motioned to the table.

It took everything Cynthia had to squeeze away the tears welling up in her eyes. Joey led her over to the chair at the head of the long table, and everyone stepped up to their places.

Tim was hiding a limp, she saw, and Jenna was sporting a burn scar on her arm. Silas's right shoulder looked stiff, and Anjali held Quinn closer than ever. Cynthia could have wept.

For the past week, she'd only thought about Cal. But the others had been nursing their own wounds. She didn't want to imagine what the fighting had looked like on the ground. In addition to the marauding dragons, Moira had sent over twenty other mercenaries to attack the plantation. The grounds were scarred by several, long charred lines where dragon fire had scorched the earth, and countless patches of dirt had been torn up in the throes of a heated shifter battle.

But everyone was all right, thank goodness. Tired, but happy. They were hopeful, too. Like Tessa, who showed off her growing baby bump for the first time, and Kai, her mate, who wouldn't stop fussing over her. Keiki, the cat from next door, wound between Silas's legs and purred loudly. Almost as if promising that Tessa's baby was just one of all the wonders the future held in store.

Cynthia sat slowly, taking it all in. Cal sat to her left, and Joey on the right. Beyond them sat Dell, Anjali, Silas... Well, everyone. The table seemed to go on and on, and the scent of jasmine and lemongrass rose from the feast laid out on the table. The doors at each end of the barn had been left wide open, framing the majestic Maui landscape. The party lights strung from the barn rafters complemented the fiery sunset building in the sky outside.

"This is beautiful," she said, struggling to put her emotions into words.

"It is," Dell agreed, grinning at the meal he'd prepared.

"Perfect," Hailey said, looking at the candles she and the other women had set up — or at least, that was Cynthia's guess.

"Gorgeous," Cal murmured, looking right at Cynthia.

She bit her lip. For all the times when life seemed hopeless or depressing, there were other times when pure beauty was all around. Right now, she could find dozens — no, hundreds — of things to celebrate.

Connor looked at Cynthia. "Eat first, talk later?"

She nodded. Considering she could barely put two words together, that seemed best.

Dell started passing platters, and before long, the barn was alive with chatter, laughter, and the quiet chime of silverware. The pineapple-glazed ham was so delicious, Cynthia found herself licking her fork clean. The warm rolls slathered in macadamia nut butter were sinfully good, as was the kula green salad, the garlic shrimp, and all the other dishes. Dell had pulled out all the stops, and Tessa had brought over her best recipes from Koa Point. As good as it all tasted, though, Cynthia spent most of the meal looking around. Not too long ago, most of those men and women had been perfect strangers. Now, they were close friends.

More than friends, her dragon decided. *Family.*

Her mother would have scoffed, because Silas was the only one who came from noble dragon stock. Most came from ordinary or even disadvantaged circumstances. A few weren't even pure shifters, "just" humans turned shifter by their mates. Plus, they represented so many shifter species — bears, wolves, lions, dragons, and tigers. She could scarcely imagine a more ragtag group. But there they were, dining and laughing together. Living as one community, looking out for one another.

For a moment, she wished for a camera, then dismissed the idea. There was no lens that could capture that moment, let alone her emotions.

"Dessert, anyone?" Dell called.

A dozen hands shot up, but Connor shook his head and glanced at Cynthia. "How about we save that for a little later?"

She took a deep breath and nodded. The platters had been picked clean and most of the glasses drunk dry. It was as good a time as any to discuss the unavoidable.

"So," Connor started slowly, then trailed off, glancing between Cynthia and Cal.

She cleared her throat and followed his cue. "There are some things we should discuss."

Everyone looked on silently, giving her time to find the right words.

"There are a few things I've been meaning to tell you," she said at last. "Starting with my name, I suppose."

"I knew it," Dell cried out. "Your real name is Esmeralda!"

206

Everyone laughed except for Anjali, who play-smacked his arm.

Cynthia laughed too. Leave it to Dell to loosen things up. "No, I mean the *Brown* part. My real family name is Baird. Cynthia Baird."

Officially, it was Cynthia Berwyn Elizabeth Victoria Rhydderick Baird Brenner, but no one needed to hear that mouthful.

Everyone looked stunned — except Dell, Cal, and Silas, who already knew.

"Baird, as in, *the* Bairds?" Connor asked.

She nodded slowly. "Yes, those Bairds." Then she took a deep breath. "As long as I can remember, my family taught me we were special because of our bloodline. Our wealth. Our traditions. Not for our accomplishments, our bravery, or our loyalty." She looked at Connor, then around the table. "But you have taught me how wrong they were. Pride should stem from your own accomplishments, not the deeds of your forefathers. You've taught me that it doesn't matter where or how a hero is born. What matters is the heart. The effort. The sacrifice." She looked at Cal until she was close to tears. Then she turned to Joey and attempted a joke. "We're going to have to redesign some of our homeschooling lessons, sweetie."

"No more spelling?" Joey's voice rose in hope.

Everyone laughed, and she touched his beautiful red hair. "I mean history."

"But I like history. It has ballistas and other cool stuff."

More chuckles sounded, though Boone, the wolf shifter from Koa Point and father of twins, looked thoughtful as he patted the infant sleeping on his shoulder. "Never would have thought of fighting a dragon in human form, I have to admit."

Chase, one of the other wolves, nodded.

Cal stuck up his hands. "I can't take credit for the idea."

Connor snorted. "No, just for the execution. No pun intended."

Cynthia swallowed the lump in her throat, thinking of Barnaby.

"Indeed, heroes can come from anywhere," Silas announced, raising his glass toward Joey. "They come in all sizes.

207

And from all species." He nodded at Cal. "And even, occasionally, from the old bloodlines." He swung his glass toward Cynthia, and then motioned all around the table, indicating everyone. "To our heroes, no matter what families they come from."

Everyone clinked glasses, and Cynthia couldn't stop gazing at the people gathered there. Each of her shifter friends had defeated ruthless enemies in the past. But now, they'd worked together to conquer the greatest enemy of all.

"Hey, it's shining again." Cal motioned to her necklace.

His voice was just a whisper, but everyone quieted down, staring at her pearl.

Chapter Twenty-One

Cynthia couldn't see her pearls, but she could feel them — or rather, the one in the middle. In one practiced movement, she swept her hair aside, undid the clasp, and held the necklace in her hands.

"Mine is shining back," Anjali whispered, holding out the single pearl strung from the necklace she wore.

"So is mine," Jenna added.

Sophie and Hailey followed suit, each revealing a pearl of a different color.

"All right, Cynth." Dell threw up his hands in mock exasperation. "What other surprises do you have for us?"

"Believe me, this was a surprise to me too."

"One of the pearls of desire?" Silas asked quietly.

She gulped, touching the middle pearl. "I never suspected. But yes, I believe it is."

"It has to be. Look," Jenna said, motioning around.

Every pearl shone as if lit from within, and faint beams of light crisscrossed the table, connecting the pearls.

"A pearl of what?" Cal stared.

"One of the pearls of desire," Anjali explained. "I can't believe you've had the last one all along."

"I can't believe it either," Cynthia assured her. "It's never done this before."

"I've felt mine lots of times, but it's never given me as much power as it did this time," Jenna murmured, touching her pearl. "Like it knew everything was on the line."

Hailey nodded somberly, as did the other women. Cynthia took a deep breath, thinking how close it had all been. She never would have been able to hold off Moira's guards as long as she had without the power of the pearl. She held it higher, fascinated by the crisscrossing bands of light that connected her pearl to the others'. Never had she felt more like a sister to the other women, nor so grateful to be part of such a special pack.

"It's like the legend says," Anjali added in a hush. "Nanalani, daughter of the shark shifter king, called forth the spirit of the sea to put a spell on her pearls so she could experience love."

"Desire, baby. The word is desire," Dell joked.

"Love," Anjali insisted.

"Passion," Tim said, smiling at Hailey.

"Yearning," Chase whispered, pulling Sophie into a hug.

"True love." Cynthia looked at Cal, feeling like her heart might burst from joy. Then she looked around at the others, and a new thought struck her. Maybe it wasn't just Cal she'd been wishing for, but a feeling of belonging. The desire for friends and family that came without strings attached.

Got all that — and more, her dragon whispered. *A nice, safe home. A pack to belong to, not just to rule.*

It was amazing, how so many treasures could rain down on a woman at one time.

"True love," Anjali agreed, giving Dell a stern look. "Eventually, Nanalani threw her pearls back into the sea where they would wait to be reawakened and inspire great acts of love again." She laced her fingers through Dell's, tilted her head against the baby's, and sighed. "Just like the legend says."

"The question is, what stirred it now?" Silas mused.

Anjali chuckled. "Isn't it obvious? After all, it is a pearl of *desire...*"

She stressed the last word, and the women flashed knowing smiles. Most of the men, on the other hand, looked stumped.

Cynthia blushed crimson and glanced at Cal, who appeared totally blank.

"I don't get it," Dell said.

Anjali rolled her eyes. "Doesn't it make sense that a pearl of desire would awaken when its bearer felt... well, desire?"

She shot Cynthia a *sorry-not-sorry* look. "I mean, when she gets a second chance at true love?"

Cynthia's mouth hung open. "How did you know?"

She glanced at each woman in turn. How did any of them know? She thought back, sure she'd never allowed herself to mention Cal.

Anjali flashed a smile. "Call it intuition."

Dell rubbed his hands together. "Well, well, Cynth. I can see us getting a lot of mileage out of this."

"Don't you dare," she said dryly.

"Mileage out of what?" Joey asked.

"Um...um..." Dell hemmed and hawed, a moment Cynthia might have enjoyed immensely if she hadn't been worried about what he might say.

"Mr. O'Roarke is teasing me for being in love," she explained before Dell gave away anything else.

Being in love, not falling in love, she said into Cal's mind.

Falling in love all over again, he replied.

"Oh." Joey looked at her, then at Cal. Cynthia held her breath. What would he say? A moment later, Joey shrugged and turned to Dell. "Are we having dessert soon?"

Cynthia stared. Could it really be that easy for her son to accept a new man in her life?

Dell stood with a huge grin. "Good plan. Come and help me bring it over from the kitchen, will you?"

Joey stood, as did Sophie. "I'll get the coffee."

Anjali smiled as they left, then motioned to Cynthia's pearls. "Where did you get that necklace in the first place?"

"This was a gift from my mother." Cynthia touched the warm, smooth surface of the central pearl, wondering if her mother had known what that really was. She doubted it, though.

"And where did she get it?" Anjali asked. "Was your mother ever in Hawaii, where the pearls got their power?"

Cynthia pursed her lips, thinking of the legend of Nanalani, who had imbued the pearls with her magic.

"No, she was never here. My mother got them from her mother. But where my grandmother got these pearls, I don't know." She thought back, picturing the ivory jewelry box her grandmother had kept in her bedroom. "My granddad would pick something out from his treasure hoard once in a while as a special gift for her." Then she winced, realizing how that must sound.

Sure enough, Cal snorted. "Treasure hoard, huh? My grandfather had a junkyard."

Tim laughed. "Never know where you might find a real treasure, you know." He looked in Hailey's direction, and his eyes shone with love. "I found mine in a mall."

"On a plane," Connor murmured, looking at Jenna.

"At a smoothie truck," Chase whispered, looking as giddy as he'd been the day he'd met Sophie.

Cynthia couldn't help getting a little dreamy-eyed herself, and she murmured, "On the side of the road at night."

Cal rubbed his thumb over her hand, and for a moment, the world faded away until it was just the two of them gazing into each other's eyes exactly as they had so long ago on a quiet Adirondack country road. She could almost hear the leaves rustle and feel the crisp autumn air.

But then someone cried out in glee, yanking her out of her reverie.

"No way. You picked this guy up on the side of the road?" Dell laughed, prancing up behind her with a stack of dessert plates. "Did that bike of his break down? Do tell, Cynth."

She grinned. "I was the one with the broken-down car. Cal was the one who picked me up."

Picked you up... Laid you down... Made you mine, Cal whispered into her mind, making her go all warm and achy again.

Luckily, Dell made a second run to the house, and Hailey leaned forward, pointing to Cynthia's pearl. "Funny, I always thought it was white, but it's tinted with blue now."

Cynthia nodded. "That started happening a little while ago."

"When Cal got here?" Anjali asked.

"No, a few weeks before." She looked at Cal, who was studying the pearl.

"About the time I left the East Coast to find you," he mused.

She stared at him, then at the pearl, which seemed to wink as if to say, *Yes, I already knew.*

"What does blue in a pearl symbolize?" Jenna asked.

Cynthia opened her mouth, about to explain. But then the meaning struck her — really struck her, and the words stalled out on the tip of her tongue. When Cal squeezed her hand, checking if she was okay, she got herself back together again.

"My mother told me blue means *you will find love,*" she whispered, looking at her mate.

Cal's lips curled up. "Found that a long time ago."

Briefly, the sorrow of the past years threatened to well up again, so it was a good thing Dell, Joey, and Sophie came back.

"Coffee, anyone?" Sophie asked.

The rich aroma wafted around the room, and everyone shot a hand up.

"Plus, we've got a mango tiramisu and a pineapple upside-down cake," Dell said.

"I helped make them," Joey announced.

Everyone oohed and aahed, but Dell just waved away the praise and pointed outside the wide-open doors. "More importantly, check that out."

Everyone turned, but no one noticed a thing. No one but Cynthia, whose eyes caught on Cal's motorcycle, parked over in one corner. Her pink scarf was still tied to the handlebars in a gritty reminder of the past. God, she'd been so young when she'd given it to him. But even if she'd known about the struggles to come, she wouldn't have changed a thing. Not now that all her pain and sorrow had led to enduring joy.

But she doubted Dell meant that, so she searched beyond the Triumph for some clue.

"What?" Connor demanded.

Dell shushed him. "Listen."

Everyone strained for a moment, but there was nothing — nothing out of the ordinary, at least.

213

Dell cracked into a grin. "Yep — nothing. Isn't it beautiful? No enemies swooping out of the sky. No sounds of intruders. Just peace. Real peace."

Everyone listened in a whole new way, and Tim nodded gravely.

"Wow. You're right. Peace like never before."

"And the best part is, it's here to stay," Dell added.

"Well, we still have to keep an eye out for trouble," Connor said, but even he sounded a little dreamy.

Cynthia looked around, fully prepared for a shiver of foreboding to run down her spine. But Dell was right. The world seemed at peace in a way she'd never sensed before.

"You can never really be sure," Cal murmured, rubbing a hand absently over his ribs. "But with Moira out of the picture..."

Silas made a face. "And Kravik." He shook his head. "All this time, we were focused on Moira. I never thought Kravik would join her to launch an all-out attack."

"Who exactly was this Kravik guy?" Connor asked.

Silas's face darkened. "The head of a dragon clan I've heard rumors about for quite some time. Old blood, but bad blood, if you know what I mean. They left Europe — or were driven out — a few years ago, looking to establish a new shifter empire." Silas's eyes locked on Cal's. "Mr. Zydler, we owe you more than we can ever repay."

Cynthia watched Cal meet Silas's gaze. His face gave nothing away, but she could see pride shine in her mate's eyes.

"The prophecy," she whispered without thinking.

"What prophecy?" Hailey asked.

Cal winced, and Cynthia did too. She hadn't meant to share his secret, even if he'd always refused to believe in it.

But Silas spoke before either of them could. "A prophecy of a warrior who would come out of nowhere and accomplish great things." His eyes never left Cal. "A warrior who would extinguish overwhelming evil and herald in a new era of peace in the shifter world."

Cal shrugged. "Oh, you know. Old wives' tales."

"I think not, Mr. Zydler," Silas insisted. "I think not."

214

For a moment, no one said anything, and Cynthia's heart swelled. Cal had always been an outsider, but at heart, he was a powerful alpha. The type of man born to live a life among highly accomplished shifters, not to roam on his own. She looked around, squeezing his hand. Yes, Cal would fit in perfectly here. Then she searched his eyes. Would he agree to that?

Cal cleared his throat and looked around. "The thing is, I was getting a little tired of the dragon-slayer gig."

Silas crooked an eyebrow. "Is that so?"

Cal nodded. "Yeah. Honestly, I was thinking of settling down." He glanced around, and though his voice was all casual, his hand tightened around Cynthia's. "And I got to thinking that Maui might suit me. For a while, at least."

Silas turned to the others. "Any objections?"

Everyone broke into wide grins, and Connor spoke for them all. "No. Not as long as you stay on our side, man."

Cal laughed and jerked a thumb at Cynthia. "No problem. Not as long as you stay on her good side."

"I don't know." Tim rubbed a hand over his beard. "It's kind of handy, having a dragon slayer around." The nod he shot at Cal was one of pure respect. "What about the rest of Kravik's clan?"

Silas shook his head firmly. "My contacts on the mainland report that his associates are beating a quick retreat back to Europe."

"Good," Connor grunted. "Let them stay there. I just hope there are enough reliable shifters over there to keep them under control."

A secret smile played over Silas's lips. "From what I hear…" He broke off, leaving that mystery for another time. "But we digress." He reached for his glass, raised it in Cynthia's direction, and grinned. "I have a proposal, Ms. Baird."

She glanced up, having ducked her head to loop her necklace around her neck again.

"Yes, Mr. Llewellyn?"

"Seeing as we've had several new members join our group lately…" Silas waved his glass toward Cal then to Sophie and the others. "I feel it's time to reorganize how we run things here."

Cynthia sat perfectly still, dreading the worst.

"There's the matter of a certain property I own on Maui," Silas went on. "A plantation I'm quite fond of. But my uncle left me so many properties..."

Jenna's eyes went wide. "No way, Silas. You can't sell this place."

His smile grew, though everyone else looked shocked. "Of course, I can. Though I would only sell to someone who would take better care of it than I can. Ms. Baird, what do you think?"

Cynthia stared. Was he proposing she buy Koakea from him? But how? The place was worth millions, and she didn't have a cent.

Then her inner dragon puzzled it out. *With Moira eliminated, Joey is safe. You don't have to hide your identity any more.*

She smacked a hand over her mouth. "My inheritance." She could step forth and claim her full inheritance—

Silas grinned. "And Barnaby's. And Moira's. After all, you're the last of both family lines."

Everyone stared. Dell smacked her on the back. "Holy crap, Cynth. Are you rich?"

She blinked a few times. "I suppose you could say that."

A hubbub broke out as everyone reacted to the news, but Cynthia could barely move. Eventually, she pulled Joey into her lap, hugging him and Cal at the same time.

"An inheritance is all well and good," she whispered. "But truthfully, I have all the riches I need."

Cal wrapped his arms around her and kissed her on the head. "That's what I love about you. Well, one of many things."

Cynthia closed her eyes and listened to the steady beat of his heart while her fingers played over the soft strands of Joey's hair. She was lucky. So, so lucky, and a huge inheritance was the least of that. Still, the thought was thrilling, because it meant she could stay on Koakea forever. Not only that, but she could take care of her new pack the way she'd always wanted to.

Finally, she collected herself and raised her glass in reply. "Mr. Llewellyn, I accept. But only if everyone agrees."

Connor snorted. "It's your money, you know."

She shook her head. "It's our pack. So, what do you think? The deed might have a different name on it, but everything remains the same. Well, mostly the same." She smiled, cozying up to Cal.

"Works for me," Connor announced.

Dell hooted. Tim and Chase exchanged high fives. Anjali and Sophie hugged each other, then rushed over to hug Cynthia.

"I can't believe it."

"This is amazing."

"It is amazing," Dell added. "Do I get a raise, Cynth?"

She pinned him with her best stare, but he just laughed.

"Okay, okay," he gave in. "I'll settle for dessert. Anyone else?"

Cynthia laughed along with everyone else but didn't raise her hand. Resting against Cal's chest had given her dragon all kinds of bad ideas, and suddenly, she was burning for her mate. Cal's eyes were glowing with the first hint of desire as well, and when Joey slid out of her lap to accept a plate of tiramisu...

"I'd love dessert, but... um... " Cynthia fumbled with her napkin.

Cal stood, putting a hand on his side. "I'd love some, but my ribs are killing me."

Cynthia nearly snorted when he pulled her up with his usual rock-hard power. Dell's eyes flashed with his latest, greatest line — a tease he held back, thank goodness.

"You must be exhausted." Anjali tut-tutted, shooing Cal away. "Cynthia, you'd better go along in case he needs a hand."

Cynthia stood, and Cal slid a hand over her rear, out of sight of the others. "I definitely need a hand. Or two."

Cynthia followed him, trying not to blush. "Well, if you insist..."

"Don't worry. We'll bring Joey over in an hour," Hailey called.

"Or two." Anjali winked.

Cynthia turned away, keeping nice and close to Cal, feeling his body heat rise. Yes, an hour or two would be nice.

"Thanks for dinner," Cal called.

As eager as she was for a little private time with her mate, Cynthia paused at the barn door and turned back. Everyone hid his or her smile, knowing exactly what she and Cal were up to. But there was one more thing she had to say.

"Thank you." She gripped the doorframe with one hand and Cal with the other. "For everything."

The smiles grew broader, and Connor spoke on everyone's behalf. "You're welcome. Now, get out of here and take care of your mate."

Oh, she planned to, all right.

I sure do, her dragon said in a sultry whisper, pulling her mate out into the night. The fresh air didn't do a thing to cool her passion, and the stars — bright, happy, uncountable — all seemed to cheer her on. She and Cal barely made it around the corner before crashing into a huge, hungry kiss. Her hands flew over his body as the pearl warmed against her skin. His fingers threaded into her hair, holding her like he never planned to let go.

That's because I never will, he murmured into her mind. *Never, ever again.*

Chapter Twenty-Two

Three weeks later...

"Like this?" Joey asked, wiping a wrench with a greasy rag.

"Yep. Just like that." Cal nodded, leaning back to admire their work. After neglecting his Triumph for far too long, he and Joey had finally tuned everything up.

He smiled at the shining chrome. That bike had been the one constant in his life from the time he was nineteen, and it had seen as much mileage — and change — as him. At first, the bike had been his ticket to freedom, and he'd roared in and out of towns all the way across the East Coast, usually one step ahead of trouble. The whole time, he'd sworn to never, ever get hitched. Then, one fateful night, he'd met Cynthia and experienced true joy for a while. True sorrow too, not long after. But now...

He closed his eyes and sniffed deeply, registering more than just the sweet scent of tropical flowers on the fresh, salt-tinged air. Cynthia was nearby, and her natural fragrance worked on him like a balm — especially now that it carried a hint of his own scent.

Mate, his wolf rumbled in satisfaction. *My mate is finally mine.*

In the distance, the ocean rolled slowly over the shore, adding to the feeling of calm. Even the Thruxton — a master-piece of engineering that screamed *speed* and *power* — seemed content to kick back for a while. The tattered scarf that hung from the handlebars was the only part of the bike that wasn't shining in the sunlight, but that was okay, especially since it was no longer his sole reminder of Cynthia.

They had spent just about every hour of the past weeks together — eating, sleeping, and working side by side. They'd filled last night — like most of their nights so far — with hot, hard, and extremely quiet sex, what with Joey slumbering in the next room. Then they'd drifted off to sleep, and Cal had gotten to hold his mate all night — nice and tight, as if she was the ultimate prize for a warrior who'd finally found his way home.

Sometime in the morning, Cynthia had woken with that sixth sense of hers, and they'd sleepily pulled on some clothes — just in time for Joey to trundle in and cuddle up on Cynthia's side of the bed. Which was nice too. Just lazing there for a quiet, sleepy hour was great — and not only for the contrast to some of the more miserable mornings of Cal's life, spent far from his true love. He luxuriated in the quiet. The calm. That unfamiliar sense of peace, inside and out.

Peace. A word he'd never truly understood until now.

"Looks good," Joey said.

Cal considered his reflection in the chrome. *Looks happy,* he nearly joked. Instead, he settled for murmuring, "Sure does."

"Do you think Mommy will like it?"

Cal laughed and tousled Joey's hair. "I think she'll love it."

The little redhead glanced around then whispered, "Do you think she'll let me ride it again?"

Cal cracked into a huge smile. The previous day, Dell, Connor, and the others had helped Cal talk Cynthia into letting him take Joey for a ride. The world's shortest, slowest ride that took them around the plantation a few times. He'd never seen a kid as thrilled as Joey during that ride.

"I'm sure she'll let us ride again. We're partners, man."

Joey smiled and gave the muffler one more swipe with the cloth. "Partners."

Cal nodded. *Partners* worked for both of them, because Joey had already had a great father, and Cal would help him cherish the memories for the rest of his life. Besides, Cal wasn't so sure he was ready to be called Dad. *Partner,* on the other hand, helped each of them transition into their new roles.

Gravel crunched, signaling someone coming around the corner of the barn.

"Wow. It looks great," Cynthia called.

Cal whirled, grinning even before he spotted her. Whatever he was about to retort got stuck on the tip of his tongue, though, because seeing her knocked him out every time.

Looks great, his wolf practically whistled.

The sun backlit her long black hair, giving her an ethereal glow. Her smile was soft and full of wonder, as if she was witnessing a dream come true.

Cal gulped. It shouldn't be possible to fall even deeper in love than before, but there he went. Cynthia seemed the same way — happier, calmer, and more beautiful than ever. Was that all in his mind or was there something slightly different about her? Something he couldn't quite put his finger on, like a faint glow.

He cleared his throat and pointed at Joey. "All thanks to this guy."

Joey beamed, and Cynthia smiled. Her gaze lingered on the scarf, then on Cal, and he warmed.

"Still looks pretty old to me," Dell cracked as he walked by.

Cal snorted. "It's vintage, man."

"A little like you?" Dell chuckled.

Cynthia patted Cal's shoulder. "More like a fine wine. Now, if you'll excuse us..."

When Dell took the hint and sauntered on, Cynthia motioned to the hillside behind her. "Are you two ready to go?"

"Sure. Been waiting for you," Cal said.

Within minutes, he and Joey had cleaned up and joined Cynthia, who pointed up a path that disappeared behind a coffee grove.

"Where are we going, Mommy?" Joey asked, taking her hand.

"To the place I wanted to show you and Cal."

There was a hint of a tease in her voice, but Cal was too busy admiring the tiny scars on her neck to pay much attention to her words. A week after she'd given him the mating bite, he'd returned the favor at the climax of another sizzling night. A rush of fire had swept through his body as her dragon essence mingled with his wolf blood.

Cynthia glanced back at him, suddenly flushed. *Would you cut that out?*

He grinned. Was it his fault lust hammered through him at the memory?

Cynthia was trying to look prim but failing miserably.

Like you don't think about that too, he challenged.

Constantly, she admitted. *But right now. . .* She jutted an elbow toward Joey.

Cal took a couple of deep breaths. That was the hard part of being mated — the constant need to bond with the woman he loved. But taking a walk was nice too, and Cynthia was clearly excited about whatever lay ahead. So he pushed lust toward the back of his mind and let curiosity slide to the front.

"What exactly is up there?"

"You'll see," she said, all coy.

The path meandered this way and that, rising and falling with the contours of the plantation. They skirted the coffee grove then descended into the cleft cut by the creek. Cal sniffed, catching the scent of frangipani, ginger, and lion — after all, Dell and Anjali lived right around the bend. Then they climbed back up the other side, ducking branches as they went. Ahead of them, the foliage thinned out, and Cal couldn't help imagining how incredible the view from the top must be. Cynthia crested the next rise before him and looked back.

"The path needs a little clearing, but. . ."

She gestured to the open sweep of land that lay ahead. As Cal's gaze crossed the rich green landscape, his wolf sighed. *So much space.*

That slope was a little corner of paradise unto itself, angled in a way that hid it from the rest of the plantation. The sea breeze wafted over the area, making the tall grass dance in a manner that drew his gaze from one little detail to the next. There was a rocky outcrop over on one side — the perfect place for a wolf to howl to the moon, or for a dragon to launch from.

A cluster of six trees on the far side formed a little orchard, and over in the middle of the area...

Cal stood still, staring at the perfect little house. A low white bungalow built back when folks still took time to carve gingerbread eaves and set squares of stained glass into frames. The window beside the front door was one big field of green surrounded by little panels of yellow, blue, and red, while the window on the north side gave yellow center stage, with multicolored panels marching around it on all four sides.

"Nice place," he murmured.

Cynthia's eyes filled with hope. "It is nice."

A veil lay over her thoughts, but Cal guessed her train of thought was something like, *Nice enough to live in.*

"Oh! I know this house," Joey said, skipping ahead. "Tim let me check the roof with him. I even got to crawl underneath."

Cal hadn't been paying much attention to the bear shifter's movements, but now that he thought back, he could recall Tim disappearing in this direction several times.

"Should we have a closer look?" Cynthia said, oh so casually.

Cal nodded and followed her, wondering why the white picket fence didn't fill him with the urge to turn and run. Fences like that were for guys who wanted to settle down. Ease up. Spend weekends on home repair instead of tearing down highways on their motorbikes. Guys whose thoughts might even go as far as starting a family someday.

His wolf thumped its tail a few times. *Our own little den.*

Den wasn't exactly the word — not for that sun-drenched porch or those wide, cheery windows. But it did match the cozy feeling of the place.

"The best room is in the back," Joey called, yanking open the front door and rushing in.

"Wait. Sweetie—" Cynthia cried out, then stopped.

Cal could feel her warring with herself. Who would win — the overprotective mother who'd been through so much? Or the mighty she-dragon with enough faith in the world to give her son a little space?

Frankly, Cal couldn't help tensing up a little himself. But then he remembered what the guys always told Cynthia.

Loosen up. . . Let the kid be a kid. . .

It was hard to loosen up when something as precious as a child was on the line, but Dell, Connor, and the others were right. There wasn't a hint of enemy dragon in the air, nor a whiff of unknown shifters slinking in for another attack.

"Never mind," Cynthia said, letting Joey gallop on.

Cal followed her up the creaky front steps. The screen door squeaked as they opened it and stepped into the house, where Joey was running from room to room.

"That's the biggest room, and this one has a giant cobweb. This one has a closet that makes a pirate hideaway." Joey rambled on, pointing out every feature of interest to a kid.

Cal looked it over with different eyes. The wallpaper was peeling, and the bathroom fixtures looked about a hundred years old. But, wow. The place had potential.

"What do you think?" Cynthia whispered, holding his hand.

He looked around. "I think it needs six solid months of work to get into livable shape. But, yeah. It's a nice place."

"Six months is more than enough," Cynthia murmured.

Briefly, he wondered what her deadline was based on, but the view out the front distracted him. All that ocean, practically on his doorstep. All that space. At the same time, the rest of the pack wasn't any farther away than they were from the main house. Dell and Anjali's place was over by the creek, and Connor and Jenna lived at the edge of the cliff that formed one bookend to the view. Still, the bungalow had a feeling of privacy the main plantation house could never offer, not with the shared kitchen/living area on the ground floor.

He glanced at Cynthia. Was she thinking what he was thinking?

"It is pretty perfect," he said, trying to speak casually despite the fact that his wolf was growing more enchanted by the minute. If he didn't watch out, the beast would start running in circles, chasing its tail along with those thoughts.

Our own place. Our own yard. Our own home.

"Perfect for...?" Cynthia asked.

Her words floated in the air, and he sensed her holding her breath. Was he really ready for a life like this?

Hell yes, his wolf barked.

He didn't even have to think it over. "Perfect for us."

Cynthia caught him in a huge, teary hug. The kind that spoke of deep, boundless hopes instead of dark, unspoken fears.

"It is perfect," she said, pulling herself together to motion around. "Lots of space for all of us."

He smiled at *all.* Three people didn't add up to much, really. But she was right. That big room would be perfect for him and Cynthia. The back room suited Joey, and...

His eyes strayed to the third room, and his heart thumped harder.

"Lots of space for all of us," Cynthia repeated, sliding a hand down to her belly and giving herself a pat.

At first, Cal nodded casually, but then the gears finally clicked into place in his head.

All of us... Six months being plenty... The tender way she'd touched her midsection.

His jaw dropped. "All of us?"

Cynthia nodded. "All of us. You, me, Joey..." She took his hand and guided it to her belly. "And her."

Cal sucked in a deep breath. He'd attributed Cynthia's inner glow to being a freshly mated shifter. And part of it was, for sure. But when he examined her scent closely, he found something totally different wrapped around the rest, like a vine of tiny white flowers. Something sweet, fragile, and totally innocent.

A baby? So soon?

His inner wolf grinned proudly, muttering something about virile canine blood.

He loved the idea, but it flabbergasted him. Most shifters — even destined mates — took ages to conceive. He and Cynthia had only been mated for a few short weeks.

Cynthia's eyes went all bittersweet as she let her dragon speak into his mind. *More like years.*

A stab of sorrow cut through him, but a flood tide of elation immediately washed it away. He swept Cynthia off her feet, spinning in a circle of joy.

Joey ran up clapping in excitement even without knowing what they were so happy about. "Me too! Me too!"

Cal released Cynthia long enough to spin Joey around, laughing the whole time. He pulled both of them into his arms, tucked his cheek against Cynthia's, and breathed in her scent. Beams of light streamed in from the windows — yellow, green, and red. There was even a blue beam, shining in from yet another small room on the right.

"Maybe there's even space for more than one baby," Cynthia whispered, teasing but not teasing at the same time.

Cal grinned and kissed her, long and deep. "Lady, life is one big maybe. And I mean that in the best possible way."

Sneak Peek: Fire Maidens

New series coming soon!

The shifters of Koa Point have vanquished their mightiest foes, but danger remains — if not on the sunny shores of Maui, then thousands of miles away. The remnants of Kravik's power-hungry dragon clan have crept back to Europe, where they plot to seize power in the grandest, most glamorous cities — Paris, London, and Rome. But the guardians of old have summoned a new generation of shifter heroes to protect the castles, cathedrals, and cobblestoned streets of their ancestral homes — and to seek out the last of the Fire Maidens, women coveted by the dark lords for their royal blood. Those women are absolutely off-limits to the young warriors tasked with protecting them. But destiny, of course, has other ideas...

Stay tuned for Anna Lowe's FIRE MAIDENS series, coming in 2019!

Books by Anna Lowe

Aloha Shifters - Pearls of Desire

Rebel Dragon (Book 1)

Rebel Bear (Book 2)

Rebel Lion (Book 3)

Rebel Wolf (Book 4)

Rebel Heart (A prequel)

Rebel Alpha (Book 5)

Aloha Shifters - Jewels of the Heart

Lure of the Dragon (Book 1)

Lure of the Wolf (Book 2)

Lure of the Bear (Book 3)

Lure of the Tiger (Book 4)

Love of the Dragon (Book 5)

Lure of the Fox (Book 6)

Fire Maidens - Billionaires & Bodyguards

Fire Maidens: Paris (Book 1)

Fire Maidens: London (Book 2)

Fire Maidens: Rome (Book 3)

The Wolves of Twin Moon Ranch

Desert Hunt (the Prequel)

Desert Moon (Book 1)

Desert Wolf: Complete Collection (Four short stories)

Desert Blood (Book 2)

Desert Fate (Book 3)

Desert Heart (Book 4)

Desert Yule (a short story)

Desert Rose (Book 5)

Desert Roots (Book 6)

Sasquatch Surprise (a Twin Moon spin-off story)

Blue Moon Saloon

Perfection (a short story prequel)

Damnation (Book 1)

Temptation (Book 2)

Redemption (Book 3)

Salvation (Book 4)

Deception (Book 5)

Celebration (a holiday treat)

Shifters in Vegas

Paranormal romance with a zany twist

Gambling on Trouble

Gambling on Her Dragon

Gambling on Her Bear

Serendipity Adventure Romance

Off the Charts

Uncharted

Entangled

Windswept

Adrift

Travel Romance

Veiled Fantasies

Island Fantasies

visit www.annalowebooks.com

About the Author

USA Today and Amazon bestselling author Anna Lowe loves putting the "hero" back into heroine and letting location ignite a passionate romance. She likes a heroine who is independent, intelligent, and imperfect – a woman who is doing just fine on her own. But give the heroine a good man – not to mention a chance to overcome her own inhibitions – and she'll never turn down the chance for adventure, nor shy away from danger.

Anna loves dogs, sports, and travel – and letting those inspire her fiction. On any given weekend, you might find her hiking in the mountains or hunched over her laptop, working on her latest story. Either way, the day will end with a chunk of dark chocolate and a good read.

Visit AnnaLoweBooks.com

Made in the USA
Columbia, SC
07 August 2021